Dignity

Otter Lieffe

WWW.ACTIVEDISTRIBUTION.ORG

Copyright © 2020 Otter Lieffe
First Edition published 2020 by Active Distribution, Croatia / UK
Cover design: Zoe Langer
Editor: Liv Mammone
Proofreader: Natalie Kontoulis

www.otterlieffe.com
www.activedistribution.org

During years of state repression, I felt isolated and betrayed by the movement I grew up in, I felt like any grassroots or revolutionary struggle to change things was ultimately weaker than those with power and control, I felt small and vulnerable - but plants remind me that they are on our side. All the plants, animals and ecosystems in the world want recovery, they want freedom, they want health - and with them as allies, we are never alone.

Nicole Rose

Imposing

Just a few years ago, I hadn't yet found my voice. I could barely write, much less stand up in front of people and tell my stories. I felt—because people told me—that I had nothing useful to say.

I've heard that imposter syndrome is something we're supposed to push through. It's all in your head. You can do anything you want.

But in reality, those insidious messages—that I'm not good enough and that my existence is an inconvenience to everyone else—come from outside of me. In a world that demonises femininity and discards trans women, that blames poverty on its victims, that consumes our experiences and repackages them for someone else's profit, these messages carry the specific intention of making us feel like we're imposing.

It's the guy on the underground who stares at my make-up, his hands clenched into fists. It's the woman who had me removed from a women/lesbian/trans space on my first day in Berlin for wearing the wrong shoes and for being the wrong kind of trans. It's the near total lack of access for working-class, trans women in a publishing world built on privilege.

And that's why people living in the margins are so fucking amazing. To survive in this world, to push past a culture that hates us and subcultures that sometimes hate us even more, and still be who we are... that's everything. It takes resilience that many will never know. It gives us super-powers.

Writing and political organising is all about allowing myself to dream. I dream of dismantling imposter syndrome and the culture that creates it. I dream of creating new spaces and alliances that actually meet our needs. I dream of us lifting each other up instead of shutting each other down.

Dignity

Just over a year ago, I stood in front of two hundred people and announced that I was founding a new organisation, Trans Feminism International, working to meet material needs of trans women. Now that my 'writer's block' of several decades has passed, stories are pouring out of me. I have stepped into my power in so many ways.

Around twenty years ago, I worked in a care home in a small conservative military town. Sometimes I would work twenty-four-hour shifts, seventy-hour weeks, cleaning body fluids off my shoes in the middle of the night for minimum wage. The conditions for the residents—who couldn't leave— were worse.

Now I am a writer-organiser in a pandemic lockdown. I watch as society around me discards its older people, its chronically ill and disabled people, working-class and BIPOC communities, for the sake of haircuts and industry. I'm reminded that change is slow, that we have so far to go and that sometimes it seems impossible to see the destination in a journey filled with pain. Which is why I write. To imagine something else, to answer the question of what-if.

What if we were shameless in exploring, imagining and dreaming together?

What if we could live in connection with the powerful world of non-humans around us?

What if we could create something so intensely beautiful that the toxic sweetener of capitalism would lose all temptation?

What if, with care—and dignity—we could move towards something better?

Otter Lieffe, summer 2020

Acknowledgements

We did this!

I could not have imagined how collective this process would become. Yes, a lot of it is me sitting alone with my laptop: writing novels means isolation even without pandemic lockdowns. But with each new stage, there have been more people involved. As I reach these final stages with *Dignity*, I think about how many have co-created this work. It has literally taken a community. It has meant that I've never felt alone in this process—that's a lot.

A huge thanks to the many, many friends and supporters who have helped out with everything from social media to website advice, from hosting events to visiting bookshops. Thank you everyone who has supported this project financially, through crowdfunding and pre-orders. Thank you to my wonderful friends in Manchester, Basel, Brussels, Berlin. To LGBT Books to Prisoners and Books Beyond Bars UK for our wonderful collaborations and for all your hard work. To Active for getting my words out into the world. To Liz Thumb for all your fabulous help. To Keira Sinclair for your encouragement. To Pi Jem Thanachon, Sarj Lynch, Reneé Imperato and so many other loved ones, for all your tireless support. To S. Miller - you know why.

To Leah Lakshmi Piepzna-Samarasinha for the concept of emotional labour as air. *Care work* changed my life. Thank you.

I have so much gratitude for the sensitivity readers of this book—Angel, Johanna von Felten, Nicole Rose, Serafina Ndlovu—who so carefully and firmly helped me to write better about experiences that I don't have; specifically wheelchair use, fatphobia, long-term incarceration and racism. Your guidance has meant the world to me. Any remaining inaccuracies are mine alone.

Thank you to Liv Mammone for once again being with me on this journey of editing and making my writing the best it can be. It was such a pleasure, you're the greatest. Thanks, and a hug, to Natalie Kontoulis for somehow finding time to proofread, I hope I didn't drive you wild with my trans-Atlantic spellings and randomly sprinkled commas. Zoe Langer, thank you for so skilfully turning a dream into the cover of this book. The colours lift my heart.

Thank you dear sisters; Ayelet Yonah Adelman for helping me find the words to express my politics and Anja Van Geert, because you are everything. I adore you both.

As with any story, especially a political one, this novel contains scenes and subjects that might be difficult or triggering for some people. Please take care of yourself while reading and get support if you need it.

1. Freedom

Chapter one

The land was alive.

As the group made their way through the streets, even towers of concrete and rivers of asphalt couldn't stifle their excitement. Above them, the sky burned crimson with the last light of the day. Pigeons and crows soared through the streets, their calls reverberating off windows. A red deer nibbled herbs in an abandoned car park and looked up as the group passed. Their enthusiasm, at being together, to experience the night ahead, was palpable.

They had a way to go yet. The group would soon enter the commercial centre of town. The glittering offices ahead held the means of control for people like them. People who were different. People who opposed the State. They would have to quieten their voices, tone down their love, smother their care for one another. But for now, they could rejoice in the beauty of the evening and this land that clung on to life. A goshawk flew overhead and excited eyes and pointing fingers followed her path. The ground physically hummed with the group's passing. Holding the hand of her dearest friend and stepping forward breathlessly with a rare bounce in her step, Ash couldn't wait to arrive.

Chapter two

Y ou're working the night shift by yourself tonight so don't forget to clean the bathrooms, wipe the wheelchairs down and get the sandwiches ready for tomorrow."

Perfect.

"Residents one to twenty-two are in their rooms. Resident twenty-three was being difficult as usual so the nurse sedated her."

Awesome.

"Check in again before end-of-shift and if you need to restrain her, you know where the belts are."

I know where the belts are.

"Oh, and the solar panels have been playing up and the lights are set to turn off early. There are spare candles in the office. You'll need them—this place is a rabbit warren at night."

Y hadn't spoken a single word since their boss had accosted them in the yard to announce her early departure. Y stood in the middle of the triangular slab of concrete that served as the backyard of the Home; three heavy, stinking garbage bags hanging from each hand. *Would you just leave already?* Finally, the boss turned without so much as a goodbye. When Y was sure she was gone, they dropped the bags on the ground and collapsed next to them, their back against the wall. They hugged their knees and sighed.

Their body and mind were numb. This was their third double of the week and it had been days since they'd seen the sun. They looked up vaguely at the patch of sky framed by high-rises, but it could have been any time of the day, any day of the winter—a blanket of grey clouds had consumed the sunset. Drizzle fell softly onto an endless expanse of grey city and Y's hunched body was wet within minutes. Leaning against the damp bricks, their back ached, their stomach cramped and there was a high-pitched whine in their left ear that they couldn't remember ever living without. At least they had a bed to sleep in these days. Before T—resident sixteen—had died last week, they'd been sleeping on a ratty yoga mat on the floor during the night shift.

I should be grateful, they noted. *At least I get to actually go home sometimes. Anything is better than being a resident in this place.*

But Y wasn't grateful. They knew that being a carer was considered one of the worst State placements: the pay was only just enough to survive on, the hours were so long Y rarely knew what week they were in and the co-workers—and boss—treated them nearly as badly as they treated the residents. Nearly, not quite.

They turned their head back and forth, stretching their neck and trying to work out a knot that had been stuck there all day. They watched through blurred eyes as a young hooded crow landed in the yard, bounced over to the garbage bags and started pecking a hole. Within a minute, the young bird was spilling the contents onto the yard.

"That's great, thanks a lot," Y mumbled out loud. The crow paused and looked up at them curiously with jet-black eyes. Then deciding the human wasn't worth paying attention to, he continued gleefully tearing the bag apart.

Fine, go for it, little guy. Get yourself something nice.

Seeming to understand their thoughts, the crow's face emerged from a bag with a beak full of sandwich crusts. With a

gleeful craaaw—that nearly caused him to drop the treasure—
he flew off to find a quiet place to enjoy his dinner.

Y looked distantly at the mess the crow had left behind.

Tomorrow. I'll deal with it tomorrow. They rubbed their
eyes. *But wait, am I in again? What day is it actually?*

They shook their head to try to clear sleepy thoughts.

*I was last at home on Monday morning—right?—but then I
pulled a double until Wednesday and—did I sleep here that
night?*

Y knew that their brain was too tired to cooperate. Casting a
last glance at the rubbish spread all over the yard, they stood
up, closed the door and headed to the staff room.

*   *   *

Passing through a park, the group of friends paused for a
moment to rest. No-one in the City had time to visit the park
anymore—and it showed. Every bench was rusted and
moulded over. Something that might have once been a slide
and a swing set had been consumed by ivy and brambles. A
tree brought down by the last storm had destroyed a fence and
would probably lay there for a good few years before the State
would do anything with it. The park, which had been well-
manicured and busy just a few years before, was desolate,
abandoned by people. Ash loved it.

She leaned against an old oak and caught her breath. Pinar
came over and offered her a drink from her canteen. The water
tasted metallic, but Ash drank down half of it in one go and
gave it back to her dearest friend with a grateful smile.

Despite a chilly breeze, they were both sweating from the
walk. Ash took off her woollen hat and stuffed it into her
pocket. She ran her hands over her bald head and adjusted her

hoops. "Do I look okay?" she asked, fluttering her mascaraed eyelashes.

Pinar chuckled. In the decades they had known each other, she had never known her friend to care what other people thought of her appearance. They sometimes spent hours together sitting on a bed, taking turns brushing Pinar's hair—it came down to her mid-back these days and needed brushing at least twice a day. But Ash had never really shown much interest in her own appearance, except the very basics. *Feeling comfortable, yes. Expressing her femininity, of course. And she's used the expensive eyeliner tonight.*

But really caring what other people think of her? Ash is way too independent for that and fuck transphobic beauty standards anyway.

"You look gorgeous, my love," she replied genuinely. "Ready for a party?"

Ash stretched and pushed off of the tree. "Honestly, I'm much more ready for the revolution, but a party will do in the meantime."

By an unspoken signal, the group set off again. As they left the park, the family of foxes who had watched them since their arrival stepped out of the shadows, and set out for the night ahead.

* * *

The staff room was stuffy and cramped, like most of the spaces at the Home. It served as a place for the staff to rest, eat, and file their notes on the residents—usually all at the same time. The staff room was also their de facto office and sleeping space for the night shift. There were no windows and the one UV strip light in the ceiling flickered on and off. Since Y had started their placement at the Home three years before, they had never seen it work properly.

One wall was lined with creaky old chairs covered in tea stains and the other was taken up by a desk buried under a collection of mugs, a small mountain of folders, and five-times-reused pieces of paper. Even through the fog of tiredness, Y noticed that the room smelled like celery soup—in the worst possible way.

Someone should spend a few days in here cleaning up, they thought to themself, knowing full well that no one would get even an hour. Getting the residents washed, dressed, fed, medicated and back into bed again filled every minute of the Home schedule. The staff room, along with the long-forgotten 'entertainment and wellness' programme for the residents, was always pushed aside for some other four a.m. vomiting emergency or getting the living room clean enough to pass a State inspection. Y knew that every factory has an unloved, hidden back end where the inspectors never came, and this pokey little office was theirs. They stood in the middle of the room looking vaguely around. *Why did I come in here again?*

Right...schedules.

They stepped over to the desk and began moving plates and folders until they found the scrap of paper that served as their work calendar. They held it up in the flickering light, blinked twice. For the first time that day, Y was suddenly aware of their heart in their chest.

Yes! Fucking yes!

They'd almost missed it, but today—it turned out—was the third Sunday of the month. Y could have sworn it was Thursday. A yawn suddenly overtook them, their eyes blurred up again and Y knew they were as tired as they'd ever been. *I should go home, or at least curl up in T's old room for a nap.*

But they only come once a month.

Y threw the calendar on the desk, pushed their shoulders back and left the overwhelming office. No matter how tired they were, they could always find energy for the Resistance.

I'd better go wake up the residents.

* * *

They were closer now, and a hush of anticipation and caution fell over the group.

"*We'll split up here,*" Ash signed to the others. She used Universal Sign, a kind of manually encoded English which had become a second language for almost everyone living on State land. "*And let's reconvene at the Home. Just keep your heads down and we'll be fine. Just a normal evening walk for some perfectly normal people coming home from work.*"

A chuckle moved through the group. They looked nothing like a group of State workers leaving the office—far too much glitter, for one thing. Too much joy, for another. Pinar tucked a strand of dark hair behind her ear and stepped forward.

"*This is uncomfortable,*" she signed. "*But, as we all know, things have been bad recently. So, for those of you who are particularly fabulous tonight, we brought some very boring sweaters to put over your looks.*" Pinar took off her backpack and unzipped it, intentionally avoiding the gaze of her friends dressed up in their sparkling finest for the evening. She sighed audibly. "*I'm sorry, I hate it too.*"

Pinar and Ash passed around the dark clothing and once the most vulnerable in their community were ready, they broke into groups and spread out through the City's district of power.

* * *

"L, are you awake?"

L was sleeping soundly, a blanket pulled up around her neck. She was eighty-two years old, almost completely deaf and had been a resident of the Home since her family was forced to admit her. She slowly opened her eyes. "Is it morning already?" she asked, her voice groggy.

Y switched to USL. *"I'm sorry to disturb you. I thought you'd want to know..."*

"Yes?" L signed back. *"What is it, dear?"*

"The Resistance is coming."

Faster than Y had ever seen her move, L jumped up to sitting and tore off her blanket. *"Well, what are we doing here?"* she signed with bright eyes. *"We have a party to organise!"*

* * *

"How much further?" Ash asked. She felt ridiculous. Over the cute black dress she had picked out for the night, she wore baggy trousers and an oversized military sweater. If anything, she felt it made her look more obvious than her tights and pumps. "I'm not really feeling the drab costume party tonight."

Drab, an archaic word used to describe the dull clothing trans women sometimes had to wear for safety, had come back into common use recently. The State had begun repressing expressions of femininity, particularly those of visibly queer and trans people, through laws and populist campaigns. Ash and Pinar heard horror stories of attacks nearly every week.

Ash scratched at the polyester itching her arms. Just the week before, a trans woman had been attacked with a metal bar on her way home from work. She had spent three days hiding at Ash and Pinar's herbal clinic before she could face the street again. *Fuck all of that.* "I hate it, Pin."

Her friend gave her a sympathetic smile. "I know, hon. I wish we had other options."

They paused at the corner of the street, waiting for a group of men to pass by.

"But if it helps, navy blue is definitely your colour."

Ash stuck out her tongue. When the street was empty again, they continued their journey. Not far to go now.

Standing at the front door, anticipating the night ahead with a full chest and a wide grin, Y could hear them long before they came into view. Despite their best attempts to be quiet as they moved through the heavily controlled neighbourhood, the joyful sounds of the Resistance were irrepressible. Their giggles reverberated off the tall State office buildings; the creaking of crutches and the clicking of heels on cement was unmistakable.

Inside the Home too, the usually sombre corridors were filling with busy conversation, as the residents roused each other from sleep, put on their Sunday best and made their way to the living room to light candles before the electricity switched off for the night. Y would swear they even heard someone singing deep in the bowels of the building. For the residents of the Home, the arrival of their friends marked the best day in their every-day-identical calendar.

And they're here.

As they began regrouping at the doors of the Home, Y could make out some famous faces. With a racing heart, they stepped unconsciously toward the crowd and called out:

"Welcome...welcome friends. You are safe here."

And in a flush of hugs, cheek kisses, and whoops of excitement, the Resistance had arrived.

Chapter three

P in, did you bring candles? I can't see a bloody thing in here!"

Pulling ten long candles out of her backpack and laying them out on the kitchen counter, Pinar rolled her eyes in the dark. She replied to her friend with just a hint of frustration:

"Yes, dear. You literally reminded me five times. Did you bring the matches?"

"I did! At least I think so. I must have them somewhere…".

Ash dug around in her backpack, but the oversized sleeves hanging over her hands made everything more difficult. She managed to knock her bag, and the candles, off the surface with a crash.

She snorted in frustration and tried to escape from the giant, itchy sweater. Her hoop earrings got stuck immediately. "Pin, help me!"

Together, they managed to extricate Ash, losing only one hoop along the way. She pulled down the baggy pants as well, giving them a little kick away from her for good measure.

"Feeling better?" her friend asked her.

Ash ran her hands over her sequined dress and felt immediately more like herself. She bent down and picked something up out of the mess on the floor.

"I found the matches!"

* * *

The Home was abuzz. In the living room, sleepy residents in their pyjamas helped move scruffy chairs and scratched-up coffee tables to clear space for the new arrivals. Their friends in turn quickly filled the room with candlelight and laughter. A small crew prepared the corner that would serve as their stage later in the night and another pulled a banquet of snacks and home-cooked food from their backpacks and started passing plates around. As they always did, the Resistance automatically sat down in the concentric circles that defined their spaces.

Y had never seen so many people in the Home at one time.

This just keeps growing.

They knew that as State crackdowns had become increasingly violent, a new generation of its citizens were being galvanised to the cause. After a spate of evictions had given them fewer and fewer spaces to come together, the Home had become one of the last refuges where the Resistance could meet, organise and, of course, party.

It's fabulous.

Y could think of no better word to describe this gathering of *vergents*—those whose very existence defied the State's norms of body, expression and identity. As the living room filled with the smells of food brought fresh from the soup kitchens, Y's stomach growled so loudly they were sure that those sat nearby must have heard it.

I've been missing meals again.

"Eat up," said a resident in her nineties who sat behind Y holding out a plate full of vegetables. "You spend as much time here as I do, and I've never *once* seen you eat."

Resident eighteen, Y thought to themself. *Wait, no, not tonight.*

"Thanks...erm...Mary," they replied, taking the plate and flashing her a grateful smile.

"Y, isn't it?" asked Mary softly.

"Not tonight. It's Yarrow."

Of all the things Yarrow loved about these gatherings, the best for them personally was this breaking-down of roles. Tonight, they were no longer Y, the barely-paid worker who was kept so busy that the idea of 'care' had become one more task on a never-ending to-do list. And these were no longer residents, the elderly, chronically ill and designated 'unproductive' members of society that the State could find no other use for. They were all just friends, enjoying each other's company. There would be a whole night of meetings—there were always meetings—but first, food and time to reconnect.

Yarrow felt good. They felt freer than they had all week. But, as they began to eat, gulping down the food too fast to taste it, Yarrow was also worried how long this could last.

During the rare moments of freedom that the Home staff found to rest, most of them gathered in the office to eat and gossip. A week before, Yarrow had come to the office for a snack and overheard their co-workers talking in loud voices about something called the Peccatums.

"What's that then?" H, their colleague had asked. Unlike in Resistance spaces, the employees of the Home were very careful to use their State-designated names at work: one letter per citizen. Secretly, Yarrow doubted that many of them ever used their real names anymore. They were all pretty conservative.

"Well, as I heard it, it's some kind of new gender law," another colleague, Q, announced between bites of her sandwich. "Something about 'excessive femininity' or whatev—"

"Actually," interrupted K, the only man working at the Home. Yarrow had been waiting for him to jump in with an educational moment. "It's a whole *set* of new laws, including a ban on a range of behaviours that the State doesn't consider natural."

"Natural?" Yarrow asked. They hadn't heard the news in weeks.

K shrugged. "That's what they said."

"*Excessive* femininity?" Yarrow insisted, "*Natural* behaviours and bodies? Who defines these things?"

Yarrow knew they were exposing slightly too much of themself for comfort. They had come out to the staff as non-binary within the first few weeks of starting their placement in the Home. The dysphoria of being constantly called 'he' was too much to do anything else. They had asked Yarrow many, many questions at the beginning, but in the end most of the staff had come to accept that part of Yarrow's identity. Or the team were just too tired from working twenty-four hour shifts to care anymore. Still, Yarrow was careful not to express their political opinions at work. *Gender is one thing, hating the State is quite another.*

Fortunately, K ignored Yarrow's outburst and opened their lunch box. The conversation soon moved on to the weather, the increasingly dramatic winter storms, and if and when the next flood would be.

Yarrow was used to being ignored. They bit into a tasteless Nutrition bar and felt a familiar sense of hopelessness seeping into their chest.

After centuries of fighting for the human rights to love and be, the State had shown itself to be as fickle as any other. *All of our rights signed away overnight.* To Yarrow, the Peccatums felt like just another step in the State's descent into dystopia.

The boss arrived in the office and announced the end of breaktime. Yarrow stood up and went to prepare lunch for the residents. *Sometimes it's better to just stay busy.*

Looking around at the living room now, smiling residents— many wearing dresses and suits over their pyjamas—told stories with their friends, expressing themselves in several forbidden languages, among them Spanish, Arabic and any Sign Language other than the State-sanctioned USL. As they moved their hands and hips with abandon, Yarrow felt both exhilarated by the freedom of this space and deeply concerned.

If the State knew how much colour, feeling and care was in this room right now, they would have troopers at the door within the hour.

Chapter four

The yoga teacher wasn't really feeling grounded. Her self-care routine had been disturbed this week by too much work and she had been sitting in this canteen for an hour without finishing the herbal coffee she had ordered when she arrived. A waiter passed close to the table and looked like he might try to clear up her drink— she grabbed her cup with both hands and pulled it closer.

Considering how much they charge my life accounts for this weak brew, I'm going to make it last as long as humanly possible. I'll stay here all evening if I want to.

She threw the waiter a look and he continued on to the next table.

No tip for you.

She had had another long day teaching the State officials working in the building above the canteen, running yoga classes for pregnant people, for releasing office tension—and her favourite new class—mindfulness for soldiers. It was a good placement and she was pretty happy. Sure, some of the military guys were clearly more focused on her ass than her teachings and she knew that a lot of her students only came to class as an obligatory part of their placements—all part of the State's care-for-workers programme to increase productivity—but she enjoyed sharing the knowledge she had gained in India and her students in general were pretty okay.

India.

She ran her finger over the rim of her mug and allowed

herself a moment of nostalgia. It had been a while, but she missed those days when she was free to travel, to leave the State. Before the pandemics and lockdowns, back when seeing the world was as easy as booking a flight.

Well, squeezing the money out of mum and dad and then booking the flight.

She daydreamed for a while about the colourful places she had seen, the incredible people she had met on her journeys. She thought for a while about chakras and whether the throat chakra could really help lucid dreaming. She thought about the price of drinks in this place and if there was any way she could ask for a pay rise from her boss.

And what about the heart chakra, does that affect dreaming as well...?

Suddenly a loud bang outside brought her crashing back to her body.

Her mind went blank. Her shoulders were up close to her ears. Her chest forced her to breath. She released her blonde ponytail which for some reason she was grabbing with both hands.

Her first thought was that it must be a bomb. *Or something.*

She remembered that she had heard whispers in class. The Resistance have been mobilising again.

I'll never understand. Why can't they just get placements like the rest of us. Why can't they—

She looked around her and for the first time noticed that there were other people in the canteen. They all shared her worried expression. Some people had stood up and were peering up through the grates that opened on to the street. The yoga teacher joined them, but couldn't see very much except passing feet.

Her heart skipped as another bang resonated down into the steamy canteen.

Then whistles and voices and more banging.

What is this?

She began to realise that actually the banging was coming more regularly now. And it wasn't random. Maybe some kind of a rhythm?

Wait...it's drums! People are playing drums in the street— some kind of State street party. I've never seen one before!

She checked the clock on the back wall.

Still time before dinner. Well, never let it be said that I'm not ready for fun at the drop of a hat!

She ran back over to her table and pushed her yoga mat into her backpack and picked up her jacket. After slurping down the last of her tepid drink, she flew up the stairs, out of the building and towards the music.

* * *

Sometimes rhythm isn't a thing that we control; it's an objective force, an animate power that takes our hands and our hips and moves them on our behalf.

This is what Tania was thinking as she watched her hands bring out each beat on the sordo. Her heart beat at double the rhythm as the cold evening air faded away. The rows of troopers became nothing more than distant blue lines on the periphery of her consciousness. Only her hands and the sticks remained: wood and cloth held together with reused duct tape and sheer tenacity. Each beat thrown into the air lifted her heart; each tricky slip into a new break and back out again, each change of rhythm rising to a crescendo. Silent understandings passed between her and the rest of the band she knew so well, a glance, a wink.

This rhythm that controlled Tania's hands came from

somewhere else. It wasn't only in the deep belch of the sordo or the high song of the agogo. It wasn't only hiding under the skin of the tambourine, waiting to be released into existence. The hands of the maestra couldn't create it by themselves, they could only channel what was already in the air waiting for direction. Yet this rhythm was power. Drums from her homeland, hands and beats from the edges of her networks pounding out a rhythm in the streets. Beats that physically changed the troopers, how they stood, nervously gripping their weapons or unconsciously swaying in time. Beats that by some greater force had caused a standing demonstration of hundreds to become a moving sea of people, occupying the roads and blocking tram lines. But Tania barely noticed the city around her. She was under the spell of the rhythm, it was carrying her through the crowds, the flashing lights and the sheer energy of so many people. She was part of it now and hoped she would always feel this big.

* * *

The yoga teacher stepped into the dark street.

Oh, it's samba!

She had always dreamed of visiting Brazil some day; she just knew she'd love it.

Such happy people, such great parties.

As soon as she left the building, she was engulfed by the festivities. The music played and the road was filled with people dancing along, pulled forward by the rhythm, whistles and shouts and people hugging each other and smiling, great, wide smiles.

Now this is the perfect way to spend the evening.

She felt better immediately. Dancing was her favourite way

to release stagnant energy, to express herself. Alone, but surrounded by the crowd, the yoga teacher showed off her trained body, diving deep into the rhythm. She lifted her shirt slightly to make sure people would get a glimpse of her abs. She looked around, making eye contact with everyone she could. *I love this. I've earned this.*

But then something about the street party struck her as a bit odd.

Over to one side, she saw a sign that read 'Masculinity isn't neutral'. *Whatever that means.* And another with 'Vergent Power' painted in shocking pink.

At the back, somewhere near where she first entered the procession, people started chanting something that she couldn't quite make out. *That might even be one of the forbidden languages.* One of the samba bands had stopped playing to allow the chants to be heard. She took a strand of her long, blonde hair and nibbled on it for comfort. She started to look again at the faces around her.

Then the bands started back up and the rhythm caught her, pulling her along with the growing movement of bodies. *I'm just going to enjoy this. I work so hard. I deserve a break.*

She tied her jacket around her waist and started really going for it.

No more than ten minutes later, she was deeply entranced by the music. She didn't notice a rising tension coming from the back of the procession. Shouts lifted from the crowd and suddenly a trooper loudspeaker could be heard a few blocks away.

Troopers? But why?

The bands played on, but the yoga teacher was feeling less and less comfortable.

"But this is a street party", she blurted out to the person marching next to her. "A carnival, anyone can see that. The troopers must surely have better things to do."

The person returned a confused look and walked a little further away. There were sirens now, out in front of them, and flashing lights reflected off the buildings. Still the music played on.

After a while of some more enthusiastic dance moves, the yoga teacher realised that no-one else was dancing. The crowd was still moving forward but people had started walking— marching, even—and they weren't smiling as much as they had been before.

Suddenly there was a loud crash up ahead, and this time it wasn't a drum. The crowd pulled back instinctively, almost as a single organism, then regrouped and continued the inexorable push forward. Another bang and the crowd stopped all at once. A few people began to sit down in the road. The message got through and eventually everyone was sitting down on the asphalt. All except the yoga teacher. She looked around, panicked and confused.

"Get down!" urged the person she had spoken to before, who was sitting on the curb and offering her a hand. She made her decision.

This has gone quite far enough. I'm tired of this party.

She started looking for a way out.

But she was right in the middle of the street and there were too many people to get past.

And they're all sitting there like idiots blocking my path.

She tried to climb past a few members of the samba band but nearly stumbled over their instruments. She stepped on someone's foot and almost fell. Then another sound ahead of her drew her attention to the front of the crowd. Ahead of them, just up the street, there were lines and lines of State troopers. More military police than she had ever seen in her life. Horses and riot shields and things she had never imagined.

She felt suddenly, hopelessly exposed. She sat down right where she was without words for the fear inside her. From her very core, she started shaking.

* * *

It's getting dark. This has already become so much bigger than we expected.

Sitting on the cold asphalt, Tania's palms were wet. She wiped them against her jeans and tried to breathe. She felt her body, the shivers that ran up her spine, the pain of tension in her shoulders. She breathed again. In moments like these, it was all she could do to stay present.

We've got this.

She looked around her at the hundreds of her friends who sat in the road, breaking so many laws just by existing in the city, much less, blocking one of the main trainlines.

They had been building to this moment for weeks— strategy meetings, training, endless samba practice. *There's no way back from here.* Tania knew they had to see it through. These new laws couldn't pass quietly, sealing the fate of her loved ones. *And me for that matter.* She had to react. *We have no choice but to resist. This is how we survive.*

Her hands were balled into fists around the drumsticks and she consciously released them. She stood then and held the sordo up above her head. *Let's do this.*

* * *

A hundred people jumped abruptly to their feet. The samba band started up a nervous new rhythm as the crowd lurched towards the police. This time the yoga teacher didn't resist. She felt herself pulled along and even closed her eyes for a moment. A chant rose up and she joined it, not really understanding the words, but feeling suddenly part of something. Something bigger than herself. It was a feeling that she had talked about many times at work, but it had never felt like this before. She was more than her body, more than her breath. She felt endless.

* * *

Numbly, the yoga teacher watched the troopers attack the people closest to the front. There was a cacophony of shields and batons and banners and drums. Time slowed to a crawl and all the sounds of the demo faded away to white noise. She felt herself lift up and above the screaming crowd and float amongst the skyscrapers looking down over the scene, the troopers beating down with batons, the horses being pushed onwards to stomp over fallen bodies and discarded placards. She watched the violence taking place far below her and felt strangely at peace. She took in a deep breath. And another.

And then her trance was broken.

She stood alone in the road surrounded by nothing but the wreckage of the demo. She could hear screams and sirens from somewhere in the next block, but around her was just the aftermath. She rubbed dust off her shirt slowly, her mind empty, her hands feeling like they belonged to someone else. Only then did she notice blood on the concrete.

"This was...supposed to be a party", she said to herself, her words slow and sticky in her mouth. She reached out to steady herself, but there was nothing. She collapsed onto the blood-slick street.

Chapter five

Ash, the soup won't be enough. Shall we make some more flat breads?" Pinar stood in the Home's kitchen, waving a wooden spoon as she spoke. Ash was deep inside the larder moving things around. "We need to fill people up and there isn't nearly enough fruit to go around."

"Did you say something, Pin?" Ash backed out of the larder with her hands full of bags, one hoop earring slightly askew. "How can I possibly hear you with my head in a cupboard? Oh, by the way, I found some flour in here. Why don't we make some more flat breads? People are hungry!"

Pinar smiled patiently. "That's a great idea, love. I'll find us a pan."

The two women moved efficiently around the tiny kitchen preparing extra snacks for the evening. They had always been this coordinated: just as Ash needed some hot water, Pinar had already put it on the heat. Just as Pinar was looking for a bowl, Ash had already put one out for her to use. They had been making these evening visits for several years and had been cooking together for decades longer than that. Despite its tiny size and cold, industrial fittings—normal for a building that had once been a prison—the Home kitchen was one of their favourite places to spend time together. Their conversation was light, their bodies were relaxed. They rarely felt this free.

* * *

X, the yoga teacher, pulled herself up to sitting. She was still catching her breath.

She was vaguely conscious how she must look, sitting in a public street mumbling to herself. Her hair was damp, and her hands were shaking uncontrollably. *I need to go home. I need to be safe again.*

"Are you okay?"

The voice came from her left. X turned her head slowly. She smiled compulsively.

"I'm fine, thank you!" Even to her, her voice sounded too cheerful.

The person flashed a worried look.

Must be a vergent, X noticed. *A shaved head, and those ugly builder's trousers.*

"Some of us are gathering at the Clinic tonight," Tania continued. "If you need a safe place to be. It's been a hell of an evening."

X had no idea what 'the Clinic' was but she was fairly sure she didn't want to follow this person anywhere. *No...stop that,* she told herself. *We've both been through hell tonight. And this person is showing you care.*

"Thank you!" she replied brightly. "I'll be okay, I'm just going to go home and get some dinner." She stumbled to her feet. Tania offered her hand, but X waved it away.

"Sure you're okay?"

"I'm fine, no worries. Have a great evening!" X turned towards home.

As she walked through the cold streets, shivers of fear still emanating out from her belly, X couldn't remember a time when she had felt so distraught. It was all she could do to make it back to her neighbourhood. As she let herself into her home, the shivers finally subsided and sensations of her body came back again. *I'm hungry*, she noticed. *I haven't eaten all day.*

* * *

Standing in the Home kitchen, elbow deep in dough, Pinar pointed at the work counter with her hip. "Could you clean away the rest of the stuff, love? The last thing we need is for the Home to find out about our little Sunday gatherings."

Ash nodded and started putting the last of the paper bags of food back in the larder, puffing them out a bit to make them look fuller.

Pinar pressed the dough into little flatbreads. In perfect synchronicity, Ash appeared to light the fire and heat up the pan. Pinar started passing her the little patties to toast. Ash poked at them with a spatula.

"I'm a little nervous," admitted Pinar. "How do you think this evening will go?"

"It'll be okay. I would definitely like to hear Elias sing tonight and I kind of want to get Oscar drunk again."

Pinar lifted one eyebrow and gave her a look that Ash knew far too well.

"I meant the *meeting...*".

"Oops, well...yes. It will be a meeting, so you know, it'll go on too long, people will spend a lot of time talking about things and not really making any plans—". While the patties cooked, Ash leaned back against the counter and Pinar joined her. "—someone will probably bring up a decision that we already worked through months ago and we'll have to do it all over again." Ash scratched her stubble absently. "And most importantly, my personal favourite, there will be at least one person in the room who disagrees with everything and disrupts the whole thing until we collectively ignore them. At some point, Oscar will get over emotional. Someone else will complain about the food. And I'll probably have a little nap."

Pinar chuckled. "You're such an old cynic, my love."

"I'm *sixty-nine*. I get to be as cynical as I want." Ash flipped the patties and turned to face her friend with her hands on her hips—practically her signature posture. "You're no spring chicken either, Pin. You may still look like you're thirty, with that perfect skin—" Ash waved at Pinar's face with the spatula. "—and all that ridiculously luxuriant hair...but I swear down, when *I* was fifty-five, I was already as jaded as I was ever going to be."

"I remember very well." Pinar gave her friend a wink and started scooping the flatbreads into a bowl. "But my love, I also recall that many times that 'one difficult person in the meeting who couldn't agree with anyone' was, in fact, *you*."

Ash had no response to that. With a little "hmf" she picked up the bowl and swooshed off to the Living Room.

* * *

Walking down the stuffy corridor, her hands full of plates and forks, Pinar could almost physically feel the excitement from the living room. She stepped through the open door and was instantly enveloped in human warmth and the sound of the community reuniting.

"Pinar!" Elias, one of her oldest friends, shouted to her from across the room. He sat deep in his chair but pushed himself to stand up as soon as he saw her. Pinar couldn't wave without dropping her stack of plates. She flashed him a smile instead.

Elias headed over to her at a brisk pace, threading his way through the crowd. "Put all that down and hug me already!" She did so, and they stood for a while in a warm embrace. "I've missed you, girl."

"I've missed you!"

26

"This place is a shithole when you're not here."

Pinar looked around her, taking in the yellowing walls, the beaten-up furniture and the blank TV screen up in the corner that had finally burned out after being left on twenty-four-seven for almost a decade. There were no clocks of any kind. When every hour of every day was the same, it was better not to track the passing of time. "I know, love. I wish we could come more often."

"You're busy, I get it. I wish I could escape more often but I've been sick, and the staff here don't let us out much." Elias cast a glance at Yarrow who was busy helping people be seated. "I wouldn't want their job to be honest. They do what they can, but the management are total assholes. Come, let's sit down. I want to catch up."

He led her over to his favourite corner and sat back down in his armchair, releasing a cloud of dust that sparkled a little in the candlelight. "Sit next to me," he said, patting the equally old chair next to him.

"I will, I will. Let me just put the food out and I'll be right back, okay?"

Elias gave her a shady look she knew too well.

"Just when you have time, I know you're busy."

Pinar automatically looked at the floor and bowed her head. She called over to Ash who was still standing near the door looking overwhelmed, gripping the bowl of bread. She put down the bowl and came over.

"Would you be okay to put the food out by yourself?" Pinar asked softly.

"Sure thing. Oh hey, Elias."

"Hey Ash. Are you good?"

"I'm fine. Tired and old."

"Same girl, same."

"Let's catch up in a bit, there's a hungry crowd to feed and

apparently no-one else is capable of putting soup in a bowl."
Ash headed back to the food table where a queue was already
forming.

Pinar chuckled as she sat down in the chair next to Elias.

"God, the two of you together—you're just a party full of
puppies, aren't you?"

Elias ignored that and took her hand. Pinar felt that it was
cold and clammy.

"You've been sick?" she asked. *He's pale too*, she noticed.
Elias' skin was usually just slightly darker than hers and
normally shone with health. *He's not doing well.*

"I'm fine. Same old really. The staff here just want to fill me
with drugs—I complain too much and they're using meds to
shut me up."

"Do you want me to speak to someone?" Pinar asked.

Elias shook his head. "It won't help. I've been a cog in the
medical industry since they discovered penicillin. My body is
fifty percent pharmaceutical at this point."

Pinar rubbed his hand softly. "I brought you some more
herbs from the garden. Let's find a minute later to talk about
what you need?"

"Good plan."

"Are you singing for us tonight?"

Elias took his hand back and rubbed his arthritic knuckles.
"That food smells good..."

Pinar couldn't help but smile. "Let me get you a plate."

* * *

X walked through her dining room to the master bedroom.
She collapsed into bed, realising as she did, that she was too
exhausted to cook, or shower, too tired even to go to the

stretching room for her regular evening practice. *I haven't skipped a session in years. And I'm filthy.* She just wanted to sleep, to hide. She couldn't begin to process everything she had been through.

Just a regular workday. Cute soldiers. Some overpriced tea. And then everything went to hell.

* * *

Oscar sat up in his wheelchair, cleared his throat and spoke loudly. "Welcome everybody!"

The room quietened down immediately.

"And thank you, Elias, for your beautiful song. You really are something."

Oscar winked at Elias from across the room and Elias in turn blew him a kiss from his armchair. Oscar blushed and cleared his throat again.

Although he and Elias lived together as residents in the Home, they could never spend enough time together. They couldn't always be this open, but on Resistance night, they let loose.

"Ahem...thank you. Yes, so...we have a lot to cover tonight and I'm going to dive right in."

Sat next to Elias, Pinar whispered in his ear. "You two are fucking adorable."

Elias grunted and whispered back. "Can't you see there's a meeting going on?"

At the front of the room, Oscar began the meeting. His curly brown hair had grown long, and he had to flick it out of his eyes every few minutes. The more animated he got, the more he flicked it. Elias found it incredibly sexy.

"As usual, we'll conduct the meeting mostly in English and to be inclusive of our Deaf and hard of hearing members, we'll simultaneously use Resistance Sign—or what the State has come to call 'its' Universal Sign Language. As if that makes any sense anyway! As if *they* invented it for fuck's sake!"

He flicked his hair, fiddled with his fingers for a brief second and when he looked back up, Elias gave him a generous smile.

"Ahem..." Oscar continued. "Anyway, yes, unlike the State, we don't ban languages here, so use whatever feels comfortable and we will work out translation as we go."

Seated on a floor cushion in the corner next to Pinar, Ash rolled her eyes at her friend. Meetings had begun with the same agreements for a very long time. Pinar smiled back.

"I know some of you are fairly new here," Oscar said, finding his rhythm again. "For those who aren't used to being in Resistance spaces, a quick note on naming. Here we believe in self-determination, so we are free to use our *full* names, not just the State's one-letter-per-citizen system."

Following a long tradition of states and dictatorships controlling how people named themselves and their children, the State had imposed a rigid naming system on its citizens. According to their propaganda, it was to simplify life, but everyone knew that state bureaucrats simply didn't want to deal with names they considered foreign-sounding—and they certainly didn't want trans people renaming themselves. It had been bureaucratically simple—especially common names had been given additional numbers, M1, M2 etc for official use— and everyone had adapted quickly to the new system. Taking away people's self-determination had been every bit as powerful as the State bureaucrats had hoped.

Oscar flicked his hair twice. "We don't need their social

control! Why the fuck should the State decide what we call ourselves? We're not their kids or their pet fish or something! We're not...ahem..." He exhaled. "Sorry again. I guess these things still make me emotional."

Oscar looked around, making eye contact with the rest of the room. "Check consent, take care of each other, be nice. You know how this goes."

* * *

Curled up as small as she could be in her over-sized bed, in the third bedroom of her over-sized house, X felt a deep cold seeping into her bones. She rarely felt lonely, in fact she had always prided herself on her independence. She hadn't had a boyfriend in years, and she liked her life just fine.

But as she gripped her pillow with both hands, her mind racing with horrific images, X realised she felt suddenly, terribly, alone.

I want tonight to be over.

Chapter six

T his is going to be a very *special* night!" Oscar announced, looking over in the direction of Ash and Pinar. "We have the great honour of having two Resistance celebrities with us to be our facilitators..."

Ash knew what was coming and shuffled uncomfortably in her seat.

"The famous A and P—Ash and Pinar—of the Femme Riots!"

The room burst into applause; Ash's cheeks turned a dark shade of crimson and Pinar looked at the floor, waiting for the clapping and snapping to finish.

Neither of them was very comfortable with the fame that organising the riots had brought them, but Pinar knew it was well-deserved. These gatherings, even the Resistance itself, might not have existed in its present form without their decades of work in the City.

People were now actually whooping with excitement. Pinar sympathised with her friend's discomfort. Not everything about fame had made their life easier. *The increased State surveillance for one thing*, she thought, as the noise finally began to die down. Pinar took Ash's hand and the famous A and P of the Femme Riots stood up.

* * *

X sat bolt upright in her bed. Her hair was in tangles, her pillow wet with tears. Stepping into the en-suite, she saw in the mirror that her mascara had run all down her face. *I'm a mess.*

Seeing herself just made her feel worse. But, as she gripped the sink with both hands, she found it hard to look away from her reflection.

Something has changed.

I've changed.

X caught her reflection giving just a hint of a smile. She knew what she had to do.

* * *

"Thank you for that lovely introduction, Oscar." Pinar's tone was soft and controlled. *She has such a comforting voice as a facilitator,* Ash thought to herself as she wiggled in her seat. Her body was wound too tight to relax, so she gave up and sat awkwardly with one leg draped over the chair arm.

She knew her friend was much more at ease with the public recognition their work had brought them than she was. She also knew that Pinar preferred to work quietly in the background and had done that for a long time as well.

If the movement needed a figurehead, Pinar was ready to step up; as she was fond of saying: "My comfort isn't the point—I'll do whatever it takes to get the job done." As Pinar put together an agenda for the meeting, her back straight; her smile, radiant, Ash couldn't help but admire her. *She deserves all of this. She's beautiful.*

Voices rose near the corridor as a tall woman appeared in the doorway. She wore a tracksuit and her sneakers were visibly worn out, her cheeks were red and dotted with beads of sweat. She leaned against the doorframe, catching her breath.

Ash recognised the woman. *One of the Resistance runners. Which can only mean bad news.*

Chapter seven

Ash looked over to the runner who sat on the ground, pulling her fingers through thick, frizzy hair, still full of nervous energy.

She had been speaking for twenty minutes—barely taking a breath—about the violence at the demonstration. After marching all afternoon and supporting those injured by the troopers, she had been dashing between Resistance spaces to deliver the news. Ash was impressed. *I never had that much energy in my life.*

"Mercifully no one was seriously injured, just a few cuts and scrapes which we've been treating at the Clinic. Several people have been detained and are being held at a trooper station on the edge of town."

Ash knew the meeting would now stretch on much longer than anticipated while the Resistance decided on a course of action. She stifled a yawn.

"Thank you for your report, I guess we have a lot to talk about. Can someone get some food for...sorry what was your name again?"

"Julia."

"Please rest a bit, Julia. Once we've come to a decision, we might need you to carry a message to the other collectives, if that's okay of course."

Julia smiled, jumping up to get herself a plate.

Ash had the sense that she was probably happiest when running through the streets, full of purpose and endorphins.

I can't relate in the slightest.

* * *

X already felt better as she stepped into the stretching room. The new cleaner had done a pretty good job. As she switched on the bamboo lamp, the polished wooden floor glistened in the gentle light. X rolled out her brand-new yoga mat. She was glad to notice that the lilac purple went perfectly with her tights.

She dived into downward dog, enjoying the feeling of power it always gave her. *My calves are tight, this might take a while. But I will stretch all night if I have to. Tomorrow will be a big day, maybe the biggest day. Tomorrow I will join the Resistance. Tomorrow I will become a verger.*

* * *

Ash stretched. "So, to recap, there will be a solidarity demonstration at the trooper station first thing in the morning for those detained at the action today —" she looked over at the light just beginning to seep in through the curtains. "— which is in a couple of hours now, I guess. And from the evening there'll be a strike by the sex worker collective to protest this new anti-femininity law. What did they call it again?"

"Article twelve," Pinar reminded her. "The Gender Expression Neutrality Law."

"That's the one. *Awesome* name by the way." Ash sighed. "It never ends, does it? Is there anything else or can this old lady get some sleep?"

A young cis woman who had spoken several times during the meeting stood up. Her arms were crossed, and she was pouting just a little. Ash had already forgotten her name.

"A reminder that I'm *still* vetoing this action," the woman announced. "Femininity is a social construct and we shouldn't be using the State's definitions even in our actions against them."

She looked imploringly around at the people sat near her. "As a woman, I personally find the idea of femininity oppressive. I mean, if people want to express themselves that way, I won't stop them, but—"

"Yes, yes," said Ash, losing patience. *Didn't you notice that the world is burning?* "It's all in the minutes—" She looked at Pinar for confirmation.

Pinar nodded and added: "I've written it all down. Consensus minus one with the option to hold a plenary on the subject sometime in February."

"Great." Ash stretched her arms up to the ceiling and yawned dramatically. "So hopefully *after* the revolution."

Pinar smiled. Her friend was rarely diplomatic but when she was tired, she lost her filter entirely.

"Pin, anything to add?"

"Nothing else. Thank you everyone for your time."

Ash yawned again and the meeting was over. With a much more subdued atmosphere than the beginning of the night, the Resistance cleaned the Home and began preparing to go back out into the street.

Pinar walked over to Yarrow, took a look at their crumpled uniform, and asked: "Do you need some help getting everyone back into bed?"

They flashed her a grateful smile. "That would be perfect, thank you."

Ash, Pinar and Yarrow stepped out of the front door of the Home. After helping to get some of the residents into bed and giving the Home a final tidy up, they were the last to leave. "Are you okay getting home, dear?" Pinar asked Yarrow. "We can walk you if you like?"

The sky was beginning to get lighter in the east, casting a pink glow over the commercial buildings all around them. Yarrow considered Pinar's offer for a moment but shook their head.

"Thank you, but you've done more than enough for me—for all of us, tonight."

"Sure?"

"I don't live far, I'll be okay. Will you two be alright?"

Ash gave them a tired smile. "We'll be fine. Being old makes us pretty much invisible these days."

"Okay, well, thank you for everything. It's really an honour to have you, and the others, here," Yarrow waved at the Home with one hand. "This is just a crappy placement for me but being part of all this…it gives me hope."

"Good night, Yarrow," said Ash, taking Pinar's hand and stepping down into the road. "Get home safe."

"You too."

Chapter eight

F uck this, why do we live so far away again?" Ash was panting and despite the cold and drizzle, her brow was beaded with sweat.

Pinar stopped and looked at her. "We're here now, love. We can rest on this bench before we face the stairs if you like."

Ash glared at the graffitied bench in front of them, damp in the drizzle with one slat broken and the other missing entirely. Then she looked up at the nine-story building that was their home and gave one of her dramatic sighs. "Let's keep going."

As they stepped up to the front door, their neighbour, Cleo, appeared from inside, accompanied by an older white man in military uniform. They stood aside as she gave him a peck on the cheek. Throwing a shady look at Ash and Pinar, the soldier left the scene as quickly as he could. Cleo waited until he was out of sight and ran up to her friends. She was dressed lavishly, and Ash noticed that she smelled like lilies.

"Ash! Pinar! How was the meeting?"

"Exhausting," Ash replied.

Pinar rolled her eyes. "It was good, thanks, Cleo. And you? How was your evening?"

"Also fine." Cleo looked a little bashful. "Sorry I couldn't make it tonight. Gotta pay rent...you know how it goes."

"We totally understand." Pinar gave her a warm smile and touched her shoulder. Cleo responded by softly touching Pinar's hip. Ash politely pretended not to notice.

"And this was the only one who actually turned up this week," Cleo said, moving her hand now to Pinar's lower back. "I swear down, there's a special place in hell for tricks who cancel at the last minute."

Pinar laughed and tucked a strand of hair behind her ear for no reason. "I hope so. But you still have Protection, right?"

Cleo nodded. "My regular, you just met him, keeps me covered."

"Well, good," said Pinar, squeezing Cleo's shoulder just a little. "I'm glad at least one of them is doing what he's supposed to. Is that a new dress?"

Cleo nodded and smiled, looking down at the tight, black fabric. "From one of my other tricks. No idea how he gets them, it was always difficult to get cute things in my size, but these days it's almost impossible."

"You look gorgeous."

"Thank you, Pinar. You too."

Ash gave an exaggerated yawn.

"Going up?" asked Cleo as she stepped back into the doorway.

Ash nodded. "Yes please."

The three of them climbed the first two floors to Cleo's flat. The clicking of her heels echoed through the dark stairwell. As she opened her door, the smell of incense drifted out of her studio. Apart from Ash and Pinar's place, most apartments in their building were playrooms and private spaces for sex work: just another of the many open secrets in the City.

"It's not what it used to be, is it?" said Cleo thoughtfully.

"Work?" asked Pinar.

"Yeah. I mean it's fine—it keeps me fed. And having an in-call space makes things pretty easy. But don't you miss the hang outs we had with the street workers—Angel, Cassie and the others. They were so tough and inspiring to be around.

Where even are they now?"

"As far as I know, everyone was incarcerated or deported beyond the walls," said Ash, her voice tight. "Sex work has been thoroughly gentrified."

"What do you mean exactly?" Cleo asked gently.

"Moved out of the public eye," Ash explained. "As part of 'cleaning up the City' or whatever. And you know that State officials—especially those with a reputation to maintain—are invested in keeping it that way."

Cleo looked down at the floor. "I'm one of the lucky ones, I guess."

The three of them fell quiet for a moment.

"Was there anything I should know about the meeting?"

Ash yawned. "Lots. But you'll be in the sex work collective meeting tomorrow I guess?"

"I will." Cleo stepped into her doorway and said brightly, "Anyway, time to sleep—nice to see you both! Have a good night."

Pinar stepped forward and Cleo pulled her in for a hug. "Night, love," she whispered in her ear. "See you again soon?"

"Definitely."

Cleo closed the door and Ash and Pinar continued their climb. Ash's eyes were only half open.

"I'm not going to make it!" Ash declared as they both paused between floor five and six. She was panting hard, gripping the banister with both hands to steady herself. "Go on without me. I'll just sleep here in the stairwell." She gave an exaggerated wave. "Remember me fondly! Don't look back!"

Pinar shot her a look of concern.

Their tiny apartment was on the top floor, without a lift, but they couldn't afford anything better. As their financial survival depended entirely on the support of their community and donations from their herb and bodywork clinic, they barely made rent month to month. Still, Ash and Pinar were grateful to still have their independence. Most of their peers, those who had survived, had been moved into places like the Home where the State could control them even more.

"I'm sorry, love. I hate this too." Pinar looked at the yellowing linoleum peeling off the wall to reveal spots of black mould. "I'm sorry that I couldn't find us something better...I'm sorry that..."

Ash took her hand.

"I'm just complaining, Pin. You've done everything you can—it's not your fault the State is a piece of ableist dogshit."

Pinar still looked worried.

"You know what?" Ash managed to force a grin. "There are snacks and tea at the top of these stairs, I'll race you to the top!"

And with that, Ash and Pinar pushed on up to their home for a well-deserved rest.

Chapter nine

The thrush flew up to his favourite singing post. A thick old plane tree standing outside a crumbling building. Humans came and went, but standing far off, the plane tree felt like a safe place for him to sing. He did so, with all of his proud heart. His voice was a part of this land, as polluted and noisy as it had become. With his trilling song, each phrase repeated three times, he was marking his individual territory. And singing to potential mates. But his ancestors had been singing to the sky, to their community, forever and this young bird was a part of that story as well.

A human was watching him from a window in the building. He had seen this human there before, listening to his music. He sang loudly.

She was enthralled.

* * *

Ash closed the window and climbed into bed. She picked up the cup of lemonbalm tea she had been drinking before the birdsong had pulled her over to the window.

"You know, Pin? We give too much of ourselves," she declared. As tired as she was, her mind was busy again processing the meeting.

"I know, love," Pinar came back from the bathroom drying her hands on an old cloth. "But we do it because we care." The electricity was out again, so she lit a candle and climbed into their hard bed. Ash let out a loud squeal.

"Your feet are freezing! Get over to your side!"

Pinar ignored her and snuggled up closer. "So, defrost me already. You're warm enough for both of us."

Ash tried to push her friend away, but Pinar was already in her favourite position, her head resting on Ash's chest. They lay like that for a while, Ash holding her tea with one hand and stroking her friend's long hair with the other. Pinar sighed with contentment. They had saved for a few months to get a really good duvet and she appreciated it every cold night.

"*Should* we care so much though?" Ash asked, putting down her empty cup. "I mean, sometimes I have the sense that we're still holding this whole thing together, that it would all fall apart without us. It shouldn't be that way, should it? Why is it always us doing everything?"

Pinar thought for a moment. "Honestly, I think it's always been like this. Movements are maintained by people like us— the ones who are ready to put the work in. The ones who care enough for others and are affected directly by the things we're fighting against."

"I suppose so. But it shouldn't always be the poor, sick femmes and people of colour showing up."

"It really shouldn't. But it also kind of makes sense. Our existence depends on us doing the work. If we stopped building community, who would take care of us? Or Oscar or Elias? Fighting the State, building our world, none of it is really optional for people like us."

"But that's kind of fucked up, Pin. I'm tired of losing friends we thought were in it for the long-term. I'm tired of them selling out because they can and because they were never that committed." Ash's voice was raised, her hands increasingly agitated. "I mean, burn out is very real, and we've both been there. But the privilege of treating activism like a hobby that you can drop when things get uncomfortable? That's just gross."

"I agree, hon. But it's a different starting point. For us, it's survival—"

"—as opposed to research for some fucking art project."

"Exactly."

They sighed in unison and fell silent, listening to the thrush singing outside the window for a moment. As difficult as their conversations could sometimes be, being together made everything seem more possible.

"I'm glad we're still doing this though, Ash." Pinar sat up next to her friend. "I know how you feel—sometimes all our care and work feel like they're just air, invisible labour that we're obliged to do because it's our feminine destiny or something. But it's also our strength. I wouldn't have gotten this far without you, and all your very fierce support. It means a lot to have you by my side, day in day out."

"Likewise, my love. I can't imagine any of this without you."

Pinar snuggled back down and Ash sighed again, softer this time.

"Can we please sleep now?" she asked with just the slightest sass. "I think I might actually be talking in my sleep."

Pinar leaned over her and blew out the candle.

Ash had never been a good sleeper. Since she was young, she had been anxious and for as long as coffee had been easily available, Ash had been compensating for her body's refusal to rest properly. Only exercise helped a little, or time off but that was so rare, she had stopped thinking in terms of 'days off' decades ago, much less 'weekends'. *There's always so much to do. If this strike happens tomorrow, there'll be a big fucking mess. And we need to co-ordinate with the garden people about another herb delivery. Fuck. There isn't time to sleep, there isn't—*

Next to her, Pinar's breath had deepened. Each exhale had become a soft sigh. Ash felt her friend get heavier on the mattress.

Ash noticed that her thoughts were becoming incomplete. *What was I thinking about? What was the thing—?*

And she slept.

Chapter ten

The fox den was quiet. The vixen laid down on her belly next to her mate. He licked her front paws; just as he did every night.

She had cut herself jumping a barbed wire fence a few weeks before. Her pads were finally beginning to heal, but they still itched. Her mate's warm tongue was the only thing that could bring her relief.

Their cubs had left before the cold had set in and the pair had settled down to survive the winter months. They had secured themselves good territory behind an abandoned shed in the city centre. Quiet and away from humans, there was plenty of food in the little scrubby patch of land that had once been a manicured backyard. They had stayed together for two winters.

This year was the biggest litter either of them could remember—twelve boisterous cubs, squabbling and playing and demanding a constant supply of bugs, chicks, berries, and whatever their parents had been able to find in the trash cans down the road. They were exhausted.

Her mate rolled over and she licked the back of his neck as he started to doze off. There was barely space for the two of them in their little hole and even that had taken them days to dig out together back in the spring. But she didn't often think that far back. Every day brought a new set of memories. The cycles of day and night. Cold and warmth. Food and hunger. She curled up a little closer and felt the warmth of her friend.

She fell asleep then, to dream of moonlight and eggs in a nest.

* * *

Ash was just emerging from a dream—something about a catfish in the forest—her head lost in a pillow, her eyelids too heavy to open fully.

"Ash! Ash get over here!"

"Pin, what the fuck—"

Pinar stood at the window and turned to face her friend. She was pale, her eyebrows raised in surprise, or fear, Ash couldn't tell. As she climbed out of bed, she heard the absolute silence. *There should be thrushes singing, blackbirds, robins. This isn't right.*

She reached Pinar and looked through the open window.

Down in the street below them stood Elias. Even from nine floors above and in the early morning twilight, Ash could see he was distraught.

"Elias?"

"Get down here!" he yelled. "It's Yarrow—they've been beaten!"

Ash saw them, crouched over on the broken bench, hands hiding their face, covered in blood.

2. Mutual Aid

Chapter eleven

A circle formed as daylight peeked through the shuttered windows of the Clinic. It was a tiny space, wedged between an abandoned library and a semi-legal kindergarten. So many things were contained in this autonomous community centre, often all in the same day. A migrant language centre. A supply point for trans folk to get hormones smuggled from beyond State borders. An extended living room and space for meetings. A herbal apothecary. A sanctuary for many in a hostile city.

That morning, for the first time, the floors swept, the chairs pushed out of the way, the Clinic would become a direct-action training room. The instructor looked at herself in the cracked bathroom mirror, her shaved head just beginning to stubble again, her dark eyes bright, despite her chronic lack of sleep. She had the sense that she could almost hear the whispers of the hundreds of people who had passed through the space that week, that month, that year, a gentle susurro of memories that settled with the dust.

Tania stepped out of the bathroom. Without windows or ventilation, it was stuffy but at least it was fully wheelchair-accessible—the Resistance had priorities. A room full of students looked up at her with expectation, nervousness, and excitement. Tania could feel their anxiety seeping into her body, their tension and shallow breathing mixing in with hers. She found herself remembering the demonstration from the night before. Her body began to relive that fresh trauma. *So much violence, so much fear.*

I need to shut that down. Stop.

Sensitivity was one of the things that made Tania such a caring and well-respected teacher. But she also needed to maintain boundaries, especially with a group as nervous as this one. She knew she would need time to process.

But this isn't the time for that.

She got her breath under control first, dropped her shoulders, lifted her chest. She noticed a certain sensation in the room. Something just beyond her understanding. Powerful, yet familiar.

"Let's begin."

The morning developed much as she had hoped. The group focused on consent discussions, action strategising and roleplays. Laughter filled the room, people became friends, triggers and fears were faced or overcome. Two hours passed by in a blur of learning, teaching and sharing. As the circle formed for the last time to close the workshop before the workday began, she looked around the room at her students and friends. A circle of twenty Resistance members, a group as diverse as their footwear. She began to suspect that she might recognise what the feeling was.

There are times when a person is in just the right place doing just the right thing; there's a certain political clarity, a moment where everything suddenly falls into line, when the past and the future seem to merge into the moment. This was not the first time Tania had connected to the importance of her work, her place in the movement. She rested her hands on her knees, breathed in deeply to focus and continued the closing comments and questions.

Eventually the circle was broken, and the group began to leave amidst giggles, hugs, discussions, and promises to stay in touch. She scooped up her things—her shoes, empty water bottle and untouched notes—and headed for the door following the last student out.

Standing in the doorway, she turned and looked over her precious space—the stacked chairs and political posters, the dawn light reflecting off the shuttered windows and the shelves of herbs in jars along one wall.

"Thank you", she whispered and gently closed the door.

Chapter twelve

Ash threw open the Clinic door.

"Good, it's empty. Pin, get out the futon and sheets. Elias, please put some water on to boil."

Elias nodded and went to the kitchen at the back. There was no separation between the rooms, and they could hear Elias opening and closing cupboard doors looking for a pan.

"Yarrow, let me sit you down here for a moment. We're going to set everything up and treat your injuries. How are you feeling?"

Yarrow sat down in a chair, their expression empty. Since they had stopped crying on the walk to the Clinic, they hadn't made a sound. Ash gave them a worried look, then went to help Pinar set up the mattress.

"They're not doing well," she said to her friend under her breath as she stuffed a pillow into its case.

"No. But I think we have what they need." Pinar turned to Elias who was standing by the door. "Are you off, love?"

"Yes, water's on, but I'd better get back before they notice I'm missing. The Home staff don't much care for runaways." Elias nodded at Yarrow. "Present company excepted."

Yarrow didn't respond; they were picking at their fingers with a vacant expression.

"Please take care of Yarrow," Elias said softly as he opened the door. "We need them."

An hour later, lying down on the futon, Yarrow's body started shaking. Ash had cleaned their wounds, which were relatively superficial, but they were still in a bad way. Pinar sat on the other side of the futon, her face etched with concern.

"What do you need?" she asked, but Yarrow was silent. Ash lightly touched their hand, could feel the shakes rocketing through their body—still no response.

"Yarrow, you're in shock. I'm going to make us some more tea, but I'm nearby, okay? We're not going to leave you." She thought she detected a small nod but wasn't sure. She helped Pinar tuck a giant blue blanket around their body and then crossed over to the tiny kitchen.

Ash busied around, opening the jars of herbs that Pinar had collected over the years and prepared a teapot. She was worried, distracted. She bent down to get some cups from the bottom shelf.

I should have seen this coming. I mean, I don't always. But I usually know something's up. We should have walked them home, we should have—

Ash stood up and hit her bald head on a cupboard door that she'd left open. She yelled and stepped backwards knocking over a bin. She stood, rubbing her head and staring at the mess for a good twenty seconds.

"Fuck. It. All."

Pinar called her: "Are you okay, hon?"

"I'm awesome", Ash declared, pushing back tears and giving the rubbish bin a kick for good measure.

Chapter thirteen

The garden was in its final days of the year. The first frosts had come at night and even the earthworms had started burrowing deeper in anticipation of the cold ahead. Near the edge of town, people were busy on the squatted plot of land as the garden team gathered to prepare for winter.

It was an intimate process, slowing down after the frantic days of the summer. The land was quieter now. The workers co-ordinated with barely a word as they harvested sage leaves and the last remaining rose petals. Some of the vegetable beds had been planted with green manure; enriching plants that would keep the soil protected during their absence. The rest, the group covered in straw. They threw withered crops onto the smallest of three compost heaps, giving the others a stir with a fork to keep the fertile mixture aerated. Their work was efficient and quiet.

No-one could be sure if they'd be able to keep the land for another year.

No-one knew how long it would take the State to find out about what they had done here.

* * *

"Yarrow, I'm going to do some bodywork for you now," Ash said softly, kneeling at the bottom of the futon. "It'll help you to feel a bit better. I'll use this—" She held up a small cloth ball with a handle made of the same cloth tied up with string. "—We call it a herbal ball: it's herbs from the Resistance garden, rolled up in this cloth. I'll heat it up in the steamer—" she indicated the little rice cooker that was already bubbling and releasing steam through the lid "—and then kind of stamp it over your legs, arms and back. It feels good and will help unblock some of your muscles."

And reground you in your traumatised body, she thought. *When you're ready for that.*

Pinar handed Yarrow some loose trousers and a shirt. "Here are some clothes to change into—is all this okay? If you'd prefer to just rest, that's fine as well."

Yarrow looked at the clothes then looked back to the cloth ball in Ash's hand.

"Herbs?" they asked distantly.

"Rose petals, comfrey, peppermint—anything else, Pin?"

"Some chamomile and nettle, I think."

"I like peppermint tea," said Yarrow softly.

"Perfect." Ash dropped the herbal ball back into the steamer. "Then let's make a start."

* * *

Barely nine months before, the land of the garden had been poisoned and piled high with trash. Located in one of the poorest neighbourhoods in the City, the State had apparently forgotten about it, so locals had started clearing the area and growing for their own needs. In the warmer months, the garden collective had offered the space as a meeting point for a local Resistance chapter. The collective of three soon grew to ten, then thirty.

They had started by growing bioremediating herbs—sunflower and willow to absorb arsenic and cadmium. They had planted fast-growing poplar saplings to remove lead and later cut them down and turned them into building materials for the raised beds. They built compost heap on top of compost heap to bring some nutrition back to the damaged soil. The garden had grown faster than they could have imagined; the land was richer than it had been in decades.

No-one had dared hope that they might keep it for a whole growing season, but they had been organised and determined to grow what they could, to heal the soil as fast as possible. Every day on the land had felt like a blessing.

Finally, the work was done for the day, and the collective came together around the fire circle to enjoy the warmest part of the day. As they drank tea and shared food together, a curious robin watched them from an elder tree. The digging had brought worms to the surface and all the new straw would surely contain some interesting bugs. The robin took a last look at the humans to be sure they were still busy, then hopped down and went to investigate.

Spiders, worms, a particularly juicy grub. The robin was having a feast, her feet sinking into the warm straw. A sound above drew her attention and she looked up. Two lines of geese flew overhead, filling the air with the contact calls of their long migration. The sky was unusually blue and clear. It was a perfect day.

When breakfast was over, the garden workers, hushed by the quiet land, softly said their goodbyes. "Until next year," they whispered to each other, and to the land, and they headed back into the concrete of their city.

* * *

The air of the Clinic was thick with the heady scent of lavender. Yarrow's body had given into exhaustion and they were sleeping on the futon under several thick blankets.

"Ash, will you be okay if I go out for a couple of hours?" Pinar stood near the door, fiddling with her hair. She looked intently at the floorboards. "I...had a date scheduled and kind of have no way to cancel it."

Ash looked up from the steamer where the herbal balls were reheating.

"Of course, dear. I've got this."

"Thank you."

Through the cloud of steam, Ash flashed her friend a cheeky grin. "Give him my love."

Pinar laughed. "You know I won't. I'm not sure he's quite ready for my real life yet."

"After all this time..." Ash scratched her head thoughtfully. "I'll meet him one day though, Pin. Either on our side of a riot line—or his."

Pinar shifted her weight awkwardly. "I know, it's complicated..."

Ash held up the wooden stick she was using to stir the water and waggled it at her friend.

"Oh please...*life* is complicated. I can both hate the State and be happy for you dating a State-worker at the same time. Anyway, there's no good job in this godforsaken place. As long as he's still treating you right?"

"He is."

"And worshipping you as the goddess you are?"

Pinar ignored that.

Ash waved her spoon at the door. "Get out of here. Go have

some fun!"

Pinar picked up her jacket and stepped out. She heard the loud honks of geese somewhere above and looked up automatically, hoping for a view. The sky was crowded with buildings and smog.

Chapter fourteen

Their journey had begun. For the young goose, this would be his first full journey and he had no idea what to expect. He didn't need to. This morning, he had felt the urge, the tangible buzz of the flock as they woke up in the flooded fields where he and his siblings were born. The drive to leave was irresistible. There was barely time to eat before they were in the sky together, forming the lines that came so naturally to his kind.

Pushing ahead and opening the air for the others was exhausting, so each took their turn at the front of the V before moving back to rest their wings. The young goose looked briefly down. An epic grey city stretched out below them. Buildings, asphalt, walls. He lifted his head to look at the horizon ahead, and the future. It would be his turn at the front again soon. He beat his wings and pushed forward.

* * *

"Can you stand?"

Yarrow sat up and attempted a weak smile. "I'll be fine. I have to be—I have a shift this evening."

Ash stood, her hands on her hips, assessing her patient. "I'm not super happy about you going back to work so soon."

"I really don't have a lot of choice. I'm sure you know how hard it is to get a placement these days—even one as undervalued and underpaid as mine."

"Of course," said Ash with a scowl. "I mean, you're only taking care of people, keeping them alive, giving them dignity in their last years—why would anyone value that?"

Yarrow's smile turned into a grin. "I knew you'd understand."

"Do you feel ready to talk about what happened yet?" Ash asked carefully.

Yarrow shook their head. "There isn't much to say really. I think you can guess—a group of drunk guys, the wrong street on the wrong night." They sighed. "But thank you, Ash. You and Pinar turned this day around for me. I'm honestly feeling much better."

"Take care, Yarrow, and do let us know if you need anything or if you want to talk more. We won't be back to the Home until the next meeting, but you know where we live now so come find us if you need to."

"Thank you. Could we hug?"

Ash pulled Yarrow into a gentle embrace. Although she wasn't always fond of physical touch, she was beginning to feel real affection for this person, and it was a nice way to end a healing session.

"Bye, love."

As Ash opened the door to let Yarrow out, she heard voices outside—a strange conversation was taking place in the street.

Chapter fifteen

Y ou're mine."

"Yes, Mistress. One hundred per cent."

"You exist to please me."

"I do, Mistress."

The Mistress handed the younger man a piece of paper—a valuable commodity that she'd had him steal from his office.

"Read."

He knelt, bound at the wrists and ankles and dressed in the tight grey suit he wore for the State. He had to shift his position slightly so he wouldn't fall over. His Mistress tutted impatiently as he adjusted his body within the ropes, wobbled a bit and finally took the paper.

"Don't make me repeat myself."

The sub avoided eye contact, swallowed and immediately began reading.

"I exist to please my Mistress and will obey all the rules of our most up-to-date contract, of which this article forms a constituent, binding part." He inhaled quickly. "Article seven. Paragraph three. During this session, I will put aside all thoughts..."

"Slow down."

The sub obeyed and continued.

"...I will put aside all thoughts of myself, all political opinions and assumptions that I have developed before today. I will format myself as pleases my Mistress and become a tool for her use, an extension of her body, existing only for her pleasure and to meet her needs."

She noticed his hands were shaking. Excitement, nerves, who could tell? This certainly wasn't the first time they'd started a session with a refresh of their agreement, but recently she had noticed her sub becoming more nervous. Small signs, barely perceptible except to someone as sensitive as her. She had been politicising him more in the last months, increasingly finding ways for him to support her work, moving beyond using him purely for sex and kink and pleasure. And she knew—because she knew him so well—that he was questioning himself. She could sense him processing silently about how far he was willing to go, even now, tied up on her kitchen floor, eager to serve her throughout the afternoon.

She considered it a good sign in general—self-awareness around boundaries was part of what made a good sub—but doubt in the mix was always something to watch out for. She noticed that the sub had stopped reading.

He knows me well, too, she reflected.

"I'm listening. Continue."

"Yes, Mistress. Within my boundaries, established in this contract and negotiable only within the spaces set by my Mistress according to Article One, I will push myself to do the best work I can. I will not...ahem...*resist*, push back or disobey."

The Mistress smiled. Resist was one of several words forbidden by the State, only ever spoken in public between trusted friends. When she had written this particular article of their contract—or more accurately, had her sub write it for her, collared and chained to the floor, barely able to lift the pen—she had smiled too, watching him squirm as he wrote that word, marking their crime in black and white.

"I will strive to be all that I can for this purpose. And I am grateful for this opportunity to serve the..." The sub's throat closed up and he coughed once to clear it. "Sorry, Mistr..."

"Say it."

"And I am grateful for this opportunity to serve the Resistance."

"Again."

And he started from the beginning, giving voice to the binding and ever-expanding contract that had guided their years together.

* * *

"But I want to help! Why won't you let me in?"

The voice was piercing. Ash didn't recognise it.

"This is a private apartment, I'm sorry, we don't let strangers in."

That gravelly voice she knew—it was Tania who ran the Resistance kindergarten next door and organised meetings and trainings in the Clinic. *She sounds stressed.*

"Isn't this the Resistance clinic? I'm sure I've got the address right."

Ash's heart jumped. *What is this about?*

She stepped out of the door to find out.

"Who are you?" she demanded, hands on hips, her lips thinned.

"I'm X. I'm a yoga teacher."

Ash gave her a puzzled look. "Okay..."

"I want to offer my services to the Resistance!"

Ash and Tania shared a glance.

Tania crossed her arms. "Look, lady, you need to stop using that word."

X put up her hands defensively. "No, no. I'm *sympathetic*. I was in a *demonstration* yesterday and... I want to help. I would love to offer community classes or private tuition. I could even teach next door—" she gestured towards the kindergarten. "—please, I just want to be useful. I think what the State is doing is terri—"

For god's sake. Ash grabbed the yoga teacher by the shoulder and dragged her inside the clinic. Tania followed after and closed the door.

"Would you *stop* with that? If someone hears us..."

"I'm sorry. I really just want to help. I want to be an ally to the vergent community."

Ash physically cringed at the word 'vergent'.

Once a relatively neutral term for anyone diverging from a common group—neurodivergents and eventually gender divergents, sexual divergents and so on—divergent had quickly become 'vergent' and even 'verger' and used as slurs against marginalised people. As slurs often are, they had later been reclaimed by vergents themselves, but Ash still found the words difficult to hear. *As long as I've been alive, we've been finding new words to describe ourselves. Fine. Whatever. But we're still screwed no matter what we call ourselves.*

Standing near the door, Tania sighed impatiently. "Give us your address and we'll contact you if we find something for you to do. Please, you can't come here again until then."

X's face brightened. "Got it. Your secret's safe with me!"

Ash rolled her eyes.

X pulled a scrap of paper from her bag and scribbled her name and address down and handed it to Tania.

Ash opened the door. "Bye for now."

And with a little bounce, X left. Tania and Ash shared another glance.

"Well that was weird," said Tania, adjusting her black hoodie.

Ash leaned against a wall, suddenly drained of energy. "I

hope that person isn't going to become an important part of our lives. I don't think I could deal with a lot of that."

"Right? Although, I mean maybe she could be useful? It wouldn't be the worst thing for Resistance members to have some time to stretch and relax."

Ash sighed. "But you know it'll never happen. Our people have been cleaning up after her people—literally and figuratively—forever. She'll never follow through."

"Well, let's see, mate."

"Sure, let's see. And how are the kids? Is it still total chaos over there?" Ash pointed at the wall that separated the clinic from the kindergarten. She already knew the answer, she had heard screaming and crashing and squeals of laughter resonating through the wall since they arrived.

"It's okay. With all the new laws to protest, we don't have as many folk on hand right now so it's a bit wild. But the kids are good. Sometimes they even sit down and listen to each other, which must be our greatest achievement to date."

Ash smiled. "You deserve a medal. Maybe you could recruit Ms Yoga to help out? I'm sure the kids would love her."

Tania tried to keep a straight face. "That sounds great. But you know, I think she'd be much more at home here in the clinic with you. I don't know if you've heard, but yoga is good for everyone with a body! Chronically ill people especially. Everyone should do more yoga!"

"No, no. I *insist*..."

"No, no *really*!"

They both laughed.

"Well, I'd better get back to it before the little darlings start eating each other." Tania opened the door and glanced towards the kitchenette. "By the way, your rubbish bin fell over."

"Yes, thanks for noticing. Could you take it out for me actually?"

"Oh, is that an innocent child crying that I hear? Must rush—bye Ash!"

Ash closed the door behind her friend, flopped into a chair and allowed herself a little chuckle. She looked around the cramped space practically pregnant with the decades of support and care that had taken place here. She could hear a robin singing somewhere in the street. There weren't many places she felt safe in the City, but sometimes, just sometimes, this came close.

* * *

The Mistress laid back into the hotel armchair and her sub curled up on the floor, his head resting against her feet. Her chest was still heaving from the exertion of whipping him with the soft end of his own belt.

I love this, she thought. *It took some time, but this is really good.*

It hadn't always been this way. In fact, their relationship had come out of a most unexpected context—a meeting at a State accounting office. The day before, a trooper had come to deliver the message that the tax department had started looking into the finances of the clinic.

In the City, any autonomous care, especially healthcare, that wasn't sanctioned by the State was illegal. After the pandemics, mutual aid programmes had sprung up all over the city and the State was determined to stamp them out. Reliance on the State for safety and care was one of the few things that had kept it in power for so long.

As the clinic collective had finally found a new place to rent, a Protected sex worker in their networks had managed to get a signature on the right piece of paper and they had been able to make the clinic relatively official. But evidently so much coming and going at the busy little space was still raising suspicions. The tax department was demanding a full audit. Pinar had organised the meeting at the office in a fit of panic.

As her sub, now infinitely better trained, brought her a glass of water—anticipating her thirst before she even noticed it herself—and curled back up on the floor, Pinar allowed herself to daydream and remember that day.

* * *

F leaned forward and put his hands down on the glossy conference table just a little bit too hard.

"You didn't keep the envelope?"

His voice was steady, but Pinar could tell that he'd had enough. *How could I have known?* She was tired too—she wasn't used to being made to feel stupid.

"I...didn't. Was I supposed to?"

Unconsciously she moved her chair back to get a bit more distance. She had never been comfortable around male aggression, much less when the person had power over her. And F had power in spades. His carefully-ironed shirt, crisscrossed like a spreadsheet. *Those perfect brown shoes he must polish every day.* Even his eyes—strikingly blue and narrowed as she confessed her bureaucratic transgression—said clearly that he didn't negotiate. F the accountant leaned back in his chair, pushed one hand through his incredibly blond hair and sighed.

"P, was it?"

Pinar nodded.

"If you *get* a yellow envelope, you *keep* the yellow envelope. It comes with the date on which the Department of Finance sent it to you and that date will determine the process of the filing of the..."

Oh no, it's happening again.

Pinar didn't usually have trouble concentrating, but this, her first meeting with an accountant, was passing by in a blur. *Article something something needs to be filed with the duplicate copy of something else.* It meant exactly nothing to her. She was sure that F could have explained it in easier terms, but she also had the impression that he didn't want to. His job literally only existed because the State's tax laws were so confusing, and no normal person could understand the Life Accounts system.

And he knows it.

In Pinar's opinion, F seemed to enjoy the look of confusion and frustration she had been wearing for the last half hour.

He was still talking.

"...by fax to the department head of the..."

"Wait? Fax? What? Is this the eighties again?" Pinar threw her arms up, a gesture from her family she had never learned to repress. "I haven't seen a fax machine in twenty years—how does the State even have electricity for that? Are there even phone lines here anymore?"

F just stared at her.

Fuck. I've done it now.

"Look. You're in trouble, P."

She hated him.

"That's why you came to me."

But she knew he was right. She nodded helplessly.

"It's pretty serious. But I can help you."

Pinar reached for her glass but remembered that she had drunk all her water within the first two minutes of the meeting.

"We just need to...come to an arrangement. It'll take about ten hours for me to sort out this disaster you call paperwork—

" F waved a dismissive hand at her carefully organised pile of papers. "And you already know my hourly rate."

No. Impossible. Ten hours!

"I'm so sorry. I don't have that kind of money. I mean, you saw that I don't earn much. I'm sorry that I threw away the yellow envelope. I'm sorry that I didn't tick the box of article twenty-five—"

F took a sip of his water.

"Twenty-six."

Pinar knew she looked ashamed. She knew that F could sense her panic. She had come into this meeting with so much hope and such determination to not get frustrated with the ridiculous bureaucracy of it all. She'd thrown that away now and if she wasted this meeting, there was no way they could afford another one. Ash, and the clinic, were relying on her to get this right.

F continued. "But as I said, we can come to an arrangement."

"Okay..."

"You mentioned that you've done sex work in the past."

Pinar swallowed hard.

"Yes. But not for a while and besides there's nothing wrong wi—"

F showed his palms defensively.

"Not at all. I respect that work."

"Okay, so..."

"It's more that I imagine you might have some services that I could use..."

Pinar noticed her shoulders were aching and she let them drop a little. She inhaled deeply. "You're proposing some kind of exchange?"

F nodded and looked down at the table. He started playing with the condensation on his glass and for the first time, Pinar saw something of the little awkward boy in him. The teenager who was too good with numbers to be accepted by his classmates. The husband who bored his wife with stories of accounting and State tax law until she left him for a rugby player. The man who earned too much, had too much control over people's lives and secretly just wanted to be tied up and smashed.

"Yes...precisely."

F continued playing with his glass. Pinar could see the little circles of sweat under his armpits had expanded.

"My proposal is this: I would like to exchange accounting assistance and help you out of this mess—" They both unconsciously looked again at Pinar's pile of papers. "—for your hourly rate, of course...plus the 19%."

"For the VAT?" asked Pinar.

F smiled for the first time since the meeting had begun. "For the VAT."

Twenty minutes later, after he had dismissed his secretary and freshened up in the bathroom, F came back into the conference room. Pinar was waiting for him, reading through the consent list. She had made him fill it out in triplicate, just for fun.

"Close the door," she ordered, feeling slightly unreal. He closed the door.

"Strip."

For whatever reason, he started by untying his shoes and placing them carefully to the side of the room, perfectly aligned.

Like he does every night before bed, I can just imagine it.

He took off his socks—*grey, of course*—folded them and lay them over the shoes. He started fiddling with his belt, but Pinar had had enough.

"If this is going to work, you need to move a whole lot

faster—" She rechecked the checklist of words they had both consented to using. "—sub."

F complied and in thirty seconds he was naked. He stood next to the messy pile of clothes he had torn off—even his shirt wasn't folded. He smiled just a little and said:

"Ready, Mistress."

"Stop talking."

And F the accountant had stopped talking.

* * *

Years later, things had developed considerably. Their relationship had deepened beyond what either of them could have predicted. F no longer counted the hours of work he invested to help the Clinic. And Pinar had grown to look forward to their encounters.

"Using" her "sub" at their regular hotel marked a complete departure from the rest of her life of service to Ash, her friends and the Resistance. During these sessions, she could relax, be creative and most importantly get exactly what she wanted, exactly when she wanted it. She learned quickly that F wasn't as rich or as powerful as the illusion he had projected in that first meeting, but he often brought her gifts—which she diligently shared with those around her—and she had him trained well enough that, for those short hours together each week, she could forget her responsibilities, the endless pressure of holding her community together under fire, and just enjoy herself.

It worked well. And now it was time for Pinar to get back home.

Enough decadence for me. There's a revolution to organise.

* * *

Ash locked the clinic door with one hand and held the bag of garbage in the other, as far away from her face as she could manage.

She took the bag over to the top of a pile of other rubbish bags that had accumulated at the street corner. Her nose wrinkled at the flies and stench—her bag of old herbs and tea didn't smell nearly as bad anymore.

I guess the State's too busy evicting people and outlawing minorities to actually deal with little things like garbage collection.

She dropped her bag with a sigh and a small rat jumped out of the pile, gave an annoyed squeak and ran into the alley.

Back when the State had still cared about international diplomacy and its reputation, it had instituted a clean-streets system. Ash remembered the day after the policy was put into law—even the street outside her house in one of the poorest neighbourhoods was tidy and scrubbed clean. For a while, the City had some of the most bleach-shined streets in Europe. She also remembered hearing that all garbage was exported, taken beyond the City walls on a solar train and dumped out in the forest.

Which makes sense. Everything about this place is toxic. And where do they even make plastic bin bags in this day and age?

Ash rubbed her hands on her dress in a futile attempt to feel clean. Touching her clothes reminded her of the new law, and the risk it had brought.

Quickly, she tucked the frilly edges into her pants, put her hoops in a pocket and zipped up her long, grey coat to hide any sign of bright colours or what the State would surely consider 'gender-inappropriate clothing'. She turned away from the clinic, and safety, and headed out into the city. The short winter day was nearly over. A cold wind was blowing, the sky had completely clouded over.

Chapter sixteen

A wren called as he flew through the forest. His call echoed and hit resonance in the wood of an ancient oak. This oak who had been here for ten centuries. This oak who grew up in a time when the forest seemed to have no end. When the slightest of movements through the bushes gave away the presence of a wolf on the search for a new hunting ground. A time when the rivers ran clean and were slowed only by the life's work of beavers. When fish were so many that a kingfisher barely had to wait. A time when the land that this oak still remembered in the rings of its heart, was dark green forest from shore to crashing shore.

But too soon, the flying wren ran out of trees to sing to and had left the darkness. He looked back at the tiny island of forest surrounded by roads and abandoned car parks on all sides. This was his home now.

* * *

Walking through the city, bundled up against the cold and damp, surrounded by crowds of people in dull clothing, busy in their lives, Ash felt suddenly alone. This wasn't a new feeling for her—sometimes she felt so lonely, her chest so compressed by the city, that she found it hard to imagine the next breath.

She would shake sometimes. Her head would pound with the inescapable feeling of isolation pushing down on her. She had never slept well but when she felt like this, she knew another restless night awaited her at the end of a day that would be too long to bear.

It didn't always make sense. She had a community—as flawed and precarious as it was. She had a best friend, her literal partner in crime, who she knew beyond knowing, would always be there for her when she was in need. And yet, the feelings came just the same. A smothering sense of vulnerability, a naked danger that left her feeling too small, too alone to get through it.

She had her coping mechanisms, of course. She could throw herself into her work. She could dive into her friendships, caring for those around her, to distract herself from the pain. But her sensitivity meant that people also overwhelmed her. So many needs and demands and dominating energies vying for her attention. She could end a meeting—even just a social gathering—feeling like nothing more than food, picked apart by a thousand hungry fish.

She never felt those things outside the city, neither loneliness nor social overwhelm. When she was surrounded by more-than-human nature, when she was in contact with actual land, things felt different. She could find real connection outside, losing hours looking for bugs and mycelia under logs or watching sparrows building their nests in a dense bush. When she sat watching a storm roll in over the horizon and painting the sky in oily black, she felt as whole as when she was seven—one of her earliest memories, sat outside her small family home, her heart racing with every distant crack of thunder, waiting for lightning with timeless anticipation.

But knowing that the land was her place, that isolation and overwhelm were just temporary companions she could leave behind if she wanted to, didn't make them less painful. Like so many people she knew, she had built her life in cities for sheer survival. To be near others that were, ostensibly, just like her, for support and some sense of community. But she knew she was compromising.

Today, watching the drizzle turn to rain, falling soundlessly onto asphalt—not dripping down through forest leaves, not flowing in little rivers down the bark of trees, not creating new life deep down in the soil—she couldn't help but ask herself if survival was actually enough.

* * *

The solar train pulled up to the platform with a squeak of its brakes just as the rain started getting heavy.

This will be the last one for a few hours if those clouds don't clear.

Ash pulled herself up the steep steps and, carefully avoiding eye contact with the driver, held up her wristband to be charged the fare. The driver's hand-held scanner beeped a long, low note and an LED flashed an angry red in Ash's face.

"Not enough credit," said the driver, in a voice that suggested he no longer cared about anything, much less about one more elderly person having to walk in the rain.

Ash didn't bother to respond. She turned and tried to get out of the door. But she was blocked by wet passengers pushing their way in out of the cold. She pushed again but there were too many of them. The feeling of being trapped in a small space, of being surrounded by human bodies on all sides made her panic.

"I need to get out! Let me out!"

She gave a final hard shove, managed to dislodge the mass of bodies, nearly stumbled down the last step and was back out in the rain.

Muttering to herself, Ash pulled an umbrella out of her backpack and pushed the button to open it. A gust of wind turned it immediately inside out.

Great, just great. Fuck these people. Fuck all of this.

After stomping through puddles for two blocks, still struggling to get the umbrella the right way in the wind, she'd had enough. She threw it hard against a wall and the plastic handle, already fractured from so many years of use, split right up the middle. Ash stood and stared at it.

"My only umbrella", she said slowly.

I can't even pay to get on the damned train—how will I ever get another one?

She cried then. Sobs of rage pushing up through her chest and throat. She sat down on a step outside someone's house and covered her eyes with her hands.

Is this what it's come to? Depression? Fighting with everyone? Shouting and breaking my precious things?

Sitting there, tears running down her cheeks, Ash knew with perfect clarity that the State no longer needed to pass laws forbidding femininity or unsanctioned care.

It won't take a trooper's boots to kick the softness out of me.

To survive in the city—like so many others—Ash was already losing the most important parts of herself.

I need to get out.

I need to get up.

* * *

Ash's chest heaved. She hadn't run this much in years. Like many streets in the City, the alleyway she was climbing was so steep it was lined on both sides with steps. The rain was relentless, and she slipped several times on the slick concrete.

A chill wind blew down the narrow street and she shivered from her very core. But she pushed on. Her mind was clear, her goal fixed. *I need to get up.*

And then, sooner than she expected, panting and sobbing, she reached the highest point of the city. One of her favourite spots. It was a tiny park, really just a bare patch between buildings with a few conifer trees and one spectacular old oak that had seen several centuries and somehow avoided the State's chainsaws. The view made Ash's tired heart leap every time. She stepped over the ancient roots pushing up out of the ground, walked up to the railing and held on with frozen hands. The whole City was laid out before her, from the town centre cluttered with skyscrapers out to the distant line of imposing walls that marked the boundary. To the east, the crashing sea. Beyond the walls in every direction, the forest.

Around her, the rain continued to fall and Ash was distantly aware that she was standing in a puddle and that her socks were soaked. But she was already as wet as it was possible to be. Despite the cold, the exhaustion, the frustration of this grinding, isolating city, Ash began to laugh. She looked up at the dark clouds and cried with laughter. Her whole body shook. She coughed and laughed and cried and released and released and released. Then a flash of realisation and she was gone.

Chapter seventeen

She stood in a shadow. Beyond the shadow was light. It was evening and sunny. She was warm, it was dry. *What—what?*

Then the understanding came back to her, as it always had.

I'm not where I was, I'm not when I was.

It's been so long this time.

She looked around her, trying to get her bearings. Her thoughts came slowly. *I'm in shade, but it's a sunny day. It isn't raining. And what's that fucking racket?* She heard yelling and...gunshots...she turned automatically towards the sound with a gasp. She was right next to a City wall, tens of metres high, blocking all light and a good part of the sky. Her eyes moved to the top of the wall, dotted with watchtowers. Her head spun so quickly that she nearly fell down.

It's illegal to be this close to the wall. What am I doing here?

She heard sounds from behind and she whipped back around.

Maybe twenty or thirty people were marching towards her, banners held high. Someone was shouting through a cracked old megaphone.

"Let them in! Let them in!"

Then, as the demonstrator lowered the megaphone for a moment, Ash saw a face that she knew almost as well as her own. It was Pinar. She looked furious: a look of intense power played over her usually soft features.

Ash locked eyes with her. Pinar's face flashed with recognition moving into concern. That was when Ash felt the ground shake, when she finally noticed the smell of horse shit on the breeze.

Then Pinar, still marching towards her, saw her best friend disappear.

* * *

A blackbird brought her back. Despite the pounding rain, his song was rich and clear. Ash wiggled her fingers and instinctively turned to look at the source of the song. She smiled at the small bird calling from his perch in the oak, his yellow eye rings bright in the greyness of the day.

Then it came back to her. *Pinar. The wall. I need to go.*

Her body shivered uncontrollably. She couldn't stop coughing.

Right now.

Chapter eighteen

C leo shivered in her bright pink raincoat. The wind blowing through the community garden was picking up and the rain was pattering out a rhythm on the ground and plants.

She stood by a piece of ground that was demarcated by lines of stones and overgrown with metre-high licorice plants and a thick carpet of alfalfa and red clover.

"This bed is doing so well!" she exclaimed. "We have enough transition supporting herbs here to keep the Clinic stocked up until the summer."

Julia, a new member of the collective who Cleo was just getting to know, stood near her with clippers and a bag and smiled. "Impressive, right? I love how the land keeps supporting us even in the winter."

"It's amazing," said Cleo. She tried not to stare at Julia or to notice her toned legs. *The plants aren't the only thing that's impressive around here.*

The queer herbal collective had arrived at the community garden a few hours before and despite the wind and rain pushing through the exposed piece of land, they were hard at work in the muddy field. The herbal support collective had formed in the summer. For Cleo, bundled up against the wind, the land still held those warm memories. Although the main garden collective had disbanded for the colder months, there was still a lot to do to keep the trans clinic stocked, herbs and pollen to collect, roots to dig up.

"Erm...didn't you tell me once that the plants here have some other purpose as well—something about the soil?"

"Yes, let me show you," Julia knelt down in the mud and pulled a little red clover seedling out of the soil to demonstrate. "See these little balls here?" She carefully wiped soil off the seedling to reveal tiny nodules spread all over the roots.

"I see them."

"They contain nitrogen-fixing bacteria."

"Nitrogen-fixing?"

"They take nitrogen from the air and put it out into the earth. Which is something that normally only lightning can do. The nitrogen enriches the soil." Julia sat back on her heels, apparently oblivious to the cold and the dirt. "So next year we can grow vegetables in these beds, and we won't need to use fertiliser other than a bit of compost."

Cleo looked closer. "All because of these tiny things. Nature's amazing."

Julia smiled. "It really is. All these herbs are helpful for people in hormonal transition. Clover, alfafa and licorice contain phytoestrogens which have a similar effect to oestrogen in the body. They aren't as effective as medical hormones, but when we can't get those across the border, these are a good back-up."

How does she know these things? "And the pine?" Cleo indicated the group standing around a pine tree, snipping off some of the cones into bags.

"For the pollen. Pine pollen contains testosterone and other phyto-androgen hormones, while willow catkins are rich in oestrone, which is an oestrogen. They never used to flower at this time of the year of course, but now that we don't have real winters here anymore, we can start collecting early."

"Everything changed, didn't it?" Cleo's waterproof trousers

86

made a scrunching sound as she sat down near Julia.

"It did. I never saw a real winter here, but my parents used to talk about it a lot. Snow for weeks. Even the inland lakes would freeze over." Julia unconsciously adjusted her thick hair out of her face. Cleo found herself wondering what it might smell like. "And the summer never got to more than about thirty something celsius. Can you imagine?"

A cold breeze blew over them. Cleo's teeth rattled and she got onto her knees. "I think I need to move a bit to warm up. Shall we work a bit more and...erm.."

"Yes?"

"Maybe get a drink somewhere or something after, if you have time that is...I mean, no pressure."

Julia smiled and moved just a little closer. "I would love to."

* * *

Pinar had just finished making the bed she shared with Ash. She had cleaned the whole kitchen and was ready to prepare another meal. A pot of red clover tea was reheating on the fire.

Over the sound of the bubbling water, she heard someone hacking and coughing outside the building. She stepped over to the window with a sponge still in one hand and looking down, saw Ash running to the front door—she was soaked. Pinar threw the window open letting in a gust of cold, wet air.

"Ash," she called out. "I'm coming down!" But Ash was already inside.

* * *

Cleo and Julia stood and stretched and lifted their bags

filled with herbs. They had forgotten about the cold entirely.

"That was great!" Cleo announced. "It's so good to get out and do something with my body."

She caught Julia looking her over, just a little.

"You have a great body, you know?" Julia blurted. Her expression changed suddenly. "Sorry, fuck. That just slipped out. I actually don't know if you like compliments like that...I'm not sure if..."

Cleo touched her elbow, softly at first, then a little stronger.

"I love them. And you're right. In a city of skinny people, my body is smoking hot."

Julia relaxed her shoulders and allowed herself to take a long glance at Cleo's curved form. Even under layers of pink plastic and with a hood that hid half of her face, she found Cleo incredibly sexy. "Couldn't agree more."

* * *

She appeared at their door moments later, soaked and sneezing.

"Are you okay? What happened? Where's your umbrella?"

Ash pushed past her friend and collapsed into bed. She couldn't stop shivering. Her lips were disturbingly blue.

"Ash?" Pinar closed the door and hurried over to tuck a blanket around Ash's shaking body.

"I'm—I'm okay." Ash's teeth were chattering. "I...journeyed."

Pinar's eyebrows shot up, before she composed herself. "Let me get you a towel and I'll put some hot water on. You're frozen."

When Pinar returned with all the towels they had bundled over one arm, Ash was bent over, coughing violently into a pillow. "Oh love. Get those wet clothes off right now."

"Something's...something's wrong."

"Yes, you've been walking around in the middle of winter when you should have taken the train. And not even using your umbrell—"

"Pin. Be *quiet* for a minute, would you? The State, the wall. There was a demonstration, and I think, horses."

Pinar sat down on the bed.

"Tell me everything."

Chapter nineteen

The bulldozers were the first to arrive at the garden. The horses, dogs and soldiers followed closely. They came from every side, moving in from the streets and surrounding the perimeter in lines.

A less organised group would have been captured immediately, put through a legal system that only protected the rich, or locked up in State prisons. But the herb collective was prepared for this. This work, this life, meant never being able to fully relax.

"The orchard!" Cleo shouted. The group grabbed their tools and backpacks and dashed towards the tiny grove of saplings in the east corner.

The ground was even wetter there and Cleo's boots disappeared into the mud immediately. Behind the budding fruit trees, partially obscured, was a wire fence that opened onto an abandoned garage. Midway along the fence was a hole; the emergency exit. The first gardeners had cut open the fence and resealed it with wire to make it look untouched. Cleo took a pair of pliers out of her pocket and efficiently snipped off the wire ties as the rest of the group reached her, already sinking in mud up to their ankles. She pushed open the improvised gateway and one by one they slipped through, lining up along the back of the garage that stood between them and the next street.

Behind them in the field, they could already hear the bulldozers in action, tearing up their year of hard work and love. Cleo peeked around the corner of the garage then turned back to Julia and the rest of the group.

"Th*at was close*," she signed, her fingers shaking with adrenaline and cold. She looked again. "*Okay, time to go.*"

* * *

What can we do?" Pinar sat at the edge of the bed, heart pounding.

"Just watch and wait, I guess. As usual I have no idea when I was. Just that we seemed to be in a great deal of danger."

Pinar sighed. "It's happening again, isn't it?"

"Yes."

"I really hoped things were getting better..."

Ash rolled her eyes and Pinar shrugged.

"I know, I know. You think that the whole idea of improvement is a myth—"

"—a myth for people whose lives are getting better at the expense of the rest of us—"

Pinar reached for her hairbrush and started working it through her long hair. It was one of the few things that helped her calm down. Although she hid it well, anxiety was her constant companion. "I don't know," she said distantly. "I just hoped things wouldn't be so bad forever."

"Well..." said Ash lightly. "I also hate hope."

Pinar smiled. "I know, hon."

"All the work we put in, all these decades of fighting and we're right back where we started." Ash sighed and took the hairbrush from Pinar. "Here, let me do that."

Pinar turned slightly to give Ash a better angle. She sighed, out of contentment or frustration, Ash couldn't tell.

"You know," Pinar said after a quiet moment. "I think that's only partly true. The Resistance isn't back where it started, not really. Like, yes, we're still super fractured and we still can't get through a meeting without someone derailing—"

"—always—"

"But there was a point in Europe when people like us couldn't even gather in radical spaces, we couldn't celebrate our achievements or support each other in public. I mean there were movements that centred people like us, we were in some of them, but everything was under the radar and just so fucking marginal."

"All part of the plan, I guess." Ash broke up a knot in Pinar's hair with her fingers. "Imagine if we'd had the resources that everyone else seemed to throw around. We could have done so much! The thousands of mutual-aid projects that sprung up during the covid years could have survived. We could have built some real change, we wouldn't have lost so many. We—"

Ash put down the hairbrush and slumped back against the wall. Pinar turned and could see her friend was holding back tears.

"It's okay to feel it, my love. We have to mourn sometimes."

Ash shook her head.

"It's fucked up, Pin. We've tried so hard for so long and nothing gets better."

Pinar took her hand. "It's hard. But, I don't know if you noticed, but things *are* changing. We're better than we used to be. For example, infighting isn't such a thing anymore."

"Yeah, fuck that." Ash looked distant for a moment. "Everything we could have achieved if we had stayed focused on fighting our actual enemies."

"Instead of each other, over and over for decades."

Ash took her mug of tea from the bedside table. "I'm not sure we were even 'fighting each other' though, Pin. I think it was mostly people like us being attacked and evicted from spaces that *we* built." She sat up straight, her eyes wide. "We, who most needed those spaces, who most needed safety, were always the first against the wall, evicted, out of work, into the streets." Ash's voice wavered from fury and she gripped the handle of the mug. "It wasn't accountability—I never got to have accountability for any of the shit that happened to me. It was violence through and through."

"It was awful—we were all so hurt we couldn't stand to be in a room together without triggering each other in an endless cycle of trauma." Pinar paused and looked at the back of her own hand for a moment. "But I think it got a bit better, right?"

Ash sniffed dramatically and Pinar handed her a handkerchief. "Well. At least the enemy is a lot clearer these days."

There was a loud knock on the door.

Ash shrieked, spilling half her tea over herself.

"For goodness sake!" she shouted. "What is it now?" Pinar took her cup and set it down. Yelling disturbed Ash's lungs and she folded over in a fit of coughing.

"I'll get it."

She pulled a throw over her shoulders and answered the door. It was Tania, dripping wet.

"Pinar, I'm so sorry to disturb you..."

"Come in and get warm. Here, let me get you something to stand on."

Pinar laid down an old supermarket bag on the floor. Tania stepped onto it, closed the door and started taking her boots off. "Thank you." She noticed Ash on the bed, half hidden in blankets. "Mate, are you okay?"

"I'm—great. Got caught out in the rain." She sneezed as if to emphasise her point.

"Epic, right? It's been a while since we've had rain like this.

Did you hear the news...about the wall?"

Pinar shook her head. Ash sneezed again and pulled yet another blanket over herself.

"I just came from there. A group of refugees arrived last night, as far as we can tell—flooding up on the north coast again—and the State isn't letting them in."

Pinar put her hands on her hips in an unconscious mimicry of Ash. "Fucking outrageous! They must have travelled a hundred kilometres through the rain. The State *has* to let them in!"

"According to one of the runners, all the main entrances in and out of the City have been closed."

"Then we need to do something!"

Ash blew her nose in the handkerchief.

"Pin, no! Remember what I told you? The wall, the horses..."

Pinar gave her a soft smile. "But now we're prepared."

"I still don't thi—"

Pinar turned to Tania and said defiantly, "We have a demonstration to organise. Ash will you be okay here?"

"I'll be lying around sneezing and worrying about you, but if that doesn't bother you then, yes, I'll be fine."

"Love...." Pinar stood by the door. "I won't go if you need me. But with, erm...what you saw—" She glanced at Tania. "—I feel like I should go and do what I can."

"I know Pin...and actually, this decision has already been made." Ash shrugged. "We know how this goes, there's very little we can do."

Tania looked confused. "Mate if you're sick, Pinar or me can totally stay with you."

Ash shook her head. "Go. Demonstrate. I'll see you there, Pin."

Pinar gave her a smile and Tania looked even more perplexed.

"You two are so mysterious sometimes." She turned to Pinar. "Ready?"

Pinar reached for the door handle.

As Pinar and Tania left the apartment, Ash looked unconsciously over to the window. The clouds were finally clearing, and the setting sun was shining bright. The sky was turning burnt orange.

"This again," she mumbled to herself and pulled the duvet up over her head.

Chapter twenty

An hour later, there was another knock on the apartment door.

"What? What?" Ash's voice was muffled by blankets. "Can't I get a second of peace?"

The pounding continued.

"Oh my fucking god!"

Finally, Ash managed to extricate herself from the bed and stumble over to the door.

"Who is it?" she demanded.

"Ash, it's Cleo. Can I come in?"

Ash opened the door and sat back down on the bed. She looked disapprovingly at Cleo's muddy boots as she stepped onto the welcome mat and started unlacing them.

"There really has to be a better way to communicate than knocking my door down every five minutes—Pinar isn't here by the way."

Cleo looked uncertain as she stood in the doorway catching her breath.

"Well, come in! You're letting in a draft."

"I'm—I'm sorry to disturb you, Ash."

"Come in already!"

Cleo stepped in and closed the door. "I was sent to find you. I'm sorry that—"

"I get it, you're sorry. There's a towel in the bathroom. Dry yourself off, then sit down—" Ash patted the bed next to her. "—and tell me what's worth waking a sick old lady from her nap for."

* * *

As Pinar and Tania made their way through the city, towards the wall, they paused along the way to pick up other Resistance members from their houses. As their group expanded, their excitement, nervousness and fury grew too. Tania and Pinar could both feel it.

"Feeling okay?" asked Tania carefully. "You look tired."

Is it that obvious? "Thank you," Pinar said as a reflex. She thought for a moment. "I guess I'm worried. Worried about Ash. Worried about how this is all going to work out. You know, just worried."

Tania smiled. "Intense times, right? I mean nothing new, but I feel like in the olden days we at least had a day to prepare for a demonstration. These days, everything is spontaneous, and we barely have time to breathe."

"So true," agreed Pinar. "Although I'm not sure I remember those olden days." *And you're quite young.* "Haven't we always just been in a state of emergency?"

Tania sighed, then said brightly, "Last stop. Julia's place. Shall we pause here for a bit and make some signs?"

Pinar gave her a quizzical look.

"I mean we have no idea what we're doing with this demo", laughed Tania. "We might as well at least have something pretty to wave around!"

* * *

"—they destroyed everything. The beds, the compost piles,

probably the orchard too by now. Honestly we got out just in time—"

Ash was gripping the bedsheets. "Go on."

"There's no good news," Cleo continued, her hands increasingly animated. "Runners from across the City have been bringing in similar reports. There's some kind of refugee crisis at the wall."

Ash nodded. *I heard about it.*

"And vergents all over are being taken into custody."

"Where did this come from?" she asked, trying to calm her breathing.

Cleo shrugged. "It's been building for a while, I guess. As we know, the Resistance has been getting stronger and the State aren't happy about it. There are at least three demonstrations happening today that we know about—even one at the wall. With the crackdown in full force, they're all in danger."

"The wall..." Ash stood up abruptly, her pillows knocking over the teapot on the bedside table. "Pinar! We need to get down there." The sudden movement hurt her lungs again, and she curled up coughing.

"Ash, forgive me, but I don't think you should be out in the cold today."

Ash gave her a glare but nodded.

Cleo waited for Ash to stop coughing. "We've sent runners to all the demonstrations with a message to regroup at the clinic. If you like, we can go there together. If you're up for it? It's a lot closer and probably warmer than your apartment, no offense."

Ash stood up and grabbed her jacket. She swallowed hard to stop herself from coughing again.

"Let's go."

As they headed down the stairs, with Cleo leading the way, Ash suddenly froze, her hand clinging to the banister to stop herself falling.

"Ash?" asked Cleo, running back up to her. "Are you okay?"

"No." Ash's face was pale, her eyes wide with panic. "It's all...wrong."

Chapter twenty-one

There aren't enough of us.

Despite the chill wind, Pinar was sweating. She brushed hair out of her face and tried to calm her nerves. The group was walking from the nearest solar train station, carrying their signs as discreetly as they could.

Pinar knew they were close when the group started unfurling their banner. Passers-by did their best not to notice the gang of angry protestors, or their message. *Living in a totalitarian state will do that*, Pinar thought. *People are incredibly good at focusing on their own needs, ignoring everything else that might get them into trouble.* A few made the effort of shouting at them from their balconies. Pinar was grateful the wind was too strong to hear the words.

Finally, they turned the last corner and at the end of the street, they could see the monolithic City boundary. Pinar couldn't help but look up to the watchtowers.

They really took this Fortress Europe thing to heart.

The walls around the City were ancient but in the last decades, following economic crises, pandemics and the effects of climate change, the State had increasingly withdrawn from the world. Europe never really recovered from the pandemic of 2020 and some borders never fully reopened. The borders separating the rich and the poor grew stronger every year. And every year, the State built the walls that separated the City a little higher.

As Pinar, Tania and the other twenty protestors reached the open space of concrete that separated the neighbourhood from the gate, they could already hear the shouts from the other side.

She lifted the ancient megaphone with reverence. *You've served me well old friend, since the very first days of the Femme Riots.* She inhaled deeply and shouted to the wall and beyond: "Let them in! Let them in!"

Instantly, the crowd around her repeated her words.

We have to get them in somehow. But what can we do? We didn't have time! Once again, we're just reacting to stuff that happens. Once again, we're—

Then she was there. Ash. Just as she had described. Right next to the wall—illegally close in fact. Standing with a confused expression where before there had been only empty space. They locked eyes and Pinar couldn't help but smile.

I'll never get used to this.

Then Ash turned to look suddenly to the side.

So it's time.

Ash was gone. The horses, troopers and all the state violence they could muster appeared in the distance to replace her.

That's our cue to get the fuck out of here.

"Go!" Pinar shouted. And as quickly as they could, the demonstrators turned and ran back into the city.

Chapter twenty-two

H ome was a thick rose bush in a quiet street. Thorny branches and twigs to protect them from hungry aerial hunters. An exposed trunk to keep them out of the way of foxes and cats. Still, they always came here as a group. In a world of threats, doing everything together was the only way sparrows could feel safe.

The whole quarrel—over a hundred adults, yearlings and youngsters, fluffed up against the cold—were crammed in along every branch, flirting, pecking and squabbling for the best spots. Calling to each other as they settled down for the night, they shared their most intimate feelings in a thousand ways with their family, neighbours and partners, their best friends and most hated enemies.

In the summer they had hopped around together under the bush, chirping loudly to stay connected. The adults had taught the new fledglings how to dig and scrape their feet into the sand to create sparrow-size hollows in the dirt. The challenge was to get the belly in as far as possible and toss the sand— under the wings and over the back. The more dust was thrown, the fewer parasites were left over to itch their sensitive skin. Few things felt better to a young sparrow than a warm dust bath in the sun with their friends.

Now that the cold had returned, the damp sand was less enticing, but the last magenta flowers of the season still attracted some interesting bugs to snack on. Protected by thorns, and jammed full of their community, the rose bush was a perfect place to live.

One alert nervous system picked up the sound of humans approaching.

Footsteps, strained voices.

A sharp warning call from the pit of her stomach and the whole flock knew.

In less than a second, they were gone.

* * *

"Have they gone?" Pinar whispered to Tania. They were crouched down inside a rose bush that had grown wild over the years. It was full of thorns. Her hands and knees touched cold sand covered in bird droppings.

Tania looked around as well as she could between the scraggly old branches. The streets seemed to be empty—most people knew better than to be outside on an evening like this, with troopers on patrol.

"*I don't see them.*" Pinar could see Tania's hands were shaking as she replied in USL.

"*Let's wait a bit longer.*" Pinar adjusted her position slightly and the sleeve of her jacket caught on a thorn, tearing a long hole.

"Fuck," she muttered under her breath, then switched back to signing. "*We should never have come here.*"

"*I know. But what choice did we have? We had to do something.*"

"*We're more strategic than this. This was too much of a risk.*"

"*I agree. But at least some people saw us. At least we got the message ou—*"

"*Wait,*" signed Pinar urgently with a flash of her eyes.

They both froze then and soon Tania could hear the

troopers' voices as well.

* * *

"I think we've lost them. Fucking vergers. What did they think? That they could break down the gate and let those people in?"

"Who even knows? They've just got nothing better to do I guess."

"But if we find them, we pretty much have free reign. They're calling it the Improvement, you know—all the new laws, all our new freedoms. This city is about to get a lot cleaner. I'll tell you that."

The second trooper grinned and kicked a rock.

"Then let's find them."

* * *

Pinar had a cramp in her hip. She tried to breathe through it, but it was just getting worse. She was breaking into a sweat again.

Don't move.

Tania sensed Pinar's panic and gave her a look of concern.

Just hold on.

Now the thorns were cutting through Pinar's sleeve and cut into her skin as well. She held her breath, wishing for it to be over.

Don't fucking move.

Chapter twenty-three

Pinar couldn't hold it anymore; she dropped down on the ground and rubbed her hip vigorously. As it released her, the bush rebounded back up shaking its leaves. In the quiet street, it was surprisingly loud. Panicked, Tania pushed carefully forward into the thorny bush to get a view of the troopers. They were just turning a corner. One looked back for a brief moment. She held her breath.

Then, shaking his head, he joined the other trooper and they disappeared into an alleyway.

Tania dropped back and turned to Pinar.

"*Are you okay?*" she signed. "*Can I help?*"

Pinar was too busy stretching her leg to reply. She nodded. After she had finally soothed the cramp, she sat up and signed.

"*Let's get to the clinic. We need to reconvene with the others and find out if anyone was hurt.*"

"Your arm..."

Pinar looked at her scratched, bleeding wrist. "Forget it, let's go."

As they emerged carefully from behind the rose bush that had quite possibly saved their lives, they stepped into the street and merged into a group of people disembarking a solar train. As they followed the crowd back into town, Pinar shook her head silently.

This was too much of a risk. What were we thinking? And

those people are still outside the walls.

At the end of the street that marked the line between neighbourhoods, Pinar suddenly felt something deep in her gut. A heaviness, a cramping pain. Overwhelming awareness stabbed through her body as her mind caught up with reality. It was then that she tasted the smoke.

The street was full of people, the air was unbearably thick, acrid, violent. Pinar's eyes watered. Tania gasped and grabbed her shoulder.

No...no...

Pinar thought she would throw up or fall. She screwed her eyes closed. But she already knew that the horror of the Clinic going up in flames would never leave her.

3. Survival

Chapter twenty-four

S moke, something totally new for the young bat, was filling her world. Some of her family had already left, calling to her as they took wing away from the danger. She held back. This was the only home she had ever known. Hidden in an unused attic where the humans never came, she had come back here every morning of her short life. She wasn't ready to leave yet, but her nervous system was buzzing. The air was getting hotter. Her eyes stung. Finally, with a pump of her powerful wings, the bat let go of the oak rafter where she was born. She pushed through the tiny hole between the tiles and drainpipe and with a frustrated squeak, took flight.

*** * ***

Tania took Pinar's hand. "I'm so sorry…"

Pinar was silent. Tears from smoke and rage ran down her cheeks.

They knew we were out. They planned all of this.

"I…" she attempted, but couldn't force the words past her throat.

"I'll be right back." Tania stepped into the road. "I have to go check on the kindergarten."

Pinar stared at the fire rapidly engulfing the building. Her body and mind were numb. Distantly, she heard her name.

"Pin! Pin!" Pinar turned slowly to the voice. Ash, wrapped up in several brightly-coloured throws, ran over to her, closely followed by Cleo. "Look what they've done!"

"Ash?"

"They knew if they tried to evict us, we'd have half the Resistance here in an hour. They just waited until we were all out and—"

Pinar touched her friend's forehead. "You're sick."

"What? Pinar, don't you understand?" Ash paused then to look at her face. Her eyes were glassy and vacant. Ash took both of her hands. "Oh honey, you're in shock. Here, sit down."

Ash sat Pinar down on a curb and joined her. Her friend's hands were shaking.

"Was it the demo? Are you okay?"

"They...they destroyed the clinic," said Pinar very slowly, her tongue thick in her mouth. "All our work. All the herbs..."

Ash opened up one of her blankets and put it over both of them. She stroked her friend's hair with the back of her hand. "Yes, honey, I know. I'm so sorry."

Pinar sobbed one last, deep sob then turned away from the flames to look deep into Ash's eyes.

"They're going to regret this."

* * *

Within half an hour, both the clinic and the kindergarten were fully ablaze. Resistance members arrived from all over the city to try to douse the flames with buckets and even bottles of water, but it was hopeless.

Ash returned from where a mass of people was huddled in the street. Pinar still sat on the curb holding a cup of tea Cleo had brought her; Ash couldn't begin to imagine where it had come from.

"Pin, the kids are safe. Apparently, they were all out in another demo outside one of the prisons. Honest to god, sometimes there are so many demonstrations on the same day that I can't even keep up."

Pinar nodded but couldn't take her eyes away from the flames. Ash saw that the cup in her hands was shaking.

Cleo spoke. "I heard from Julia—you know, the runner— that some folk even went to the fire department to plead for help, but I guess they were under strict orders not to intervene."

"The State created this fire," said Pinar, her voice flat. "They won't come until there's nothing left to save."

Cleo could see beads of sweat on Pinar's forehead.

"Are you okay?" she asked. "There's more I'm afraid."

"Continue."

"Julia confirmed what we'd already heard—people have been taken in an operation all across the City. Dozens of queer, trans and disabled folk, people with the HIV tattoo—they've all been locked up without charge under something they're calling the Improvement. The sex workers have called another strike, and some have got in touch with their Protectors. But so far, nothing seems to help. Shit's getting serious."

"The City is burning." Pinar stood up. Her eyes stung, her head was spinning. "We have to get somewhere safe."

Chapter twenty-five

H ome. That's what they called it. It probably had some other State designation, but everyone, for as long as anyone could remember, had called it the Home. Like everything in the City, since corporate and state power had been merged into one totality, the enterprise was run for profit. Families were forced to surrender their parents, siblings, lovers to the Home and were charged dearly to keep them there. Much of the management was ex-military, they all worked for the State. It was far from safe; it was far from being a wise choice. But they were all out of options. So that night, just after lights went out, almost the entire City Resistance descended upon the building that served as a hospice, and dumping ground, for those the State had declared to be without value.

Home. Yarrow stood in the doorway with their arms wide open, their expression a mix of worry and surprise. Soon the dark corridors of the decrepit building would be filled with voices and care and community again. Yarrow was ready.

* * *

Finn stood in the middle of the road, watching the flames in awe. Even from where he was standing, he could feel the heat, penetrating the fabric of his suit. *Fuck.* A few people milled around in the street and Finn approached a person he had never seen before.

"Erm...excuse me?" Although he still felt awkward around people he didn't know, Finn had gotten better at being polite to strangers. *My Mistress has taught me so much.* "Is, erm...P here?"

"Pinar, you mean? Hang on a sec." The stranger looked distracted as they frantically packed a backpack. They turned to another individual who was dashing by with a bucket of water. "Don't worry about that now!" they shouted. "I think we've rescued everything we can. Head over to the Home, the rest are already over there!"

Finn stepped slightly back from the raised voice.

"Wait," said the stranger, remembering that he was there. "Who are you again?"

"A friend of P...Pinar's."

The stranger looked at his suit dubiously. "Okay, well she's not here, as you can see. Everyone's reconvening at the Home. Sorry, I've really got to go."

Finn thanked them and walked away. *The Home. The care home, I guess. I know where to go now.*

* * *

"Okay, okay, everyone please calm down." Elias sat deep in his dusty armchair, barely visible in the crowd, but his words commanded respect. The living room fell silent. "This is an unprecedented day. The Improvement is in full swing and we are—all of us—in grave danger."

Elias ran a finger across the faded green fabric of the chair as he collected his thoughts. The room waited patiently.

"I also want to emphasise that we are in this together, despite our differences. Those most at risk will also be the most protected by the Resistance. Those with more privilege...we're expecting you to show up." He sat a little taller, his voice booming. "No performativity. No fishing for credit." He looked around at the packed room. "Shit is real today."

There was a murmur of agreement.

"We have about ten hours before the morning shift and management arrive. And we have a lot to get through. Here are my proposals for the night ahead..."

And so it began. Rarely had so much of the Resistance been gathered in one place—disability activists, sex workers, former prisoners and working-class organisers. Those who experienced racism, fatphobia and oppressions of all kinds. The sick and elderly, queer and trans folks who had all been rejected from State society. And dotted among them, those who, though relatively unaffected by State oppression, knew that their struggles were connected.

Ash was sat near a window pouring tea from a giant teapot.

"Can I help?" asked a blonde woman with bright blue eyes.

Where do I know you from? Ash nodded politely and passed her two cups. "Sure, that'd be great, thanks."

"No problem," the blonde woman replied in a sing-song voice. "I just want to help!"

Oh, Ash thought to herself. *Now I remember you.*

As Elias stopped speaking, and the room broke into caucuses and working groups, he noticed how fast his heart was beating. A cup of tea was passed across the room, hand to hand until it reached him. He took a sip and a moment for himself.

Why is it that we only really come together like this when shit hits the fan? He looked absently around at his friends and

116

comrades as they split into groups and dived into conversations. *Fuck hoping that things will get worse—throwing the most marginalised of us away—to provoke some great revolution. But sometimes, out of the most sinister of situations, hope does grow.*

He took another sip of his tea. Rose and lemonbalm, he noticed, and he felt his heart relax.

Sometimes we respond so well to this trauma: that which didn't quite kill all of us, making us stronger. But a world without all that trauma in the first place? I'd take that any day.

"Elias?"

Elias opened his eyes. He hadn't noticed that he'd closed them.

"Is everything okay—are you tired?" It was Yarrow.

Elias rubbed his eyes. "I'm fine. Just pensive, I guess."

"If you like, Oscar has offered to take over facilitating the main sessions for tonight." Elias glanced over to where Oscar was cuddling a puppy that someone had brought in from the street. *He's so fucking cute.*

"Elias?"

"What? Yes, yes. Fine. I'll go help with the prisoner letter-writing group. It's in the office, isn't it?"

Yarrow nodded. "Do you need help getting there?"

Elias looked at the solid mass of people sat on the floor between him and the door.

"Clear the way!" he shouted. And they did.

"That's how you do it," he told Yarrow with a grin and made his way through the parted crowds to the office.

Chapter twenty-six

Even here, she could grow.

She had been the tiniest of seeds blown into the prison yard, over walls and fences and barbed wire. All here was cement and the cracks were lined with weed killer. The managers of this place were so determined to keep out life, to eradicate hope.

But she had found a good place. Just next to the fence where the weed killers hadn't thought to look. She had touched down and let go of the little parachute that had brought her from the fields far away. Now her roots ran deep, tapping into the soil below the concrete, drinking from the energy of the land. She filled herself with water and nutrition and pushed out her jagged leaves in a perfect rosette. Soon, she would flower and be host to bees and beetles, maybe even moths or butterflies. She would bring colour to this lifeless place.

And one day, if things worked out, her flowers would turn to seed and she would release her own little parachutes on the wind to reclaim other places like this.

Concrete, fences and poison wouldn't be enough to stop her. She was infinite.

* * *

"Elias, come join me." Ash waved him over to sit next to her. She had cleared the oversized desk of papers and files and had replaced them with a stack of envelopes. Elias pulled out a chair and sat next to her.

"Just you?"

Ash sighed. "Looks like it."

"Are these all from prisoners?" Elias asked, picking up an envelope.

"Yep. And there will be even more people to support after the last few days."

Elias turned the envelope in his hands, pressing the corners into the flesh of his index finger. He sighed a little.

"Ash, I know this is important, but—"

Ash looked at him directly. "But?"

"There's so much to organise. So much to react to. I don't know..." Elias put the envelope back down on the table. "Is this the best use of our energies?"

Ash didn't respond. Instead, she took the envelope and opened it. The letter was hand-written, the paper, lumpy, recycled and reformed several times. She started reading.

"Dear A and P,

Thank you for your letter. I don't know how you keep getting them to me—this place is so controlled—but I'm so glad that you do. It sounds extreme, but you're keeping me alive. Since I arrived, here in the men's section, (although I have never been a man) things have been difficult. As I mentioned in my last letter, I haven't been able to get hormones here and my body is changing. I'm sick a lot. I don't want to tell you all the stories, but I have been beaten twice and put into solitary 'for my own protection' afterwards. This week more trans women arrived here. I don't know why we have to suffer this.

P, thank you for sharing your knowledge about plants and for the leaflet, 'A Prisoner's Herbal' that you sent me. Since I received it, every time I am allowed out into the yard for an hour, I have been collecting dandelions and yarrow and chickweed. I hide them in my bra—when I'm allowed to wear it—or in my socks. I've been making tea or, when I can't get to the kitchen, I just eat them like that. I found them disgusting to begin with, but now I kind of like them. You can't imagine how bad the food is here otherwise.

I did as you told me and chewed up the yarrow and put it on a cut on my leg. It healed right up! Thank you. I don't know if I feel the connection to plants that you talked about yet, but they've been keeping me well—or as well as I can be—and that's already a lot. I even dreamed about a dandelion the other day. I like how fluffy they get when they have seeds. One day, if I ever get out of this place, I want to help you in the clinic—"

Ash paused and swallowed hard. Elias put his hand gently on her arm.

"—and to grow herbs for myself and to help others like you do. That is my dream, A and P. To be with you on the outside someday, amongst flowers, drinking tea and getting our hands muddy together.

Thank you for staying in touch with me. It means everything,

Yours,

D."

Ash put the letter back down and wiped her eyes. Elias reached over the table and took a pen and paper.

Chapter twenty-seven

I just want to say that I'm so grateful to be here with you all tonight. It's such a pleasure to meet you all. Long live the Resistance!"

Oscar tried very hard not to roll his eyes. *Who even is this person?*

"Ahem...thank you. X, was it?" He sat up in his chair.

X nodded.

"But did you have a response to the question that we're discussing though? You know this is the security planning meeting, right?"

X replied with her warmest smile. "Of course! No, nothing specific to say, just that we are stronger together and with enough positivity we can—"

Oscar cut her off. "—Sorry. Can I ask who invited you here? Security meetings are invite-only."

"I'm friends with Tania from the kindergarten! And Ash too."

I highly doubt that. "I see," said Oscar softly. "I wonder, X, if the wellbeing meeting might be a better place for you. You mentioned that you teach yoga?"

X smiled again. "I do! And that's a great idea!" She jumped up enthusiastically.

"Down the hall, to the right—bedroom fifteen."

"Thank you everyone!" X put her hands together and bowed to the room.

When she had left the room, Oscar exhaled loud enough for

everyone to hear. "My goodness."

The group chuckled.

"Now…where were we?"

* * *

Elias sealed the envelope and put it on the pile of letters ready to be passed, hand by hand, until they reached their destination. He rubbed his own arthritic hands together. He had made it through five letters, and he couldn't write another word.

Ash's face showed sadness, rage and most of all desperation. She looked up as if she felt his gaze on her.

"It's not enough," she declared, putting her pen down and stretching.

Elias picked up his cold tea. "I know, but is anything, really?"

Ash picked at a nail.

"But this work does have value, right?" Elias asked between sips.

"Yeah, I mean, people literally tell us that it helps them. And not everyone can be out fighting troopers and burning down the prisons."

"And not everyone needs to be, Ash. You do so much. And honestly, neither of us is twenty anymore."

"And not every twenty-year-old can do those things either."

"True enough."

Ash folded her letter, pushed it into the many-times-recycled envelope and added it to the pile. She touched Elias' hand lightly, then signed discreetly in USL: *"Let's go back in? I'm sure we have a lot more meetings to get through before the night is over. These kids never sleep apparently."*

Elias smiled. She had just used the wrong hand to sign the word 'kids'.

Although everyone in the State had been using Universal Sign Language as a second language for over ten years, Ash still made occasional mistakes. USL, and its predecessor, Resistance Sign, technically weren't real sign languages: distantly based on Manually Coded English, USL was far simpler than the sign languages that grew out of Deaf communities. It had had a complicated history, developing from a tool of inclusivity of a diverse resistance movement to being appropriated by the State in a failed attempt at gaining prestige.

Ash had never gotten completely used to it and Elias noticed her making more mistakes when she was tired. His sign on the other hand was flawless. He had always been a linguist, speaking three languages and signing two others. All of them, except English and the State's corrupted version of Resistance Sign, were illegal.

"If we're lucky, there might be more food at some point," he replied. *"Some yoga teacher promised us some of her home cooking."*

Ash chuckled at Elias' improvised sign for yoga teacher. He had put his hands together, above his head and plunged dramatically to the side.

"Yes, she seems super reliable. I expect lots of follow up from that one."

They both sighed in perfect unison and left the office.

* * *

Oscar was still facilitating the security session in the living room, which was in deep discussion about plans for the coming days.

They needed to simultaneously find somewhere to move to before the Home management returned in the morning and wanted to organise some kind of solidarity action with those already taken by the Improvement—not to mention the refugees who were presumably still gathered outside the City walls. Pressures for action were lining up and the energy in the room was tense. People were tired, frustrated. No-one seemed to be able to find a way forward and the threat—and reality—of State violence had everyone on edge. Oscar looked overwhelmed and exhausted, but he smiled as Elias arrived and squeezed in as close to him as he could.

"*Good to have you back,*" he signed discreetly.

Elias returned his smile. "*How's it going in here?*"

"*Stressful. I have no idea how we're going to get out of this.*"

Elias offered his hand and Oscar took it and held it against the armrest of his chair.

"We'll get out of it together, that's how."

The meeting came to an end and the group got ready to break back into caucuses to dive deeper into their decisions.

"Thank you everyone," said Oscar. He flicked off his brakes and rested his hands impatiently on his wheels. Elias knew what that meant. "I'm going to take a break for a few hours. Elias, would you mind helping me get into bed?"

There was a murmur of amusement around the room. Everyone knew that given enough time, Oscar could get into bed just fine by himself.

Elias scowled at them sitting down, crammed between Oscar and the door.

"Well, get moving then!"

* * *

Elias closed the bedroom door behind him. He saw that a wheel had gotten caught on Oscar's long, sequined jacket.

"I'm stuck, babe."

But Elias was already on one knee detangling the wheel. At the beginning of their relationship, he was much more careful and checked for consent whenever he touched Oscar's chair. But over time, touch between them had become something unconscious, intimate. Oscar would sometimes rub his hands through Elias' hair, or stroke his leg to wake him up during a meeting. Elias in turn would randomly squeeze Oscar's muscular arms, or give his chair a push when needed.

"Do you actually need help getting into bed tonight?" he asked, still kneeling. "Or was that just a ploy to get me in here?"

"Help would be good." Oscar took Elias' hand in his. "And babe, do me a favour?"

"Yes?"

"Get your fucking clothes off already. I won't wait another minute to be inside you."

No matter how many times they had done it, the manoeuvre of getting into bed could still be complicated. Sometimes Oscar would leave a leg behind, tangled up in blankets, and the chair would roll away. Sometimes Elias would suddenly get a cramp in his calf and would hop around the room until it passed while Oscar made fun of him. Nearly every time they would collapse together in a heap on the over-soft bed, sweating and giggling. It was the best kind of foreplay in the world. Within minutes they were under the sheets, making out like teenagers.

Elias' heart raced. He laid back on the floppy Home pillow as Oscar, curled up against him, traced his fingers through the dark hairs on his lover's chest.

"You're amazing." Elias' voice was barely a whisper.

Oscar lifted his head and smiled. "You."

"Really. I feel so good with you."

Oscar grinned. "Well, you don't get to my age without learning a thing or two. You weren't bad yourself, babe."

"Kiss me?"

"Always."

I love this, Elias thought. *Soft, passionate.* Oscar's finger drew a line down his lower back. Elias quivered as it reached even lower. "Please fuck me," he whispered, and Oscar was inside him.

After staying too long in the same position, Oscar needed to stretch. First light was just beginning to show through the heavy curtains.

"We should get back to the meetings. It's nearly morning."

"Let the children argue among themselves for a bit longer. Please."

"They respect us—and they need us, Elias."

Elias sighed in the world-weary way he was so well-known for.

"Why though? Why are we always expected to be the elders of this community?"

"Because we're literally older, not to mention experienced?"

"You're not even fifty!"

"Which is kind of old these days for people like us." Oscar pulled himself up to sitting. Unconsciously, Elias handed him a pillow.

"I don't know," said Elias softly, running a sticky finger over Oscar's nipples. "Why is it like that? I mean, why are there so few of us? I feel like there must be more old people out there. Did everyone just sell out when they could?" Elias looked up. Oscar watched him with a serious expression. "Why are we the last radicals of our generation? That doesn't seem right."

Oscar stroked his hand over Elias' greying stubble, enjoying the rough sensation on his fingertips. "Because we're poor and marginal as fuck—people like us die young, babe. Remember Anne and Diamond...even poor old Pigeon. How many old, sick and incarcerated people we lost to coronavirus, to poverty, to State violence—especially during the collapse. The people who survive to old age are still around because they're rich, or privileged, or safe. And so of course they're more conservative. They benefit from all the crap that destroys people like us."

"But *we're* still here..."

"Because we have the Resistance. We have community—as messy as it is a lot of the time. And people like Pinar and Ash wouldn't be here either without that. So yes, I'm an elder at forty-seven, and that isn't right. But at least we're surviving."

Elias nodded. He was close to tears.

"I love this. Here, with you I mean."

Oscar curled back up and put his head on Elias' belly.

"Me too, my love. Me too."

They kissed. "Let's go again?"

Chapter twenty-eight

She was screaming, as she always did. Although the noise she made during sex could easily attract a predator—a passing fox, a hunting owl—she couldn't help herself. In the shadows of the Home patio, between a wall and a trash can, the hedgehog was finding her rhythm when she felt her partner tense up. Then she heard it too. A human walking nearby, crashing through fallen leaves and cracking sticks.

The hedgehog uncoupled from her partner and led him deeper into the shadows so they could continue. She wasn't going to let one noisy human get in the way.

* * *

Ash was tired, confused and deeply overwhelmed. She couldn't begin to unpack everything that had happened in the last twenty-four hours—the Clinic, the Improvement—and suddenly she was surrounded by almost the entire Resistance crammed into a decrepit care home that smelled of mould and boiled cabbage. She had spaced out for most of the last meeting. Now, she needed a break.

She squeezed out of the living room and wandered down the corridor looking for Pinar, until she remembered that her friend was still in the caucus for femmes of colour. Ash decided that she really needed a quiet room to herself for a while. She chose a bedroom at random and knocked gently on the door. It was empty, as nearly all of them were that night. She stepped in, leaving the door open and went straight to the armchair next to the window. The fabric was as ratty and dusty as every other piece of furniture in the building, but she collapsed into it with a contented sigh. She pulled open the curtain. The sky was still dark but there was just the beginning of light reflecting off the tall buildings.

She yawned and rubbed her eyes. She could already feel her nervous system slowing down, finally getting some space from so many people with all their hectic energies and frantic planning.

After a bit of daydreaming, Ash noticed moaning and squeaking springs from the room next to her. *Oscar's room if I'm not mistaken.* She smiled. *Well, the revolution is pretty romantic, I guess.*

A man appeared in the window, pushing his pale face up to the glass. Ash screamed.

Chapter twenty-nine

Who the fuck are you?" Ash stood up, staring, arms crossed, heart pounding.

The man looked just as surprised.

"Well?"

"Oh my god, I'm so sorry," he said. His voice was husky. "I...I knocked at the door, but I guess no-one could hear me."

"Who are you?' Ash repeated. "I've never seen you here before."

Despite how bad Ash believed her memory to be, she was pretty good at recognising faces if not always connecting names. After so many years organising in the city, she knew almost everyone in the Resistance by sight.

"I...I'm F."

"That doesn't help me. Are you State?"

"State? Erm...I do work for the State, yes, but..."

Ash took a step back. She was ready to run for the door. She grabbed a candlestick from the bedside table and held it up, trying to look as threatening as she could.

"I may look old and sweet," she warned him. "But unless you're here with a squadron of troopers hidden out there in the dark, you really should leave immediately."

"I'm looking for Mistr—ahem, I'm looking for Pinar." The man blushed.

Understanding dawned on Ash. *Oh, I see.* She put down the candlestick and grinned.

"You're Finn!"

Finn continued to blush. "I prefer F, but erm yes. I guess you might be A?"

"Ash."

"Ash, right, sorry..."

Finn ran his finger through some condensation on the window. "So...erm...here we are."

Ash flashed him another smile. "Pin said you were cute. Okay, wait, let me go find her and we'll let you in. She'll be very surprised to see you."

"Maybe I shouldn't have come?"

"That's up to her. Wait there."

* * *

"Mistress Pinar."

Pinar stood in the doorway of the Home with a look of total confusion. Finn was on his knees in his ritual greeting. *What's happening?*

"Stand up!"

Her sub obeyed and Pinar took a step forward. "What are you doing here?"

"I heard...I was told that something happened at the Clinic," Finn stood uncomfortably, moving his weight from foot to foot. "I went over to check that you were okay and someone there, a younger guy, I don't know, maybe not a guy, told me you had all come here to the Home. I guess he thought I was, you know... with the—" He signed the word for 'Resistance' discreetly as he looked over his shoulder.

Well, I guess activist security culture has gone to hell today.

Julia arrived then, in her familiar black running gear. She paused near the door to catch her breath.

"Julia?" asked Pinar. "Everything okay?"

Julia shook her head. "Not even close. Is there a meeting happening? I need to deliver some bad news."

Pinar sighed. *Isn't it always bad news?*

"In the living room," she said softly. "I'll meet you there."

Julia stepped in. Pinar returned her attention to Finn, who was still standing awkwardly in front of her.

"Mistress, have I made a mistake? Please don't be angry."

Pinar was furious with him. She was confused. She was also ever so slightly delighted.

"Are you alone?" Her sub nodded.

"Then come in and close the door behind you."

* * *

Ash was returning to the meeting when she met Oscar and Elias in the narrow corridor.

"What have you two been up to?" Ash teased.

Oscar blushed and Ash gave him a wink. "I'm happy for you both—we all are."

Elias reached abruptly for the door handle. "Excuse me. We have a meeting to attend."

As they returned, the living room was in uproar.

Ash quickly learned that even with four hours to go before the management returned, they were no closer to finding a solution. As each hour passed, it seemed less and less possible to move the entire Resistance to a new place, but it was also clear that none of them were safe by themselves tonight. Everyone was desperate and uncertain. Julia entered the room holding a glass of water.

"It's all bad I'm afraid," she announced as she sat down next to Ash. She was still catching her breath and her face was damp—but from rain or sweat, Ash couldn't tell. "Basically, the State is done with us. After the demo inside the wall today, or yesterday, I guess—" she looked unconsciously towards the window. "—word got out. State citizens were lining up at the admin buildings demanding to move them on."

Ash's attention drifted. There was only so much she could take at once.

She tuned out the human voices and noticed a scratching sound somewhere above them, a rat or a mouse, she couldn't be sure. She brought her attention back; Julia was still reporting.

"—with all this Improvement business, the State's propaganda machine is stronger than ever. Migrants and vergents are being blamed for everything from climate change to the price of nutrition bars. And the people are buying every word of it."

Ash wasn't surprised. She knew that history was littered with examples of marginalised folk being used as scapegoats to reallocate blame. She remembered reading online that, in 2014, after floods devastated towns and cities in the Balkans, and killed at least fifty people, rather than mentioning climate change, senior figures in the Serbian Orthodox Church claimed it was a punishment by God because drag artist Conchita Wurst had won Eurovision.

The awesome power of drag queens, she thought to herself.

"Everyone likes a scapegoat," muttered Elias.

"Troopers at the watchtowers were given the order to fire rubber bullets." Julia's voice was tired, stretched. "And the refugees were forced to move on. We know how long it is to the next town."

"Fuck," said Ash, louder than she meant to. The room murmured in agreement. "What can we do?"

Julia shrugged. "I hoped you'd all have some solutions by

now. Any ideas where you'll all go? I'd offer my place but it's barely big enough for me and my cat, much less the Resistance."

Elias looked around the room, his arms crossed. "We still don't have a plan, right?"

People avoided his gaze or shook their heads.

Oscar sat up and cleared his throat. "Actually, I might have an idea…"

* * *

"So that's how it stands, sub," Pinar told Finn, standing next to him in the kitchen. He was avoiding eye contact and Pinar lifted his chin gently with her hand and held his gaze. Her expression was deadly serious.

"You need to hear this. The State set the fire. Their so-called Improvement is in action all across the city. We only have a few more hours before the management comes back here and we haven't been able to decide on where we can all go at such late notice."

Her sub nodded. "I understand."

"You can't possibly. But I do need you to show up tonight. This is getting very real. And we are, all of us, in danger. I wouldn't have involved you, but now that you're here, you're a part of this." Pinar's palms were sweating. Her head was spinning.

Talk about worlds colliding.

"So, what do you say?"

"I serve you, Mistress. I will do everything I can to protect you and your friends. Please let me be useful to you."

Pinar allowed him just a small smile.

"Right answer. My friends won't trust you immediately, but

after everything we've done together, I know that I can. Stay here for a minute while I go and catch up. And sub?"

"Yes, Mistress?"

"I'm going to need fifty sandwiches prepared, and fast."

Finn reached for the chopping board.

* * *

Pinar stepped into the living room, everyone was talking at once. The noise was overwhelming. *"What did I miss, Ash?"* she signed to her friend.

"All kinds of drama. Let's step outside for a sec." Ash took Pinar's hand and led her back out of the noisy room. "So, Finn came to visit..."

Pinar smiled. "He did."

"Is he staying?"

"He is."

"Because if he isn't, he's got about thirty minutes to get out."

Pinar gave her friend a quizzical look. "But don't we have a few hours before the management returns?"

"Yes, my love. But..." Ash paused dramatically. "We'll start barricading ourselves into the Home well before that."

Chapter thirty

Pinar stared at her friend for a long moment. Ash grinned, waiting for the news to settle in. "It'll be just like the old days," she said with a chuckle.

"Ash...we can't. Can we?"

Her friend shrugged. "I mean, we need to go back in and finish the consensus process but basically, it's decided. Those who aren't up for it or are at too much at risk—including some of the more vulnerable residents—are heading out in a few minutes. One of the 'allies'—" she exaggerated the air quotes in the air "—has a place just out of the centre and they're going to stay there until it's over. Maybe they'll also organise some support outside the Home."

"Because we might be in here for a while?"

Ash was still grinning. "Exactly."

"Why are you so happy about this?" Pinar tucked a strand of hair behind her ear, it fell forward and she tried again. "This could be really dangerous."

"It could. And Pin, I'd totally understand if you'd like to leave. Get some rest at home, see how things stand tomorrow..."

Pinar put her hands on her hips. "If you're staying, I'm staying."

"Okay good," said Ash, obviously pleased. "Because between you and me..."

"Yes?"

"I'm in the mood to occupy the fuck out of this place and

create the queerest, most gloriously emancipatory care home the State has ever seen."

Pinar couldn't help smiling. Ash took a step towards the noisy meeting hall.

"One thing, Pin?"

"Yes, love?"

"Is your sub any good at construction?"

* * *

Cleo and Julia passed them in the corridor.

"Hey you two. We're heading out", Cleo announced. She was wearing a heavy backpack over her winter jacket. Her hair and make-up were immaculate.

"Not in the mood for an occupation?" Ash asked with more sass than she intended.

Julia took a patient breath. "We can be of more use out there. Don't worry, we'll be doing what we can to support."

"I'll show you out," said Pinar and accompanied them to the front door.

Cleo hovered near the door. "So, this is it."

Pinar nodded. "Yes. Are you going to be okay out there?"

"No problem. I'm still Protected, for now. And I feel like I can be more help out there, organising food packages for you—"

"—and helping me keep watch on the State." Julia stood a little closer to her friend. "The first sign of trouble and I'll get back here to warn you."

Pinar sighed. "Thank you. I have a feeling we'll need that."

They stood quietly for a moment. Residents and a few others left the building, on their way to more secure locations.

137

"Well," Pinar said softly, putting her hand on the door handle. "Stay safe."

"And you too." Cleo leaned in to give Pinar a kiss on the cheek. She turned to Julia who was pulling on her own backpack. "Ready?"

"Ready."

Pinar watched for a moment as the women walked away. She pulled the door closed and locked it. *Time to build some barricades, I guess.*

* * *

"So, what happens next?" Cleo asked Julia as they turned the corner and left the Home behind. "Should we already start connecting up with the food distro people?"

Julia looked thoughtful as she pulled her hand through her thick hair. Cleo noticed that whenever she did that, the light caught her stud earrings in a certain way. *Beautiful*, she noticed. *She's magnificent.*

"I think we should watch the Home for a bit. Word will get out quickly once the occupation starts and we should be ready for anything."

Cleo sighed. "It's going to be messy, isn't it?"

"Probably, but it's better to give them as much notice as possible."

"So how do we do it? I mean, we're already too far away to see anything back there."

Julia smiled and took her hand. "I know a place."

* * *

Pinar returned inside and saw Ash was still standing awkwardly in the corridor.

"Are you alright?" Pinar asked her.

"Nervous, excited. Gonna pop back in for the rest of the meeting. And you?"

"I'll go check on Finn—I gave him some tasks to do in the bathroom."

"I'm sure you did," Ash said with a wink.

Pinar poked her in the arm. "Go already. I know how much you love a meeting."

After Ash left, Pinar paused in the corridor for a long moment, staring at the carpet. She knew she should be feeling more nervous than she was. Every decision they were making would be critical. *This is big stuff.*

But she was beginning to realise that her tight chest and shaking fingers weren't only a result of anxiety. *I'm actually excited. This could be fun.* She lifted her chin and walked down the corridor to find her sub.

"All done here?" she half-demanded as she stepped into the cramped bathroom.

Finn stood back and admired his work. With tools he had found in the basement and a whole lot of aluminium foil from the kitchen, he had managed to block off the air vents into the bathroom in case the State tried to send gas through the pipes.

Because the lives of old people and sick people mean nothing, Pinar noted.

"Done, Mistress."

She put her hand on his arm. "Just call me Pinar for now. This is weird enough as it is."

Pinar climbed into the bath to inspect his work. *He's pretty good actually.* She flashed a look at his polished brown shoes, the tie he had rolled up in his pocket. *Who could have guessed?*

Standing in a giant, industrial bathtub, surrounded by sponges, hammers and rolls of duct tape, a sense of unreality was creeping into Pinar. She wasn't completely in her body. She inhaled and steadied herself. *Not now. I'll make time for that later.*

"There's another vent that needs blocking," she said with authority. "Going out of the staff toilet at the back of the building."

Finn smiled. "On it, Mistr—Sorry...Pinar."

He climbed out of the slippery bath and offered his hand to her as she stepped out and back on to the carpet. She gave his hand a little squeeze. *This can work.*

*   *   *

"How much further?"

Cleo's breath was coming in puffs and pants. They had been climbing for a while up a dark stairway that smelled like mould and dust. She needed to take a break. *I may be a proud fat femme, but that doesn't mean I'm built for climbing epic towers. And why does the State hate elevators for fuck's sake?*

Julia stopped and turned. "Sorry. I'm going too fast, aren't I?"

Cleo held onto the stair railing. "It's okay. It's just...we have very different bodies."

Julia sat down on the cold step, pulled out a blanket from her backpack and laid it down for Cleo to sit on. "Let's rest a bit?"

Cleo followed her lead and sat down on the blanket. Julia offered her some water and Cleo took a sip and passed the bottle back.

"What else do you have in that magic bag of yours?"

Julia gave her a wink. "You'd be amazed."

* * *

Meetings completed, the Home was beginning to fill with the sounds of drilling and hammering. Pinar, Finn, Yarrow and dozens of others ran back and forth through the corridors blocking doors and barricading windows. Tania was doing something with wires hanging from a socket that Ash couldn't begin to understand. *This is so not my thing.*

Some of the residents were rediscovering the skills they had learned in their former lives, before they'd been locked away to watch the walls for their last years. She stood for a long moment in the corridor as people rushed past her, equipped with materials they'd produced out of nowhere, tool belts, and sensible shoes. *Where did any of this even come from?* Even Elias passed by with what looked suspiciously like a flat-packed bookshelf, taken apart, and turned into barricade material for the windows.

Ash stared at the hammer in her left hand. *What was I even thinking?* She bent down and put it back on the carpet and stepped away as if it might be dangerous. Dodging busy builders of every gender and age, she made her way back to the empty kitchen and put some water on to boil. *Well, I know how to make tea. I'm not entirely useless.*

* * *

I think I'm going to be sick.

Cleo stepped out onto the glass floor, trying not to look at the roofs of other high rises down below them. As if being at the top of the highest building in the State wasn't enough, the wind blowing in from the sea was buffeting her body from all sides. She felt as if she was stepping out into nothing. *Which of course is the point.*

Back when the City had been one of Europe's major tourist destinations, bringing millions of visitors every year to its coastline, its bustling cosmopolitan streets, clubs and social centres, this rooftop had been created as a viewpoint, a stunning vista for selfies and model shoots—for those who could afford the entrance fee to the bar. Half of the roof was covered in chairs and tables firmly attached to the cement to survive the winter weather. A rusting sign that read 'The Jewel of Europe' hung on the wall at an angle. The rest of the roof was a dizzying glass floor leading up to the railing and a fence that ran around the entire building.

Why would anyone pay for this? Cleo asked herself as she walked out over the transparent floor, putting out her hands for balance. She shuffled slowly until she reached the railing with a sigh of relief. *Ah. Now I see.*

The view was incredible. The financial district spread below them was impressive enough from this angle, but the sea stole the show. Whipped up by the wind, the water was dark blue with crests of white. Spectacular cliffs dropped down to miles of beach, all but abandoned except for a few windswept shelters set up as temporary homes. *All of this used to be prime tourist real estate, but no-one visits us anymore. The walls are higher every year.*

"Are you okay?" Julia asked her from where she stood holding the railings. With the wind blowing through her hair, and the sun picking out her green eyes, she looked radiant. *I never get tired of seeing that face.*

Cleo smiled as she joined her. "Once you get over the utter

terror, it's pretty nice up here!"

"It really is," Julia agreed. Hand over hand, she moved along the rail a little closer and put her hand over Cleo's. It felt warm, protected from the cold wind. They stayed like that for a moment, enjoying the view and each other's presence.

"Shall we get to work?" Cleo asked.

Julia turned to take off her backpack. She pulled out two pairs of binoculars, a flask of tea and some chipped tea cups.

"Sure thing. Snack first?"

Cleo took a cup. "The State isn't going anywhere."

* * *

"Elias, sit down and have some tea."

It was a command, not a suggestion. Elias sat down obediently and took the cup from Ash. He was slightly out of breath, but he looked better than Ash had seen him in a while.

"Having fun?" she asked.

"You know? I am. It's nice to see everyone coming together like this. Nothing ever happens here, except watching the dust. Unless you all come visit and we get to stay up past our bedtimes for an interminable meeting or two."

Ash found it curious that Elias sometimes made the distinction between the Resistance outside and the residents inside. *You're as deep into this as anyone I know.*

"Well," she replied. "Meetings are important, but there is definitely such a thing as too much talking."

"Agreed."

They sat quietly for a while, drinking their tea, listening to the sounds of construction filling the corridors.

Elias leaned in with a conspiratorial whisper.

"So, tell me about Pinar's new person."

* * *

"Can you see the Home?" Cleo asked. She peered through the binoculars, leaning against the cold rail. Her hands were frozen even through the thick winter mittens she had put on. Julia on the other hand didn't seem to notice the cold at all. She was wearing a denim jacket over her running gear, no gloves, no scarf. Cleo couldn't help but notice how good she looked in it.

"Yes, it's there, I think. Two buildings down from the tall tree—do you see where I mean?"

Cleo looked again. *Tall tree? There are a lot of tall trees.*

"Here, let me show you." Julia moved in closer and with one hand on Cleo's shoulder, she pointed to where the road ended, and the old Home building stood alone in its small yard.

"Ah yeah, I've got it." Cleo took in a deep breath. *How does anyone smell that good?*

Another gust of wind made Cleo shiver.

"Cold?"

Cleo put down the binoculars, nodding.

"If you want, I can stay out and watch. I think from the windows on the other side"— Julia indicated the abandoned bar inside— "you should be able to see the East wall. It might be good to keep an eye on that as well."

Cleo gave her a coy smile. "I mean that's one option to stay warm..."

"Let me try something else," said Julia softly. She took Cleo's hand and pulled off the glove. Holding her fingers up to her mouth she blew, warm, sweet air over them. "Better?"

Another shiver ran through Cleo, but this time it wasn't from the wind.

"Erm...yes, that works."

"Glad to be of service," said Julia with a wink. "Is your mouth cold too?"

* * *

"She calls him her sub. They've been playing forever. But between you and me, it might be just a bit more than that."

Elias looked surprised. "Really?"

Ash allowed herself a small chuckle. "Bi-erasure, Elias? I thought I knew you better than that."

Elias poked his tongue out at her. "That's not what I meant, and you know it. Wasn't she seeing that woman who lives in your apartment building?"

"Cleo, yeah. It's always been open though."

"Oh. Open is cool, I guess." Elias didn't sound convinced.

"And you and Oscar?"

"I'm the jealous type, Ash, you know that." He showed the palms of his hands. "What can I do?"

"You seem happy together though?"

"We are. Anyway...this sub?"

"Finn..."

"You said it's been going on for a while?"

"A very long while. I'm surprised she hadn't mentioned him."

"She's very private about some things. We've known each other forever, but there's a lot she doesn't share with me."

"It isn't personal. She's guarded about some things."

Elias nodded. "And do we like this Finn person? Is he State?"

Ash shrugged. "I just met him, and yes he is. But he also seems good with a hammer and that's what we need right now. It's not like this night could get any weirder though."

"Ash, I guess I'm asking if he's solid? He's not going to freak out, is he?"

"People get to freak out, Elias."

"Sorry, I mean is he going to make trouble for us."

"I have no idea. But I trust Pin. She's the best judge of character I know."

Elias shrugged. "I mean, she likes *us*, right?"

Ash laughed but her expression became serious again and she looked unconsciously towards the window. "I'm nervous Elias. This is big."

Elias swallowed. "It is. But there's no group of people I'd rather be locked in here with. The State has no idea how powerful we really are

* * *

The floor of the bar was dusty, even sticky in places and they couldn't have cared less. Cleo rarely felt so good in her body. She felt a distance sometimes, between what she desired and how she felt when she got it. She had been taught to hate her body, her curves and that made it difficult to connect with another person or to her own pleasure; to the sensations of a body that sometimes felt like it wasn't a part of her. *But not today.*

Between rusting table legs and fallen ashtrays, taking turns to hold each other down and losing their clothing as they went, Julia and Cleo were lost. They couldn't get enough. When one of them climaxed, they both did. And then again. They barely had to touch each other anymore. It was turning out to be the most intense—and loud—session Cleo had had in years. *I don't want this to end.*

In that moment, Julia locked eyes with her. Cleo recognised

a look of guilt—even shame.

"What happened to us?" Julia asked as she pulled away. "We need to get back out."

They both looked unconsciously towards the window. Far below them in the street, a group of people were moving towards the Home. The management were arriving for the morning shift.

Chapter thirty-one

They're coming!"

The message passed through the Home within seconds. From the women standing guard, peeking through the barricaded windows, to the kitchen, the living room, to the bedrooms where some of the older residents were napping despite the chaos. It had already been an impossibly long night and they all knew that more was to come.

No-one could have believed that in just three hours they would have gotten it all done. Both doors to the building were blocked with sofas, desks and bedside tables. Windows were covered in slats of wood nailed to the walls.

"Ash, it's time." Elias' voice was heavy, but determined.

Ash pushed her shoulders back and took his hand as she stood up. "Let's get Pin first. I can't do anything without her."

Elias nodded. "None of us can."

He picked up the battered megaphone he'd been keeping near him dramatically. "Time to let them know."

* * *

Pinar pushed open the hatch up to the roof of the Home. She stepped out into the sunshine, squinting. Finn climbed out behind her.

"We'll need to block this on the way back in."

Finn nodded. "Yes. It locks on the inside. I've already been looking at ways to secure it."

Pinar smiled. "Good. Anticipating my needs."

"That's what I'm here for." He turned and offered his hand to help Ash and then Elias up the last step. They stepped out and joined them on the roof.

Ash gave Pinar a poke in the ribs. "You're very cute as a domme, Pin. I've never seen this side of you before."

"Oh, be quiet." Pinar stepped towards the edge of the roof.

She turned to face the three of them. "Ready?"

They all stepped forward to join her.

* * *

"We have taken the Home!"

Pinar's voice was loud and clear through the megaphone. She gripped the handle with wet palms. She prayed the batteries would last.

"This building belongs to the Resistance now! We stand in defiance of your maltreatment of those you declare unproductive, locked away here for their final years to turn a profit for a wealthy few."

On either side, Pinar felt the support of her friends, pushing her on.

"We stand in solidarity with those turned away at the gates and for all those imprisoned under the State's so-called Improvement. The State makes us out to be the enemy, but the *real* enemy is a system that thrives on oppression, on profit and the militarisation of what we once proudly called the Jewel of Europe. Walk away or join us, but this is *our* Home now."

Pinar put down the megaphone and looked down at the four management staff members staring up at her with bewildered expressions. "Well, that's done," she said, turning to her friends. "Time for breakfast, I guess."

Ash took her hand. "Great idea."

Chapter thirty-two

C leo and Julia re-emerged onto the glass rooftop. The wind had died down and this time they both stepped out easily to the rail. Again, Julia pulled out the binoculars and handed one set to Cleo. *Sticky fingers*, Cleo noticed. *That was so hot.*

As Cleo tried again to locate the Home, running her view up and down streets and getting lost in some car park somewhere, she heard Julia inhale suddenly.

"What? What is it?"

"We need to get down there right now."

Finally, Cleo found the big tree, the cul-de-sac street. And the mob of people with banners and sticks marching towards the building.

"Go. Run!" Cleo's voice was tight. "You need to get to the Home. I'll make my way down in my own time and alert the others."

Julia stood at the door of the bar, looking uncertain.

"I don't want to just leave you here. We can go down together. I can...wait for you."

Cleo touched her arm. "You're a runner, so run. I'm not some damsel, honey. I'm surviving in a world that hates bodies like mine and that makes me pretty hardcore. Maybe I can't run across the city at a million miles an hour, but I have plenty of other things to bring. One of the security group is also in the sex worker collective, he lives nearby. I'll let him know and see if we can pull a counter-protest together or something."

Julia took her hand. "I'm sorry. It came out wrong. That's not what I meant."

Cleo gave her a generous smile. "I know. You're all good. Go, they need you. I'll find you later, somewhere."

Julia reached in and gave her a full kiss on the lips before turning and dashing down the stairs.

* * *

The Home had fallen quiet again. Since the announcement had been made and the management had gone, an air of domesticity had descended over the building. Residents napped in their chairs and others went about their day, collecting laundry and sweeping the floors as if nothing out of the ordinary had taken place. *This is kind of surreal*, thought Ash as she walked into the living room looking for something to do. She crossed her arms immediately.

"Deep inhale and reach for the sky. Very good! You're all doing so well!"

What the hell?

"And back down to rest in downward dog."

X bent down and pushed her bottom up towards Ash.

Ash wasn't impressed. "Ahem...breakfast is nearly ready."

X looked at her through her legs, her cheeks red from exertion. "Oh wonderful. Perfect timing—we're just finishing up here. So kind of you to make food for us!"

"It was a team effort," Ash declared as she retreated back to the kitchen.

* * *

Julia's heart was pounding; even as well trained as she was, her lungs were pushed to capacity. As she reached the bottom of the stairs, she felt her legs force down into the concrete and push off in the direction of the Home. A flash of the mob she had seen through the binoculars came back to her. *They're in danger. I need to go faster. So much faster than this.*

* * *

"Ash, could you get the plates ready for me?" Pinar called from inside the larder. "Finn and Elias are going to wake up the rest of the residents." Ash opened a cupboard and started noisily piling up plates and bowls. Pinar appeared with a bag of Nutrition bars. "Did the security meeting finish, do you know?"

"Nothing happening in the living room but a lot of lycra and reaching for the sky."

Pinar raised an eyebrow. "Lycra?"

"Ms Yoga."

"Ah." Pinar opened the cutlery drawer.

"I don't trust anyone that happy or flexible."

Pinar chuckled. "She might not be so bad you know. We're all under a lot of pressure. Some exercise probably isn't the worst thing, especially for some of the residents who've been left to rot in their rooms for who knows how long."

Ash tutted. "Sure, Pin. We're barricaded in, with a million people to feed and care for, waiting for the State to respond to our little occupation. What we need right now is definitely some stretching and positive vibes from someone who only heard of the Resistance five minutes ago."

Pinar gave her a patient smile. "Finn is also new. And he's been quite helpful."

"Well…" Ash poked her with a spoon. "At least he's hot."

Pinar didn't respond to that.

"Well, come on then," said Ash, picking up a stack of bowls. "Brunch won't serve itself, you know."

They had barely started eating when the living room window imploded.

Chapter thirty-three

Ash stared at the brick that lay on a moth-eaten rug, surrounded by broken glass.

Her brain was just beginning to catch up.

The State doesn't throw bricks—

—we do.

And why wasn't this window secured yet?

She watched as Elias moved people away to the back wall of the living room. Sensations were flooding into her beyond her control. She heard terrified voices from throughout the Home and yells of anger from outside. The smell of something burning in the kitchen. A robin singing. She couldn't really focus on anything. Then one voice penetrated the fog. A voice that Ash found extremely annoying. It was X.

"Oh my god, oh my god, oh my god," she shrieked, stepping backwards from the window and nearly colliding with Oscar who dodged out of the way. "Oh my god, oh my god, oh my god, oh my goooooddd."

Ash saw Yarrow backed up against a wall. Their eyes were wide, one hand covered their mouth. Several residents in the room were becoming increasingly agitated as the yelling continued.

It was enough to bring Ash back. She took X by the shoulder.

"Stop." Ash's voice was surprisingly calm. She touched X on her shoulder. "There's no time for that right now."

X stared at her as if she was speaking an unknown

language.

"Do you need a task to distract you or do you need to go hide in the bathroom or something? Either way stop screaming. It's definitely not helping anyone."

X blinked. "A task please."

At that moment, Pinar appeared. Finn followed, carrying several slats of wood and a box of nails. Ash recognised her friend's expression from countless other crises—totally focused.

"You can help them," Ash directed and gave X a little push.

* * *

Too fucking late. Julia was bent over, hands on her thighs. Her chest was heaving.

She looked up and watched as the mob gathered in front of the building. Some of them were armed with bricks and what appeared to be broom handles. Others stood around looking less certain. It was clear they weren't organised. *Which might make them even more dangerous.*

Nothing I can do here by myself. I just hope Cleo has more luck with her contacts.

With a pounding heart, Julia turned and started running again. She wasn't entirely certain where she was headed, she just knew she needed to keep moving. The thought of watching her friends being attacked was too much for her to bear.

* * *

Numb and slow, Ash stepped over to the window. She peered through the now-boarded-up slats.

"Ash, maybe you shouldn't..." Pinar warned from the back of the room, where she was comforting a resident who was hyperventilating and trying to get her back to her room.

"I'm fine", Ash replied. She could barely believe what she was seeing.

A crowd of several hundreds of people were gathered outside the Home. Some holding weapons, some waving improvised banners. If she didn't know better, she might have hoped they were there to support the occupation. *But I don't believe in hope.*

"Vergers!" she heard them scream through the hole in the glass. "Degenerate trash!"

"Get the fuck out!"

"Come face us!"

The State didn't need to send troopers to evict us. They have an angry mob to do their work for them. Ash stepped back and turned to her friends.

"Well, this was a terrible fucking idea", she declared. Then she collapsed face first onto the broken glass.

4. Autonomy

Chapter thirty-four

It was beautiful.

Ash lay face down on an expansive terrain of earth. She lifted her head, just enough to see a world of microscopic life opening up before her.

Ash could smell the soil. Infinitely small particles floating in damp air, entering her lungs and her mind. She imagined, saw and tasted the mosses growing around her. Riverlets of water running through their miniature world and raindrops glistening on their infinite branches. An iridescent beetle, gigantic before her, clambered across the river in search of a meal. Ash could hear the sounds of six clawed feet as they splashed through the rainwater, brushed over the canopy of moss and grasped the earth.

She inhaled, once, and felt a vibration she had forgotten moving through her body. A pulsing rhythm that called her home, deep into the mycelia beneath her body, out into the forest it connected and the world.

The air outside became her air inside, and Ash sensed the connection she held to every place on earth. Deserts and oceans moved through her. There was no-one and nothing her humble body was not connected to in that moment.

The beetle looked up and saw her. Ash pushed out a greeting through her mind and the beetle continued with his life.

She stood then, effortlessly, her body feeling lighter and more supple than she ever remembered.

Sunlight filtered down through the forest canopy above and Ash could see the new year's leaves were just beginning to bud. The ground beneath her bare feet was soft and spongy. The air was crisp and all around her blackbirds and woodpigeons called to each other.

Ash reached out to touch the rough bark of an ash tree. Her hand was gently caressed back. Her awareness was drawn to her fingertips as they ran over this other skin. She was at once, both the sprawling world of plants and fungi, networked across the earth in a dynamic force of community, and the tiniest sensation of skin on skin, the cells left behind, the memory of their meeting retained.

Moving smaller still, Ash explored the infinity of life living on her own surface. The wrinkles on her hands held a lifetime of fungi and microscopic companions accumulated across decades of life. The hairs billowing over her arms were the forests of mites.

She inhaled again and as she followed the breath inside her, Ash entered her own body.

The ecosystem is me, she realised, as the world of her own beings opened up to her. Her blood pulsed and in the flow, Ash saw, and felt and spoke with the viruses she had lived with for so long. *They are part of me too.*

Even her own cells—and their tightly coiled, mitochondrial DNA—resonated with the memory of her bacterial ancestors, absorbed into herself a million generations before she was born.

She dived deeper still and knew then that she could never be alone. That what she so easily called 'Ash', had no limits.

There was no clean edge between herself and the land.

No sharp line existed between Ash, her body and all other bodies.

Nothing stands between us.

The world imploded. The forest of her arms and of trees folded in on itself. The land enveloped her, and the ecosystem that she carried, curled up inside itself for protection.

She felt her face hit dirt and the taste of blood and soil was surprising and wonderful.

Chapter thirty-five

W *here am I?*
"Ash, Ash are you back?"
"Am I back?"

Pinar hovered over her friend. Her hair was up in a ponytail; she had dark circles under her eyes.

"Ash?"

"I'm back. I'm back." Ash tried to move but she was under a thick duvet, tucked into a hard bed. She managed to withdraw her hands and saw they were bandaged. Her face hurt—she had been cut by something. *Near my eye. Glass.* The pain and memory entered her awareness gradually. She looked around the room. Elias and Pinar shared a look. "How long was I gone?"

"Ash, my love," Pinar touched her knee through the blanket. "You've been out for two days."

* * *

"Elias, could you check how lunch is going...Finn, reheat some of that tea, would you?"

As she had been for days, Pinar was in full organisational mode.

"Don't worry, love," she said to Ash who was still lying in bed, rubbing her eyes. "You're back and it's going to be okay."

"Pin?"

"Yes?"

"What the fuck happened?"

Pinar sat on the bed next to her. "You took a tumble my love, into the glass of the broken window." Ash looked again at her hands, which seemed to be mostly healed. "And you were...gone, for a long time. It's Thursday lunchtime."

"Thursday?" Ash looked confused. "What day was it before?"

Pinar's concerned frown deepened. "Tuesday. Do you remember? Are you okay?"

"Pin, I never know what day it is! Stop fussing."

"You've never been gone so long. I told people you were sleeping, but that didn't make any sense either. It's different to sleep and I think some people could tell. I tried to keep everyone out, but Elias demanded to see you a few times."

"No, it's fine. I don't care. I couldn't begin to explain it anyway."

"Well, you've always enjoyed having a bit of mystery about you," Pinar said with a smile. "My temporally divergent friend."

Ash rolled her eyes. "Enough of that." She stretched and pulled off the blanket. "I need some exercise and I'm fucking hungry. Can you get that sub of yours to deliver to the living room?"

Pinar smiled again. "Sure love."

* * *

Ash's body was weak. Just standing up made her light-headed but she was determined to get back on her feet. Slowly, holding onto the wall as she went, she made her way to the living room. Lunch had just finished. There were people everywhere.

"Ash!" X practically squealed at her.

Oh god.

"Hey X, sorry I'm not really up for chatting right now. I just came to get some lunch."

"Message received," X said brightly. "I saved you a seat—" she indicated an armchair that had been reserved with a pile of books "—and I'll bring you a plate. We're down to just Nutrition meals I'm afraid. We're waiting for another food delivery this evening."

Ash shot her a confused look, but gratefully made her way over to the chair. A resident she recognised removed the books for her to sit. X brought her food and a glass of water.

"Thanks," she mumbled and took a sip.

"Sure thing! We're glad to have you back!"

Ash tried to ignore her enthusiasm as she stared at the grey slop in front of her.

Since Nutrition Corporation had become the official food supplier to the State, Nutrition meals, bars and snacks had become standard fare in the City. *One more reason to hate this damned place,* Ash thought as she took a bite.

"Isn't this wonderful?" X asked, indicating the busy room. Ash took in the space around them. It couldn't be more different to the stuffy care home she knew so well. At the other end of the room, Yarrow and a resident were busy dusting off a bookshelf and an ancient rubber plant. Resistance members and residents buzzed around clearing up dishes. Out in the corridor, the walls reverberated with hammering. Excited conversations filled the air. Sunlight leaked in through the wooden slats, making the living room brighter than she had ever seen it. The dust was gone, the smell of decay replaced with fresh air. A new energy had permeated the Home and Ash couldn't help but let it in. *This is really happening.*

"Some more?" X asked her, putting her hand out to take

Ash's empty plate. She stared at it vaguely with no memory of finishing her meal. She shook her head.

"I'm good, thank you."

X flashed her a bright smile and disappeared back to the kitchen.

Two days? thought Ash. She watched as a resident—who she'd never seen get out of her chair in all the years she'd been there—passed through the living room with a handful of cleaning equipment. *It's like I've been gone a year.*

Pinar appeared with a tray full of tea and cookies and sat next to her.

"These are the last of the cookies we made last night—I saved them for you. I know how much you love Nutrition."

Ash took one gratefully and bit into it. It was already a bit stale, but at least it tasted like food.

"Thanks."

"Are you ready to talk about what happened?"

Ash shook her head. "I don't think I could explain it. It was intense."

"I can imagine."

Ash knew her friend well enough to know she was bursting with curiosity and concern. But she wasn't ready. "Seems like a lot happened while I was gone." Ash looked up as a strange sound reached her from the kitchen. A group of people were singing. "I feel like I came back to a parallel universe."

Pinar smiled. "Right?" She relaxed into the armchair and inhaled. "It's everything you dreamed, Ash. We occupied the fuck out of this place."

Chapter thirty-six

I need to speak to someone in charge. Right now."

The reception worker looked flustered. "I'm sorry ma'am. As I said, the General is in a meeting and I don't know when he'll be free. I'll be happy to take a message for him?"

The woman crossed her arms and gave her a stern look.

"My name's B. I'm the manager of the Home. Some Resistance vergers have taken over our building—an occupation, they're calling it. An armed mob has attacked, but the vergers are still there. Now—" She adjusted her jacket. "Is the General free or not?"

The receptionist stood, her face barely concealing her shock. "Let me see what I can do."

* * *

Ash put down her empty cup.

"So what happened? While I was gone, I mean? And who were those people throwing bricks at us? Did the managers come back? The State? How are we all still here?"

Pinar gave her a patient smile. "One thing at a time, love. Let me pour you some more tea."

* * *

"Please sit down."

It was an order, not a request. The General didn't make requests.

He looked his visitor over with a wary eye. *Pant suit, expensive hair, ridiculous heels. She's impressing no-one.*

"So," he began. "You're the manager of the Home."

A statement, not a question.

B lifted her chin. "I am."

"And the mob we sent didn't work, I take it."

"The mob *you* sent?"

The General smiled for the first time and reclined in his chair. His uniform was tight over his chest and he knew his visitor would be getting an eyeful. *You should be impressed.* "But of course. I don't only control the troopers, you know."

B looked more intimidated than impressed. She said diplomatically, "Of course."

The General rubbed his gloved hands through his regulation short blonde hair, enjoying the sensation of leather on skin. He leaned forward, slamming them down on the desk. "So what went wrong?"

* * *

Pinar paused to sip her drink. *Peppermint. Perfect for telling stories.*

"Just after you...left...Finn helped me get you to bed and while I was treating your wounds, there was an emergency meeting. We decided we wouldn't—or couldn't, to be more accurate, respond to the mob outside."

Ash sat slightly forward in her chair.

"After some of the young men started throwing bricks at the building, the rest kind of retreated until there were just a few of them left. Honestly, I think they got caught up in the moment and didn't expect to really do anything. Finally, they got bored and left. Still no sign of the State, or troopers, by the way."

Ash tutted. "They'll come. Unless their new strategy is just to rile people up to do their work for them. Which, I mean, is efficient. Everyone's been waiting a long time for an excuse to attack us."

"I know..." Pinar's expression was sad as she fiddled with her fingers. "We've been preparing."

* * *

"That's what happens when you try to get the people to do the work."

The General was angry now. He was rarely relaxed, but this was a particularly bad week. *We already burned their fucking clinic. And now they're occupying State property. This needs to end, and soon.* He had received reports that the Resistance was growing. *The more we crack down on them, the more they keep springing up like weeds.* "We'll send the troopers in and smoke the rats out."

B was trying to maintain her composure. "General, respectfully...there are vulnerable people in the Home."

The General lifted one eyebrow. *Of course, that's why we put them there.*

B swallowed and pushed on. "Could we try negotiation first? I think violence might...bring more people to the erm...other side, sir."

The General grunted. *A bleeding-heart liberal. Just what I need.*

He thought about it for a moment. *She's not wrong though. If we push them too hard, we'll just make martyrs of them and lose even more citizens to the Resistance. I don't like it, but—*

"Fine. We'll try diplomacy. And if that doesn't work, I have a well-trained army on standby."

Chapter thirty-seven

Pinar and Ash sat quietly for a moment.

"In other news…" Pinar began. "It turns out that Finn is good at construction."

Ash smiled. *Always so good at brightening every conversation.* "I noticed." She looked at the window the brick had come through. Although they couldn't do anything about the glass, the window was thoroughly boarded up. "I told you he would be useful."

Pinar caught herself smiling. "He has been. Even your favourite yoga instructor has been pulling her weight."

Ash rolled her eyes. "Did any of the staff come to join the occupation by the way? I saw Yarrow, busy as usual."

"Some of them came but turned around and went home. I think they were glad to go home to their families for a few days. They work ridiculously long hours."

Ash nodded. "Makes sense. Are they okay—Yarrow I mean? After what they've been through, this must be especially hard on them."

Pinar looked thoughtful. "I've spoken to them a few times. I get the impression that this has actually been a good thing for them. Somewhere for them to put all that trauma. I guess we all needed that."

They fell silent again as they drank their tea.

"It's kind of amazing," Pinar said softly. "So many people here were either waiting for our next gathering, or to die, whichever came first. Now, with some agency and control over their own lives, they seem to have found new energy—getting each other out of the bath or washing the dishes. J, who I guess is in her nineties, has been basically running the kitchen. Apparently, she used to own a café before the Coffee Wars. I had no idea—I've only seen her sit in her chair, staring into space."

Ash put down her cup.

"I'm glad that all that happened, Pin. It's kind of the best thing we could have hoped for. I do worry though that we might be imposing some kind of ableist ideas of productivity on these people—I mean, it wouldn't be the first time."

"What do you mean?"

"Just that everyone should have the choice. I've no doubt that J was thoroughly institutionalised in this place, but maybe she also wanted to sit in her chair sometimes. I mean, people get to rest."

Pinar sighed. "I hadn't thought about it that way."

"I guess I just worry, because it's something that happened in the Resistance for so long. Everyone was racing to keep up and so many of us got left behind, forgotten about when we could no longer 'produce enough activism' or whatever. I think we have come a long way since then, but ableism is pretty insidious."

"It is," Pinar looked worried. "I'll bear that in mind."

There was a rap on the window; Ash startled, but Pinar calmly took her hand. "Don't worry love, it's just the supply drop-off." She stood up. "Want to help me unpack it?"

Ash stretched and pushed herself up out of the chair. "Well, I do love tidying things."

"Diapers...toilet roll, insulin and a tonne of food. They got the whole list!" Pinar stood in the corridor surrounded by open boxes. Ash was already organising the supplies into neat little piles.

"Looks like it was quite a list, Pin."

Her friend kneeled down and separated the perishable food items to put in the fridge with the insulin. "I was ambitious, but I didn't really think they'd be able to get it all. I hope the electricity can keep this cold enough."

Elias appeared and took the rest of the meds to the cabinet down the hallway. He made an impressed sound. "This is great! How did we get all this?"

"Cleo mostly, I guess," Pinar said, with obvious pride. "She's been pulling all her connections outside, including her tricks. I also heard something about raids on State warehouses at the edge of town, so that must have helped."

Ash smiled, just a little. "They'll love that."

Once the last of the supplies had been put away and preparation for the next meal was underway in the kitchen, Ash leaned against the corridor wall and allowed herself a yawn.

"Tired?" Pinar asked her.

"Deeply. Let's take a nap."

"But we don't have time, do we?" Pinar put her palms on her forehead, a sign Ash knew well that she was getting overwhelmed. "We have to get Mary into the bath, Finn is going to secure the roof hatch now we have this—" She held up a roll of duct tape. "Oh damn, and the laundry needs doing before it gets too dark for the solar generator..."

To Pinar, the idea of resting often just seemed like one more task on top of everything else that needed to be done.

"Pin," Ash took her hand. "There's never enough time. There's always too much. But that doesn't mean that we don't need to rest anyway."

Pinar exhaled loudly. "Okay."

"I saw an old mattress at the back of the staff room. Help me drag it into the living room. We'll throw a sheet over and just curl up and rest."

"But isn't the medical team meeting starting now? Won't we disturb it?"

"Two old ladies sleeping in the corner? I think they have more to worry about."

"But why not just sleep in the office?"

Ash smiled. "Because this is an action."

"Don't mind us," said Ash politely to the circle gathered as she and Pinar dragged the mattress across the room. "Just taking a nap."

People got up and let them through. There were several confused faces, but no-one said a word. Ash and Pinar set up in the corner, found some cushions to use as pillows and curled up together. Despite their to-do list that never ended, all the unfinished and unclear plans, all the decisions and compromises that needed to be made, they were asleep within seconds.

* * *

Julia passed a uniformed trooper in the stairwell of Cleo's building. Immediately she froze, avoided eye contact and tried to look invisible. The man walked right past her—he seemed to be in a hurry to leave, avoiding Julia as much as she was avoiding him.

When he was gone, she continued up to Cleo's apartment and knocked on the door.

Cleo appeared at the door immediately. "Oh good, it's you! I thought maybe he had left something behind."

"Your client?" Julia asked.

"My regular. He brought more coffee with him this time."

Cleo disappeared back into the incense-filled apartment. Julia stood in the doorway looking unsure. Cleo took her hand. "Well, come on then! We're way past the point where I need to invite you in!"

Julia smiled and stepped into her favourite place in the city.

* * *

Finn had finished his tasks for the moment. He leaned with both hands on the kitchen countertop, taking a second to rest. He had spent the morning helping residents in and out of the bath, had cooked breakfast for over fifty people, had helped Pinar change the sheets of Ash's bed and had rechecked the Home's defences. *I've never worked this hard in my life.*

And I love it. Serving Pinar and her friends, giving care and using his skills to help people, he was discovering a new side of himself. A sensitivity he had suppressed for years during his work with the State.

This new life wasn't without its challenges. He wasn't used to being around so many people for one. His childhood had been quiet, and he had preferred the company of his pet fish and maths homework to other children. He wasn't into team sports, or fighting for social position, and that had kept him out of social circles. His growing lust for submission, service, and powerful women had only reinforced his strangeness and he still spent most of his time alone, cleaning his apartment or taking an early morning run on the way to work. *Work. Let's see if I still have a job to go back to after this. Who knows how this will end?*

Just the hint of doubt was creeping into his mind. Until now he had been too busy to really think about what he was doing here, in a world so different from his. He stood up straight and pushed away his thoughts. *I'll see if Mistress Pinar has use for me. Things are so much simpler when I just obey.*

As he walked down the corridor and peered into the living room, Finn was surprised that everyone had left except for Pinar, curled up like an angel on a mattress in the corner. *With Ash, the woman I scared half to death.*

He had the slightest pang of jealousy, a cramp somewhere in his gut. *I've never slept in a bed with her before.* He looked at their sleeping faces. *With everything we've done together, I don't think I've ever come close to that level of intimacy.*

He pushed it away. *They've been best friends for as long as I've been alive, I can never match that. And I don't need to.*

Finn stepped inside the living room, slipped off his shoes at the door and curled up in the last empty dusty armchair to rest.

* * *

"I can't believe you still get coffee!" Julia exclaimed as she sat down at the table and took a sip of the espresso Cleo had poured her. Julia looked around, taking in all the tastefully co-ordinated wall hangings, the antique lamps, the incense smoke in the air. *Even the tablecloth is beautiful*, she noticed. *I love it here.*

Cleo stood by the stove looking pleased. "I know, right? I mean he's rude, sometimes even demanding, but he's definitely useful."

"I don't know how you do it—I could never."

Cleo stepped away from the stove, one hand on her hip. "It's fine, I got used to it. I also wouldn't want to be running around the city six times a day delivering messages. You must be exhausted."

Julia unconsciously stretched a leg out under the table. "I got used to that too. Which reminds me, are we still on for putting together another food and meds delivery to the Home for tomorrow? Through your...contacts, I mean?"

Cleo sat down on the velvet sheets of her bed. "Definitely. But can we rest a bit first? It's been another epic morning."

"Definitely," agreed Julia. "What did you have in mind? A nap or something?"

Cleo patted the bed next to her with the slightest of smiles. "Or something..."

Chapter thirty-eight

The dunnock's territory had grown in the last year. As the sun reached its zenith, he hopped onto the highest branch of a straggly rhododendron, filling his chest with air. A few months before, he had been coupled with two other males and a female. They had nested together and had many noisy chicks. The previous year he had nested with three males and two females. Every year it was different. Food, weather, territory; these were things he knew intimately but couldn't control. Despite his dull appearance, the perfect camouflage for hopping through bushes and trees, the dunnock's song was bubbling and melodious; it enchanted everyone who heard it. He lifted his beak to the sky and sang

* * *

A sunbeam filtered down through the wooden slats covering the window onto Ash's face. She yawned and stretched. She noticed that the living room was much quieter than she expected it to be. She pulled herself up to look around. Next to her, Pinar was still sleeping, her hair was in a mess over her face and Ash gently tucked it out of the way so she could breathe freely. There were people sleeping everywhere— curled up in chairs, spread out on blankets on the floor—one person had even improvised an eye mask out of a pair of tights wrapped around her face. She saw Finn curled up in an armchair; he had taken his shoes off for the first time since she had met him.

Well good, she thought as she snuggled back down next to her friend and went back in for another nap. *Sometimes rest is the most radical thing we can do.*

It turned out to be the best nap she'd had in years. There was something about collective sleeping, about rest being socially sanctioned, that made her feel safer and allowed her to drop deeper than she could remember doing in a long time.

Chapter thirty-nine

A sharp repeated sound penetrated Ash's senses. *Dunnock. Emergency call. Predators.*
She shook her friend awake without thinking.
"Pin, wake up. It's starting

* * *

X stood in the corridor holding a tray of cups. Her eyes wide with fear. There was an endless pounding on the door. *I have to make it stop.*

"Open up!" shouted a voice through the taped-up letter box. "It's time for this to end."

Oh god. X dropped the tray with a crash. She stared at the door hidden behind the improvised blockade. *That's all that stands between us and violence. Like the demonstration. The blood. No. Not again.*

X ignored the broken cups and found herself running towards the door. Within seconds, she was pulling chairs and cabinets off the pile. *I'm leaving. Right now.*

Stepping out of the living room, Ash and Pinar began running towards her, shouting.

"X! Stop!"

"What *the fuck* are you doing?"

The pounding on the door continued. The corridor was now full of people shouting for X to stop. She showed no sign that she heard them. Instead she braced her body to pull away an old wooden table.

"Out, out," she mumbled to herself. "Out now."

Ash and Pinar caught up with her and managed to grab her hands, one each.

They were barely able to hold her back from destroying what was left of the blockade. She struggled fiercely with one final attempt to pull away from them. Then her whole body froze, her hands went cold and rigid.

"Pin?" Ash asked as she released X's hand. Her face was frozen, her eyes bulging. Her mouth moved but no sound came out.

"I've seen this before," Pinar said softly as she came around to face X and took both of her hands. "X? You're okay, okay?"

"Is she...like me?" asked Ash slowly. "Is she...?"

Pinar gave her a confused look. "What? No. She's frozen. Flight, fight, appease, freeze. She's trying to process."

Ash's expression was indecipherable.

"Process," X almost whispered. "Trying to..."

Pinar looked her in the eye and spoke softly. "X, I know you're feeling really scared right now. This is going to pass. Things are going to change soon, okay?"

"Come, let's sit you down for a minute." Ash tried to lead her back to the living room, but X didn't move, couldn't move.

"Give her a minute," Pinar instructed. She pulled an old bottle of essential oil out of her jeans pocket. She screwed off the cap and held the bottle under X's nose. The fresh smell of lavender drifted up and Ash found herself taking a deep breath as well.

X's eyes were blank but finally they began to soften. A slight look of recognition passed over her face. She took an involuntary breath and her shoulders fell.

"I..."

"Don't speak love." Pinar led her to a chair. "Just rest a bit, you're going to be okay."

X hovered over the chair but didn't sit. "I...I was going to open the door. We might have been killed. I just needed to get out. Oh my god...I'm so sorry."

Ash and Pinar shared a look of relief.

"Here, take this." Pinar handed her the tiny brown bottle. "Keep inhaling it until you feel better."

X took the oil but avoided eye contact. She stared at the ragged carpet and held onto the bottle with shaking hands. Her shoulders slumped with shame.

"Pin, have you got this?" Ash asked discreetly. "I think Elias is already going up. I want to be there with him."

Her friend nodded. "Give them hell

* * *

Elias would be the last to admit it, but he was a skilled negotiator. He stood on the roof of the Home, a few metres away from the open hatch so as to make a quick exit if necessary. Surrounded by other members of the Resistance for moral support, he remembered that he had always been equipped for this.

His family had immigrated to the City from Beirut when he was very young. It had never been easy. Between the pressures of finding work in a racist market, and precarious homes that never lasted more than a year or two, his family was constantly stressed, fractured. They fought a lot and it fell upon Elias to keep the peace. One of the reasons he was so secure in his boundaries—to the point of rudeness—was that he had just had enough of holding everyone else together.

Yet here I am again.

Blinking in the afternoon sun, he stepped towards the edge of the roof. Holding the megaphone in his clenched fist, he prepared to negotiate with the very people who had treated him with such disdain since they had moved him to the Home against his will.

"When are you leaving?" shouted a woman through an equally beaten up megaphone. Elias recognised her as the one everyone called 'the boss'. "The residents need our care!" *Power suit, too well put together.* Elias had never trusted her.

He pressed the trigger-like button and spoke as calmly as he could into the plastic box.

"I can assure you that we, the residents, are doing just fine."

He knew this was only partly true. Despite the new supplies, if there was a medical emergency, they weren't really prepared. *Street medic action isn't going to cut it if one of us has a heart attack.*

"But you need medication and food—we can provide those things for you!"

"Look," said Elias, steadying his feet against the roofing felt. "If your care is genuine and you actually want to help, then yes, there are things we need." *A med school degree would be good.* "But to be clear, we're not ending the occupation."

Down below, a muscled trooper in uniform stepped forward and aggressively grabbed the megaphone from the boss.

"Now listen here!" he shouted loudly enough that the speaker buzzed and squeaked. "You've had your fun. This area is State property."

Elias took an unconscious step back towards the hatch.

"This building will be returned to State management by this evening," the trooper continued. "You choose how many people will get hurt in that process. You have three hours." He turned and walked away, leading the rest of the group.

Elias' hands were shaking so much that he nearly dropped the megaphone. Ash appeared from the hatch's opening and took it from him.

"You did your best, love. Let's head back in. We need to bring this to the rest of the residents."

Chapter forty

The living room was in uproar.

"But we can't let them bully us back into submission!"

"Easy for you to say. Some of us have no other home to go back to after this!"

"We need to prioritise the residents, not some great revolutionary action that leaves half of us behind!"

"But if we step down now, they'll know they can do anything they like. And that will definitely impact the most vulnerable first."

The conversation was going around in circles and there was so little time. Seated next to X who was calmer, but disengaged, Pinar went over the options. They would have to come to some kind of compromise. *There's no way we can fight them off. And some of us are really at risk here. But can the State be trusted to keep their side of the bargain?*

She touched X's shoulder lightly. "Will you be okay if I go get some air?"

X flashed her an automatic smile so Pinar stood.

"I'll be right back," she announced. "I just need to get some space for a minute." And I need Ash. *Where is she even?*

Pinar left the room. She vaguely noticed that the things around her had stopped feeling solid. Her hands seemed far away, the breath in her lungs felt like it belonged to someone else.

Well, that isn't good.

Pinar stood in the middle of the corridor unable to remember where she had been heading. Her body was increasingly numb. A familiar sensation got her attention.

The bathroom. And to find Ash. Or Finn. And so many other things, too many other things, I just don't know how—

Her mind froze for an instant as she stumbled and bumped into a wall. Images of the burning Clinic flashed before her eyes. She was far too aware of her heart in her chest. Sometimes it was all too much. She was overflowing, she could no longer contain everything that had happened.

She made her way to the bathroom and sat on the toilet. She looked distantly at her chipped fingernails. She knew she was dissociating. Her mind was searching for comfort. A story, a memory, anything that wasn't the Home being raided, anything that wasn't refugees being shot. She wanted to time travel too. She closed her eyes and let her mind and body do what it needed to.

Chapter forty-one

H er hair was damp, her shoulders ached. The room she stood in, fists raised, legs in fighting stance, smelled like sweat and rubber. But Pinar was enjoying every moment.

It had been six weeks and every session was the same. Through the ordered chaos of a fated universe or through just sheer good luck, out of a class of twenty, she and he were paired up again for training in Kung Fu.

He'd been doing this for years and had been endlessly patient in showing her the ropes, explaining each move, correcting her mistakes no matter how many times she made them. She was self-conscious at first, a beginner in this all-male environment, but he made her feel relaxed.

He made a lot of mistakes with his English and she laughed when he made fun of himself. She made fun of him too. Sometimes she'd forget a move she'd already practised a hundred times. He'd tease her gently; she'd tease right back. The chemistry was palpable.

There was a subtext to all this good-natured sparring. At least for her. Apart from enjoying all the subtle, complex moves and the way they were trained to respond to each other's unexpected strikes, over the last few weeks she'd come to realise that she was really getting off on punching him. It took her by surprise at first, but it was true. He was handsome, he was funny. And he had a built chest that just seemed to beg for her to practice her hits on it.

Obviously, she thought it was kind of risqué to be enjoying it and she should probably be focusing on something else, but at some point, as she was practising a chain punch on him, she just couldn't help but let it slip out.

"You know, I kind of like this. Punching you, I mean..." She tried to make it sound like a joke. She could barely believe she'd said it and she hid her embarrassment by keeping up her chain punch.

He only paused for a moment, a look passing over his face like a shadow.

"Well, I guess I like you hitting me, so that works out," he responded.

"Yeah?" She tried to keep the humour in her voice. She let her hands drop, noting that she was sweating more than usual and barely breathing. In that moment something passed between them, a glance, an understanding, some intuition that neither of them could miss, but neither could be sure of.

"Yeah...."

The motorbike ride to his house was short. Holding on to his waist, her head against his back, she was unsure how much to touch him, how tightly to hold on. The rush of traffic going by, the feel of his powerful legs against the machine and the smell of his jacket were making her dizzy but she held on. Finally, they arrived. He opened the door without taking off his gloves. She felt herself suddenly run out of patience.

The instant they stepped inside, old roles were left behind: a pile of invisible wrappings shed onto the street. Before the door even closed, she was on him, pushing him hard against the wall. Jackets and scarves and hats showered down around them as her hands grasped his curly, brown hair and her tongue found his mouth. She felt his body softening, releasing itself to her and she just needed more. In a flash, she was carrying him, his body unresisting in her strong arms as she effortlessly took him into the bedroom and threw him onto the unmade bed.

She looked down upon him, still fully dressed in his leather jacket, jeans and boots, his hair dishevelled, his expression helpless and eager. As she climbed onto him, using her knees to open his legs and pinning his arms down to the mattress, she knew they had a hell of a night ahead of them.

"I think you want more of my punches tonight, is that right?"

A look of confusion passed over his face as he understood that he was being asked for consent. Checking was a big part of his life since he'd gotten into BDSM back home years ago. But he'd always found consent discussions in the middle of a session kind of awkward. Important of course, but also confusing. This was different though. This woman had real power. And she was waiting for an answer....

"Yes." he almost whispered.

"Call me, Mistress."

"Yes...Mistress..."

He liked the sound of it, that word slipping off his tongue, and translated it silently into his language to get the full effect. She seemed pleased as she started unzipping his jacket. She pushed up his t-shirt, still damp from training and started running her nails through his tight chest hair.

Despite the rush that was filling her mind and chest, she was playing this carefully. She knew she needed to check consent about hitting him but equally she didn't want to kill the whole thing with a moment to sit down and process. *So far so good though. He seems to be getting the idea.* And having him under her—the way he bit his lip when her fingernails scratched his cute little nipples, the way he writhed with pleasure and pain as she grabbed them tighter and then released them again—had her feeling hot as hell, and her heart pulsed with excitement.

"Here it comes, then," she stated and asked at the same time.

"Yes Mistress, thank you. I'll let you know if it gets too much, but until then, please go for it."

And she landed a punch to his left pectoral muscle, nothing hard, not yet. Just about as hard as in training when they tried to pretend that they weren't enjoying it. He smiled, opening his arms and legs just a little to let her know he wanted more. And she gave it to him. Hit after hit on his well-developed chest, building up the impact just a little each time. She tried a slap to his belly but caught the look in his eye and went back to his pecs.

She paused for a moment to take in the scene before her. This gorgeous guy she'd been checking out since her first lesson, just lying there allowing her, begging her for more with his bright eyes. She nearly came right then and there.

"You've earned yourself a kiss. Nipple or lips?"

"Nipple, please Mistress," he whispered and opened his posture just a little more for her. Her tongue started its achingly slow journey up from his belly button, hidden by dark curly hairs, and slowly followed them up, crossing his surgery scars, up onto the chest that was already reddening a little from the work she'd been giving it. She came painfully close to his left nipple, circled it, and moved up to the bottom of his neck which sent waves of pleasure, almost ticklishness through his body. She felt every one of those waves running down through her breasts and stomach, making her wetter than ever.

Straddling his leg and grinding him slowly she finally took his right nipple in her mouth and his ecstasy ran right through her, almost pushing both of them over the edge. She bit into it, softly at first and slowly, methodically increasing her pressure. She looked up into his handsome face as she turned her bite into a kiss and began sucking his tender nipple. She saw that he was keeping it all in. His body had tensed just a little and he was silent. His face clearly begged for more.

She whispered into his ear, "You know, it'd really turn me on to hear you scream."

It was just the permission he needed. She heard every grunt, whine and whimper as she bit him again and again. She slapped the side of his chest, softly, experimentally, and stared into his eyes to gauge his response. His surprise became a soft smile and she went again, slightly harder. Again and again, all the time keeping an eye on his face to check he was still with her. His breathing was deep. His body shuddered with the endorphins rushing through his system.

"Turn over and show me your ass."

He obeyed, quickly unfastened his belt and pulled down his jeans as far as he could with his boots still on. He buried his face into a pillow. She removed her training clothes and wearing just her underwear began to run her nails down his back.

"Very nice. I love your body. If you want your ass spanked, you'd better get it up where I can see it."

He took the hint and gave consent, pushing his ass up towards her. She waited, drawing out the moment before landing her first, hard slap. She knelt over his leg again and started to grind him through her panties as she hit him again. Her slaps became punches and then slaps again. She listened attentively to his grunts and breathing. She grinded on him faster and felt herself close to peaking.

"On your back."

Without a word, he rolled back over, and she straddled him

again, pushed against him, firmly and totally through her soaked underwear.

She rocked them both, increasing speed and embracing the waves of his pleasure.

She hit his chest again, matching his thirst perfectly with her aggression.

They peaked, lost in endorphins and each other's shouts.

Higher still as release grabbed them. Her eyes were blurred, he began to scream with ecstasy. Higher still until there was nothing in the world but this moment and with a final spasm of giving, they released into each other, and into each other's pain. She collapsed onto him, giving up her defences and falling into his sweat, his warmth, his smell. He ran his hand tenderly through her hair and they slipped seamlessly into another state together, totally trustful and totally given.

* * *

Pinar came back to the moment and pulled up her jeans. She looked briefly at her fingers.

Good, I'm back. Now I'm ready.

Chapter forty-two

There was a pounding on the bathroom door as Pinar emerged, drying her hands on her jeans. She almost bumped into Elias.

"What's happening—is the State here already?"

Her friend shook his head. "No, but they must be on their way." He looked back towards the living room. "We've come to a decision."

"Pin, there you are! Where have you been?" Ash arrived, hands on her hips.

"I just needed a moment," Pinar replied. *And I don't really owe you an explanation.*

Ash looked displeased. "Well, please let me know next time you need to disappear for an hour. I'm barely keeping myself together as it is."

Elias politely stepped away. He didn't need any more conflict today.

Pinar squared up with her friend. *An hour? It was more like ten minutes.*

"Ash, I know this is a lot for you. It's a very stressful situation, but you aren't the only one going through it."

Ash's eyes flashed. She lifted her chin and tightened her jaw.

"I love you, I'm here for you," Pinar continued. "And I know you're here for me too. But also, it's not okay that—"

"Of course I am!" Ash's voice was raised, and her hands were held up in defence. "But it's so much Pin, and sometimes I really wish th—"

Pinar lightly took Ash's hands and lowered them. "Love, let me finish speaking."

Ash stopped mid-sentence. Her mouth was still open.

"It's a lot," her friend reflected. "The clinic, the occupation, your journeying—"

"You have no idea!" Ash interrupted. "How would you like it if you could disappear at any moment, faceplanting into glass, reliving traumatic memories, seeing hideous nightmares that you can't even hope won't come to pass because you know they will."

Pinar waited patiently.

"I hate it! You can't ever imagine what it's like to go through all that. To live with that uncertainty. You called it my 'trait' once—do you remember that? Something that made me *special*, that I was bringing to the world. Something *adaptive*. I fucking hate that too, Pin. I don't want to be special. I just want to fucking survive. Maybe enjoy the sunshine from time to time. And now here we are, locked up in this stinky building with its hideous wallpaper—"

She peeled off a strip to make her point.

"And, it's just. It's just—"

Ash ran out of words and her chest deflated. As she had done for all their decades together, Pinar pulled her in for a hug.

For a moment she felt strangely selfish for standing up for herself, for her right to take space and look after herself. *No, that's not right. We're all doing the best we can. But this can't keep happening.*

Ash was crying on her shoulder and Pinar ran her hand over her friend's stubbly head. "I love you," she whispered. "And Ash?"

Ash pulled slightly away to look at her friend's face. "What?"

"The wallpaper really is hideous

* * *

"This is not the way! We are divided when we should be coming together!"

X was feeling the moment. The sound of her voice through the megaphone. The sunlight on her face as she stood up and faced the city. *Now this, this is the revolution*, she thought to herself.

The troopers looked unimpressed.

"You use tools of violence, but we are peaceful. Why are you afraid of what we've done here? We just want to care for each other!"

A uniformed man stood forward and took the megaphone from his subordinate. He was tall, muscled, his hair clipped and blond. X noticed, with some embarrassment, that he was also quite hot. *Fuck, why does authority do that to me?*

"Now look here," the General shouted, his gruff voice echoing off the Home's front wall. "I couldn't give a fuck about your *peace* and *care*. This is State property and if you don't come out, we will evict you, by whatever means are necessary

* * *

Ash and Pinar sat on the edge of a bed. As so often happened for them, fighting had brought them closer.

"So, we're leaving?" Pinar took Ash's hand and ran her fingers over the wrinkled skin. Her voice sounded relieved and disappointed in equal measure.

Ash shrugged. "There's really no other choice. If we keep

pushing back, the State will come in with full force. There's no way we can hold them back forever. People will get hurt."

"I agree. Some of us would survive an attack for sure, but not all of us would. The risk is too great."

"I guess we knew that it would come to this. Fighting the revolution is very sexy, and you know I love the drama, but we're not the kind of movement that throws people away when they're inconvenient."

Pinar was quiet for a moment. She sat up slightly and lifted her head. "This is the right choice, Ash. We need to leave, and the residents need to stay—those that want to. Did we announce it yet? Did someone go up on the roof?"

Ash gave her a cheeky smile. "Elias is already packing his bags with Oscar. So we asked for someone else to go up there. You'll never guess who volunteered

* * *

X tried to keep her head high, tried to show she wasn't intimidated by this handsome man in uniform. But she was feeling deflated. *Why is there so much hate?*

"I..."

"Well?" the General shouted. "I'm waiting for an answer. And I don't like to wait."

X turned to look at the others who had joined her. Their expressions told her to push on.

She swallowed. "We would like to suggest a compromise."

For just a moment, the General looked confused. He regained his composure quickly.

Without waiting for a response, X took half a step forward. "The Resistance is willing to end the occupation, but we have conditions. There are vulnerable people in this building, and

196

we don't want anyone to get hurt. We must be allowed to leave in peace, and those residents who wish to come with us, must be allowed to go free as well."

The General thinned his lips and crossed his arms. A woman to his side, wearing a dark suit, whispered something to him. She looked desperate.

X kept going. "I'm pretty sure that a massacre of old and sick people in a care home isn't what the State wants. And as divided as our citizens are today, I don't think the City's population would stand for it either. Either this ends now, peacefully, or you'll have a whole lot more fires to put out."

X lowered the megaphone.

She watched the people below her and tried to interpret their expressions. The General took his time and eventually lifted the speaker, pointing it at her like a weapon.

"Eviction in one hour," he announced. "Leave voluntarily and you'll be unharmed."

The woman in the suit spoke to him again. She was insisting something, but X couldn't hear the words.

"Ahem...and those residents who wish to leave will be allowed to do so. But in one hour, the Home will be returned to State management. Mark my words, this ends here."

X turned and stepped away from the edge. Her new friends on the roof looked pleased, even proud of her. She couldn't help but smile as she walked towards them.

Time to go. It was nice while it lasted.

Chapter forty-three

They held hands as they stepped out of the front door of the Home. A human chain. United, even in their defeat.

"Are we doing the right thing, Ash?" asked Pinar, her voice tight with emotion. She already knew the answer.

Ash's voice cracked. "Leave no-one behind."

Pinar looked to her left. Elias' expression was impossible to interpret.

This must be particularly hard on him.

She gave his hand a squeeze, but his eyes were fixed on the horizon. He won't set foot back in this place.

They walked then. The whole group, a good portion of the Resistance went down the steps and into the street. The Home staff cleared the way, and behind them a few young troopers stood nervously holding their weapons.

Ash began to understand. *They're afraid of us, of what we did here. That's the State's greatest fear: that we could care for each other, build something new. Show that something better is possible without them. That's where the real power lies.*

The one she had heard them call the General stepped forward. He didn't need a megaphone for them to hear him this time.

"This isn't over for you!" he shouted.

The group paused and stood nervously in front of him. Ash had a strange feeling that she had met this person before, in a vision maybe. *Or in the future. I don't know how, but I know him.*

She didn't relish the thought.

"I promise I will find a way to rid this great City of you vergers!" the General continued, magnifying his already intimidating voice by puffing out his chest. "I will cleanse the streets of your Resistance filth. I will make the State clean again."

The group didn't know how to respond. They set off at a steady pace—not fast enough to make them look like a moving target—and continued walking until they reached the corner of the street. Ash took one quick glance back and saw the troopers getting ready to leave. She caught a glimpse of some of the residents, and Yarrow, watching them from the window.

God, I hope we're doing the right thing.

* * *

The group walked for a short while together until they reached an abandoned park. After some discussion, they began splitting up.

Cleo and Julia appeared, hand in hand, to help former residents with their bags or to get to their new homes. Several of them gathered near X who had offered her ground floor apartment to as many people as could sleep there. Elias hesitated, but finally joined them—there was no way he could stay on the top floor with Ash and Pinar.

A small circle of older residents gathered at the edge of the park and without a word left the group and disappeared into the shadows. Pinar watched them leave. *I wonder what they're up to?*

Finn approached her with his head slightly bowed. "Should I come with you?" he asked.

Pinar lifted his chin with a finger. "Your work is done here, but thank you. I'll come find you at the office if I need you."

"The office, Mistress? Isn't there a strike on?"

Pinar couldn't help but smile. "Right answer."

He passed her a piece of paper.

"My home address in case we can't meet at the hotel. If you need me. I live with my father, he's older, but come anytime."

Pinar folded the paper and tucked it into her pocket. "Thank you. And you still know my address I guess?" *From a hundred years ago when I was your client and you were my power-hungry accountant.*

Finn nodded. "I do, Mistress."

"Take care, Finn. Stay safe."

Her sub bowed his head with respect. She turned from him, took Ash's hand and headed out towards home.

The Home itself would return to normal, the occupation would become just another piece of forgotten history. But the Resistance had been changed forever. The process of running their own lives for nearly a week had brought something new to many of them, especially the residents. A thirst for autonomy and the fire of rebellion. As they headed towards home, Ash and Pinar knew that this wasn't over.

* * *

X was elated as she arrived with her new friends at her home.

"Mi casa es su casa!" she announced brightly, unlocking the door.

The former residents, including Elias who lingered towards the back, filed in slowly. Tania followed with the bags. As one, they paused in the first room, a grand, spacious living room at least as big as the living room of the Home, but wider, and infinitely better furnished.

Elias looked around the epic space with distaste. *How can people live like this while there are people sleeping in the streets and stealing food from State reserves? Why would anyone want to?*

Standing by the dining table, X spoke again with a wide grin. "You're all welcome to stay as long as you like! Elias, you can have the master bedroom of course. It's the most comfortable bed and it's got an en suite."

Elias looked confused. *Where am I?* He tried to smile politely, but knew it was unconvincing.

X continued. "I have a futon I can sleep on in the annex—there will be space for everyone. Let me give you all the grand tour!"

The former residents shuffled towards her wearily.

"But to begin with, a few house rules

* * *

Panting and sweating up the stairs, Ash and Pinar finally arrived at their flat. Ash had never felt so grateful to arrive back to their musty little home. Without taking off her jeans, she collapsed onto the bed and Pinar soon joined her. Ash vaguely remembered taking her friend's hand and the feel of their legs against each other before they both fell into an exhausted sleep.

Chapter forty-four

A group of people moved through the dark streets, leaving chaos behind them. Former residents of the Home set about sabotaging the city that had kept them locked away for so long.

Some pushed wheelchairs loaded with buckets of cement and made their way onto the tramlines.

Others crept behind the police station with bolt cutters and set about releasing the horses that the troopers had enslaved to their cause.

Some chained the doors of State admin buildings closed—a special surprise for the morning shift. As the former residents were beginning to realise, it was surprisingly easy to shut down a system when no-one noticed you.

5. Insurrection

Chapter forty-five

X was awake at dawn, making her way through the bedrooms. She wore a white dress and her hair was flowing. "Good morning everyone! Time to wake up—it's a beautiful day!"

Half buried in an overly soft pillow, Elias rolled over and stared at her through bleary eyes. If he could have told her to shut up, he would have. *But I'm in your house, in your bed. Awesome power dynamic.*

"Erm...X?" he said with hesitation. "Isn't it a bit early? We've been woken up for rounds every morning for I-don't-know how long. Couldn't we sleep in a bit?"

X paused. She looked offended but tried to hide it. "Oh, I'm sorry Elias! I need to leave soon—I volunteered to help out with food distribution this afternoon. And besides—" she flashed him a bright smile. "—I made coffee!"

Elias pulled himself up with a groan. *Well, coffee does sound good*

* * *

"Morning sunshine."

Through half-open eyes, Ash saw that Pinar was standing in front of her with a tray of hot coffee and some fried vegetables.

"Wow..." she mumbled sleepily. "You pulled out all the stops."

Pinar smiled. "I did. We deserved a treat."

Ash took the coffee mug with a grateful smile. "I don't remember the last time we could get this stuff—how did you even find this?"

"Let me worry about that." Pinar poured herself a cup as well.

Several decades earlier, the coffee plant had become one more victim of climate change, driven ever higher into mountains by warming temperatures until its ultimate extinction. No-one quite knew how the State still managed to maintain its supply, but here it was in Ash's hands and she would enjoy every sip.

"I bet it was Cleo. Her fancy trick gets her all the nice stuff."

Pinar smiled and held out her cup. "To being home—"

They clinked their cups together.

"At least for the time being." Ash took a sip. Her eyes brightened immediately as her body reacted to what she often called 'her favourite herbal medicine'.

"How long do you think it'll take?"

Ash took a moment to respond. Her body was enthralled by coffee and she wasn't ready to leave the experience yet. Pinar waited patiently.

"Wow that's good," Ash said finally. "What was your question?"

Pinar smiled. "How long?"

"You mean before the State works out who was involved and comes to smash down our door? Who knows? They're incredibly inefficient at everything except oppressing minorities apparently."

"I hate living like this. Constantly preparing for what comes next."

"Haven't we always though, Pin? I mean, I'm pretty sure my entire nervous system is wired to escape danger by this point."

Pinar nodded. "I know. We've always been trying to find

tiny patches of safety where we can, but this feels particularly bad." She unconsciously put a hand on her belly as she always did when she was feeling anxious.

"It's really fucking bad. But also..." Ash put down her coffee. "I kind of think something better is coming. I think that's what I saw when I was...gone...those two days. It won't always be like this."

Pinar smiled a little. "You sound positively hopeful, my dear."

Ash poked her tongue out.

"But in the meantime," Pinar continued. "I think we need to make a plan."

"You mean before troopers arrive at our door and we have to climb out of the window and descend nine flights on knotted bedsheets?"

Pinar giggled. The coffee was very strong.

"Well actually..." she said, flicking her hair back. "I was thinking that my hair's getting pretty long these days. Maybe you could climb down it first, and then I'll scale the bricks. I've always wanted to go rock-climbing."

They both laughed. "Perfect, that's a great plan, Pin."

"Right? More coffee?"

Ash held up her cup. "Fuck yes

* * *

"Your drink, General."

The General took the cup without a smile and placed it down on his desk. Today was not a good day. Reports had been coming in all morning about some kind of 'uprising' across the city. Even after his subordinates had restored the Home—with far more diplomacy than he had intended—the Resistance were still out there, causing disruption. The General was deeply unimpressed. He took a sip of coffee and his mood continued to spiral.

Too hot and bitter as all fuck. He looked up at the trooper who still stood at his desk.

"Well?"

"Erm...should I give my report, sir?"

The General looked the trooper up and down.

"Fine. Let's have it

* * *

Buzzing with caffeine, Ash couldn't sit still. She had been pacing the tiny apartment for a while and Pinar was beginning to lose patience.

"Love, maybe we should take a walk or something?"

Ash looked at her with bright eyes. Pinar saw her fingers were vibrating.

"A walk! But there's so much to do, Pin. We have no idea how much time it'll take for the State to work out that we were involved. And when they do, we really shouldn't be here for them to find us. Which means packing up all your junk—" She indicated Pinar's shelves of jars and herbs and knick-knacks with a dramatic wave. "—and then what? Where do we go if we can't stay here? I know Elias found a place, with one of the allies or whatever—"

"X, I think. Your favourite person—"

"I'm sure they'll get on great," Ash said ironically. "But how long can they all stay there realistically? And if he's in danger, then all the residents and former residents might be. Which reminds me—"

Pinar had stopped listening. She packed some snacks into a

bag and silently handed Ash her coat and hat.

"What? What's this?"

"It's your jacket my dear. We're going for a walk before you wear a hole in the carpet."

Ash took her coat but didn't move.

"Do we have time? I mean, the State…"

"Oh my god, Ash. Can we not talk about our oppressors for five minutes please? Let's take a walk and then we can make a plan." Pinar opened the apartment door. "Besides…I have a feeling some interesting things might have happened while we were sleeping. Did you notice that the power is out

* * *

X opened the door and looked around the room. Elias had flopped onto the giant sofa with Mary—formerly known only as resident eighteen—who looked barely awake. The others were gathered around the dining room table sipping their coffee.

"I'm going out for a bit now, but I'll be back in the evening. Please help yourselves to anything in the kitchen. The power seems to be out, so maybe start with the cheese and milk. It should come back on soon though, the solar generators in this neighbourhood are usually pretty reliable."

She held up a keychain ringed with feathers. "Here's the spare key, but once again, if you go out please be quiet. My neighbours are pretty sensitive, and I'd rather avoid questions about why the Resistance is sleeping in my bed!" She laughed awkwardly. No-one responded. "Well, have a great day! And thank you all for visiting my humble abode!" X stepped into the street with a flourish and closed the door gently behind her.

Elias pushed himself out of the sofa and stretched. "Well, I don't know about the rest of you, but I'm going back to bed."

Chapter forty-six

The General stood up, his tanned cheeks flushed red. "So let me see if I understood. Vergers are still taking over the city, but we don't know how. They've magically shut down half the power and solar trains. The life accounts system is in freefall. And the troopers are bitching because their hookers are on strike. Is that about the long and short of it?"

The trooper swallowed.

"Call in the marketing team and recruitment immediately," the General ordered. "We need to clean up this fucking mess." *The State needs a face lift*

* * *

Ash and Pinar stepped into the street.

The City had ground to a halt. The tracks of every solar train had been blocked with cement. The doors to several State buildings were still chained closed. The power had been out city-wide since the early hours and every store and office they could see was closed.

They stood silently taking in the scene. A horse ran past them and disappeared around a street corner.

"Holy fucking shit," Ash said under her breath.

Pinar exhaled loudly. "I told you they'd regret messing with us."

"This can't last though, Pin," Ash's voice was weary.

"Shh..." Pinar took her hand. "I want to enjoy this moment. We never get to celebrate."

* * *

"Okay, here it is. I'm sure you're all aware by now of the mess we're in."

As if to make a point, the overhead light flickered on and off.

"The vergers, vergents, whatever we're calling them now, seem to have been emboldened by their little occupation. The Resistance, even including some of the former residents from the Home, have taken over our city. Our attack will be on two fronts—first..." He turned to the recruitment team. "We need a lot more troopers. Resistance has been spreading like some kind of fungus and we're only going to stamp them out with enough boots on the ground. You're the recruitment team, so get to work. I want to see a significant uptake by this afternoon. Declare an emergency, whatever it takes."

One trooper in the team stepped slightly forward, then thought better of it and moved back.

"Yes, Lieutenant—something to say?"

"Sir. We've been finding it very difficult to recruit in the last few months. There are various factors, but mostly we've found from our focus groups that people are losing interest in joining the army. There are enough other State jobs and the middle-class has been resurg—"

"They still need to eat, don't they?" The General's voice was getting louder, he was gripping the handle of his coffee mug tightly. "They still want to stay in their houses, send their kids to school?"

"Ahem, yes sir."

"Then they'll join. Nutrition tokens limited to troopers or families of troopers. Entrance to schools only with proof that they have a parent in the army. We'll squeeze them and they'll have no choice but to join. Send troopers round with posters, knock on doors, visit workplaces. Get the word out."

The trooper looked surprised but contained himself.

"Yes, sir."

"Well go then, get on with it."

The team left quickly.

"Now," he turned to the marketers in their pressed suits. "How are we going to spin this

* * *

Ash and Pinar took in the surreal scene before them.

It wasn't the first time that the City had been taken over or shut down and Ash was certain it wouldn't be the last. She and Pinar themselves had led some massive demonstrations during the Femme Riots that had created widespread disruption. But after a time, they had grown tired of organising in endless response to things, and of the incredible violence that these actions inevitably provoked from the armies of police and lawyers. Visibility could feel incredible, empowering, life-changing, but the risk it brought them had finally come at too high a cost. They had lost too many good friends along the way to bullets and cages.

So they had returned to their neighbourhoods to do the invisible work that still needed to be done. Tired of demanding that the State or its corporations prioritise people over profit—something they knew would never happen in any meaningful way—they had started creating the world they needed to exist, step by step, meeting by meeting, space by space.

It hadn't freed them from repression, far from it, but it had opened up new connections and marginalised people had gotten their material needs met for the first time in a long time.

As another horse galloped by, Ash knew very well that resistance came in many forms

* * *

The General nodded as the marketers closed up their presentation.

Not bad. Not bad at all.

"—our projections show if we continue to go negative against the 'marginals' as we've designated them here, the majority of citizens, and in particular the middle-class, will turn to the State."

"So let me get this right," the General leaned forward, putting his gloved hands on the desk. "Our plan is to split the vergers down the middle. We'll integrate the most acceptable ones into the army and State institutions..."

Showing how 'tolerant' we are of their degenerate lives and bodies.

"We'll give them jobs and privileges and they'll do our work for us, throwing the 'marginals'—who are nearly all Resistance in any case—under the bus."

Keeping them down where they should be, out of the way of the rest of us. Respectability politics as we called it in the old days.

"That's right, sir."

"Good. I like this," the General said thoughtfully. "And I've seen it work before..."

After all, that's how I got to where I am. Literally my job for ten years: pinkwashing brands and governments, armies, police

forces, deportation airlines. Bringing the acceptable homos, even some of the transsexuals in from the cold, assimilating them into the system. Building our brand of diversity and tolerance and expanding markets while stamping out the radical queers until they were no longer a threat. It worked very well in Berlin and London. It'll work fine here too.

"Sir?"

The General stopped his wandering thoughts.

"Ahem. So...are we still calling this the Improvement then?"

"If you approve, sir. We believe that that branding works even better for us now. We are improving the lives of the good vergers and improving the City at the same time."

"Works for me."

As the marketing team filed out, he leaned back in his chair, watching as one particularly well-built suit filed out. *That tight ass is very distracting.* The General opened his drawer and pulled out a bottle of State gin. *Time to celebrate.*

Chapter forty-seven

A sh and Pinar could barely believe their senses. As they stood watching, at least three hundred people had filled the streets around them and not one of them was over the age of fourteen. Pinar got the attention of someone, around twelve or thirteen years old who Ash thought looked vaguely familiar.

"Excuse me," Pinar said politely. She had to raise her voice to be heard over the shouts, whistles and drums. "Can I ask what this is about?"

"School strike!" the person replied exuberantly. "Almost every school in the City is out here today."

"Incredible," Pinar said, genuinely impressed.

They smiled at her. "But it's been coming for a while, Ms Pinar."

Ash hid her grin. *Even the kids know Pin—and they should.*

"What do you mean?"

"You know, since the Resistance schools were shut down last year."

Ah, that's where I know them from. For close to a decade, the Resistance had run autonomous schools all over the city. Their popular education programmes had flourished, but the State had strict control over education—after all, it still had to produce obedient workers and troopers from the population—and the programmes were finally shut down.

"We were all split up and sent to State schools..." they explained. "It was hard at first, different than what we were used to...but, you know...we're smart. We talked to people and they talked to people. The thirst for real knowledge is strong. I think our generation will be the most radical of all time."

That's what I thought too, thought Ash. *Don't we all actually?*

"Anyway, I hope you enjoy the day, Ms Pinar." The person turned to Ash. "Ms Ash."

They stepped back towards the march and called back, "Welcome to the revolution!" before disappearing into the crowd.

You've got to love their enthusiasm. And God knows we need it. We need everything.

"Well Ms Pinar," said Ash with a wink. "Shall we continue our journey?"

Pinar took her hand. "Welcome to the revolution, dear. Once again."

* * *

Up above the demonstration, blue tits hopped between the branches of a young poplar tree. Despite the growing wind, these little acrobats were perfectly adapted to a life hanging from the thinnest branches, looking for early caterpillars.

Decades ago, this city regularly froze at this time of year and months of snow made finding food difficult. Even water had been hard to find. The blue tits had been forced to peck holes in frozen puddles just to get a drink.

But these birds had no memory of those times. They had never seen snow. For them, autumn merged into spring and caterpillars were mostly available even in the coldest months. The blue tits had adapted to the changes, but they were the lucky ones. So many birds had moved north over those years, those that could. So many insects had disappeared from the land to never return. Dangling from their twigs, calling to each other, ignoring the legions of people moving below them, the blue tits were busy with their day. This was the only life that they had known

* * *

"Let's sit here for a bit."

"Okay..." Pinar looked around. It was a fairly regular corner of a regular street, full of trash and exposed to the wind. They sat down on a curb left over from the days when cars used this road. "Are you tired?"

Ash shook her head. "Not particularly. There's just...something here."

Pinar caught a distant look in her friend's eyes.

"Are you...okay?"

Are you about to journey, she wanted to ask.

"No, no, I'm good. It's just, don't you feel it?

A plastic bag blew past them. *The wind's certainly picking up*, Pinar noticed. *But otherwise, nothing special.*

"Something happened here," said Ash vaguely. "A riot, a demo, something. A person died here I think."

"Today?!"

"No, Pin! Not today. A long time ago...was it one of ours?"

Pinar looked around her again. "No, not one of ours. I mean, nothing we organised, not directly at least, as far as I remember. There was the Femme sit-in over there—" She pointed vaguely to an intersecting street to the west. "And, of course, the riot at the bank, but that was pretty far from here..."

Ash scratched her chin. "That makes sense. It feels a lot older than that anyway. From before. But also, later. Like, it hasn't happened yet. Do you know what I mean?"

"Not entirely," Pinar replied truthfully. "I don't always sense what you can. But I'm not surprised. This piece of land has been fought over forever. And the struggle never really ends."

"Today won't be the last day the City is overturned."

"I certainly hope not."

Another gust of cold air passed through them and they both shivered.

"Let's head home?" Pinar suggested as she zipped up her coat a bit more.

Ash stood. "Yes, I'm hungry."

Pinar smiled. *Well, some things never change.*

Chapter forty-eight

R eport!"

"It isn't good news, I'm afraid, Sir."

The General repressed a smile. Despite the terrible day he was having, he always enjoyed seeing his inferiors getting nervous around him. He could practically smell their fear, their subordination. He could never get enough of that.

"Elaborate, soldier."

The trooper swallowed. "Apparently, the schools are now joining the strike, or at least the kids are. And unfortunately, we've had very limited uptake for the recruitment drive..."

"Limited?"

"Zero, sir."

"Not good enough. They should be flooding in by now. Don't they want to protect their City from this perversion?"

Or eat, more to the point.

"Sir, it seems that many of our citizens have been finding...ahem...other sources to meet their needs. There's been a big increase in people using the soup kitchens for example. And we have intel on medicines being smuggled in from outside the walls."

The General felt heat under his perfectly pressed collar. "Resistance?"

The trooper shifted his weight and tried not to look at the door out of the office. "Yes, sir."

"Didn't we burn down their godforsaken clinic or whatever

it was?"

"Yes, sir. But several more spaces have appeared in its place—some buildings on the edge of town have been squatted. And there are the pre-existing Resistance spaces— the report I gave you last month detailed some of them, sir."

"And why haven't we burned those as well?"

The trooper took a subconscious step towards the door, then caught himself and stood stock still.

"You decided that they weren't a high-priority target...sir."

"Did I indeed?" The General sat back in his chair, clasping his hands behind his head and putting his boots up on the desk. "Well, now they certainly are. Send troopers to every one. Burn them down, evict them, whatever it takes. And start following up on those addresses for the ringleaders. I want all this shit shut down today."

The trooper nodded politely. "Of course, sir. I'll get right on it. Was there anything else?"

The General looked thoughtfully for a moment at his own boots, the way the office lights reflected off the highly polished leather. It had been a very long time since he'd had a man licking his boots. The look of adoration. The sheen of spit on leather. He missed those days.

"Sir?"

"What? No. Nothing else. Get to work. I want the Resistance shut down once and for all. Half of this City will be recruited by tonight, and we'll stamp the fucking vergers out. We've let filth run our city for long enough. It's time to clean up."

The trooper nodded politely and, as fast as he could, left the General's office

* * *

Back in their candlelit apartment, Ash and Pinar were making a late lunch. Pinar had dug out an old bag of rice and was giving the dirty grains a thorough clean in the sink. Ash was vigorously chopping vegetables.

"Do we have more carrots, Pin?"

"More? But you've already cut up enough for a hundred people!"

"Trust me."

Pinar rolled her eyes, but obediently dug around at the back of the cupboard and produced a muddy paper bag. "These are from a few weeks ago, the last harvest from the community garden. They're a bit bendy—" She waggled one in front of Ash's face to demonstrate.

"They'll do." She spread them out on their cracked chopping board and started slicing.

"Aren't you overdoing it a bit? I know you're hungry, but we need to eat tomorrow as well. It looks like you're cooking for half the Resistance."

"Trust me."

Pinar sighed. Just then, as Ash was pushing the carrot slices into the soup, there was a loud knock on the door.

"Tania! Cleo! Yarrow! What a surprise!"

Pinar stepped back to let her friends in and Cleo leaned in for a peck on the cheek.

"Bad news," said Tania, holding out a piece of paper.

Pinar took the poster and read it out loud.

As of today, January 26ᵗʰ, 2035, the State has been declared an LGBT-free zone. Vergent propaganda will no longer be tolerated in our beautiful city and those who defy our laws on presentation, behaviour and identity will be exiled without delay. Those who assist in the State's efforts of Improvement will be rewarded—report suspicious behaviour to the authorities immediately.

See it. Say it. Improve it.

"Well, that isn't good."

"Not good at all," Tania agreed. "And it's getting worse. A trans woman was pepper-sprayed by some kids in the park this morning. Another had the windows of her second-floor apartment smashed in. The city is going to shit."

Cleo stepped forward and touched Pinar's shoulder softly. "That's why we're here to help you pack."

"I see." Pinar's voice was deadly serious. "Yes, I guess that needs to happen."

"But first, food!" announced Ash from the kitchen, apparently unfazed by the news.

"Amazing," said Tania. "But is there enough?"

Ash smiled and started serving up.

"Has it really come to this? I don't think I'm ready to just abandon our life here." Pinar was speaking between mouthfuls and as she usually did when she was emotional, she was eating too fast. She put down her fork and swallowed. "It was so hard just getting this place—and paying the rent. I can't think about looking for a new place for us."

Perched next to her on the bed, Ash put her hand on Pinar's lap. "Once again, Pin. I don't think we have any other choice."

Sat on the floor, nibbling on a fried carrot, Yarrow spoke for the first time since their dinner had begun. "It's time. But we're going to do all we can to find you something else. Somewhere safer—"

"But there's nowhere safe for any of us!" Cleo slammed her fork and knife down dramatically. "I mean, I have Protection, but that might not mean anything in a few weeks."

Yarrow looked sad as they poked at their food. "I'm sorry. I feel like this is my fault. Maybe the occupation was a bad idea. I feel like it's just made things worse."

Ash tutted. "No. There have been demonstrations every day for months now, wildcat strikes, the sabotage from last night...this place is ready to explode. I have no idea what's coming next, but I'm sure of one thing. There's no going back from here."

They fell silent then and returned to their food. The spectre of State violence was thick in the air between them.

Chapter forty-nine

X paused for a moment to take in the bounty that had been collected. She was busier than she ever remembered being, but she felt great. With helping the residents in her home in the morning and helping the food collective set up a new squatted food distribution centre, she had barely had a moment to rest, much less to stretch. But despite that, she felt amazing.

Connected, even. Like this is where I was always meant to be.

She saw the line of people who wanted to pick up vegetables was getting longer and had started to merge with the people distributing medicines. All of it was either raided from the State, brought in by people with more credit, or smuggled in from beyond the walls. *Through some kind of tunnels, they said. There's so much more to this city than I ever realised*

* * *

This is epic, thought Pinar as she filled yet another cardboard box with jars of herbs, twigs, tinctures and cups she'd forgotten she ever had. *How did we ever accumulate all of this?*

Ash was lounging on the bed watching her work with a smug smile. Ever the minimalist, it had taken her less than twenty minutes to stuff her tiny pile of clothes and pills into a bag. She hadn't particularly prepared to leave the house that night, it was more that she was always preparing. The security of being able to move home at the drop of a hat was as built into her as nest-building and creating comfort were built into her friend. Tania and Yarrow re-appeared at the door, their faces damp with sweat.

"How much...more...is there?" Tania asked between pants.

Pinar looked ashamed. "Just two more." She indicated the two boxes she had already filled and put next to the door, hoping that no-one would notice the small mountain of other miscellaneous items that still needed a home. At least half of it had been brought in from the street for some day when it would definitely be useful.

"It's all good," said Yarrow kindly. "What we can't store at Cleo's, we can put in mine. Or I can probably smuggle some of it to the Home on a night shift."

"How is it there now, by the way?" asked Ash.

"It's weird. I think we're all trying to pretend nothing happened. The only major change is that my boss is being weirdly nice to me and the residents. I think she's scared of us!"

Ash grunted. "She should be."

Tania sat down on a box to catch her breath. "We did what we could, and it could have ended much worse."

"It still might," said Ash with a sigh. "Not for the residents hopefully, if the State keeps its agreements. But for the rest of us." She looked around their tiny, increasingly empty, apartment.

Pinar sat down amongst her mountain of jars and books. "It might be okay though Ash, we don't know what's going to happen. Maybe we'll just spend a few days with our backpacks, this will all pass, and we'll be back here by next week."

Ash looked away. There could definitely be such a thing as too much optimism

* * *

X stepped forward to help as the mass of people started to self-organise back into tidy lines. People at the front of the queue stepped aside as a woman with a baby in her arms moved to the front and was given a box of food stuffed into an old supermarket trolley. X was impressed.

Until, what? A week ago? I had no idea people could do things like this. I thought the world was built on competition. On hoarding what we had, minus the occasional charity so we could feel better about ourselves. But this is something completely different.

She glanced at the boxes of Nutrition meals and vegetables. A hand-written sign made from a piece of cardboard was propped up against them.

This food distribution centre is built on mutual aid. Give what you can—ingredients, time, credit—and take as you need. Organisational meetings on Tuesday evenings, open to all.

X sighed with contentment and leaned against the make-shift bar. *I love this.*

A moment later a shout went up near the front door. A dozen troopers, armed with tear gas, pepper spray and batons, were coming around the corner.

Chapter fifty

M was at home taking a moment for himself, spread out on the sofa. He had barely half an hour before he needed to go pick up the kids from nursery, then groceries, then start dinner. *And I'd better clean up the flat before their mum gets home or we'll fight again for sure.* M's wife worked under the General and had been increasingly short-tempered lately.

He felt exhausted just thinking about how much he needed to do. He was already fatigued after a long day at work. *Boss breathing down my neck all the time. Minimum wage, even though I work like a dog. And we still have last month's rent to pay.* He sighed and rubbed his hands over his face.

Just then there was a knock on the door and the sound of something being pushed through the letterbox. *Odd, the post never comes this late.* M stood up, stretched and made his way over to the door. A folded piece of reused paper sat on the mat. He picked it up, unfolded it and inhaled loudly. He read it again out loud, just in case it might change what was written there.

"M, you have been selected to join the State's illustrious army. All other placements will be postponed until further notice. Access to State stores and services for your family will be contingent upon your service. Report for duty at seven hundred hours tomorrow at your neighbourhood barracks. Yours in service and protection, blahblahblah."

What the fuck is this? They're conscripting us into troopers now?

M looked around at the messy flat, the kids' toys spread all over the floor and the pile of bills next to the door that still needed paying. *Well, fuck*

* * *

The distribution centre erupted into chaos as troopers tried to break down the front door.

Boxes were dropped, spilling vegetables all over the floor. A man slipped on a turnip. A baby started crying. People raised panicked voices and started moving around, frantically trying to find a way out. X stopped. She breathed. She felt her feet on the ground as she stepped forward and called out.

"Wait, slow down. Everyone! Please, slow down. I've seen this before, and we have a plan."

It went smoother than she could have expected. Barricades were set up at the front door within minutes, holding back the newly recruited troopers. The troopers, not well-known for forward thinking, hadn't checked other entrances and the entire squat was out of the back door—the most at risk sandwiched in by the rest—within ten minutes. Boxes of meds and food were carried out and they faded away into the city while the troopers—soldiers for barely an hour—were still struggling with the front door.

X found out later that, in a fumbled attempt to pass a tear gas grenade through a crack in the door, some of the troopers ended up gassing themselves in the face. She wasn't sad.

* * *

"What's this?"

The General had left his office for the first time that day. He paced up and down the lines of booths where his many admin workers were busy. Each worked on an archaic manual typewriter, surrounded by piles of many-times-recycled paper. Even with all its power and control, the State had as many problems getting paper or squeezing enough power from the failing solar panel system as the rest of the population. Cutting ties with the rest of the world had come at a high cost.

The booth workers pretended not to hear him and tried to look busy rustling their papers.

"I said...*what the fuck is this?*" The General's day wasn't getting any better and the report that he'd found on his desk when he returned from the bathroom had made him furious.

He grabbed the shoulder of the nearest booth worker, forcing her to turn around. Her eyes were wide.

"It's a...financial report, Sir." Considering the words 'Financial Report' were written across the top of it in red ink, she hoped it didn't sound like sass.

"I know what it is," spat the General. "I want an explanation!"

The worker flinched a little but tried to stay in control of her features. "May I see it, Sir?"

The General threw the report down on her desk, knocking over her carefully piled papers. She picked it up and scanned it.

"Well, it seems that...erm...there was some kind of problem in accounting. Some mislaid tax contributions, maybe a decimal point in the wrong place. Since yesterday...ahem..." The worker cleared her throat.

"Yes?"

"Well, according to this report, sir. Since yesterday, the State is, erm...bankrupt. I don't understand all of it, I must admit. I'd need to check the numbers with my colleague. But public life accounts seem to be at zero."

The General stared at her as if she was single-handedly bringing down the system with her words.

"Sir? I'm sorry to ask but are we still going to get paid? I have kids at home..."

The General turned on his heels and stormed back into his office, slamming the door behind him. *I need another fucking drink*

* * *

Finn adjusted the sign on his office door.

"Accounting is closed due to unforeseen circumstances."

The revolution, for example, he thought to himself.

He had spent the day at his desk, doing what he did best— moving numbers around. They made much more sense now; his work was done. The State would take years to recover from his cold, precise sabotage. He stepped back in and took one last tour around the empty floor. He walked carefully past the small bonfire of papers still smouldering in the sink and, with a sigh, tenderly ran a finger over the polished desk where he had first met Pinar on that fateful day. *This is for you, Mistress.*

Finn left the office, locked the door for the last time and started down the stairs. As he exited the building, his jaw muscles ached from grinning. Only with Pinar had he ever felt this alive.

What next

* * *

"Are you ready, love?"

Pinar had already gotten her backpack on. Even after giving

away almost everything she owned, it was still much heavier than she thought it should be. *But it's also way too light. What if this is all we have now? What if we can never come back here?*

"Nearly." Ash glared at the backpack at her feet.

Pinar looked at her friend with admiration. *She's so strong. She's been doing this—picking up and moving her entire life— forever.* But she knew her best friend well enough to know she would be taking it hard. *Trans people might be experts at surviving homelessness, but that doesn't make it any less painful.*

Ash reached for her hand. "Pin, I'm actually not ready."

"What do you need?"

Ash looked away. Pinar knew she was tearing up.

"We need to...say goodbye. To this place."

Pinar took off her bag and sat down on the hard floor. "So, let's say goodbye

* * *

Ash sat cross-legged facing her friend. They held each other's hands softly, their eyes closed. Ash felt the wooden floor beneath her. The air, full of dust disturbed by their packing, tickled her nose. A treecreeper she had known for years called from the plane tree outside the window. She felt herself connecting, dropping into the moment. It was a physical sensation, but images were strong in her mind. The past and the future were like balloons swollen ahead of and behind her. She stood between them in the present, in an epic landscape of time. As she watched in stillness, the past and future emptied. Memories and worries, regrets and hopes, leaked into the present. Her moment, only this moment, filled and filled until there was nothing else. Only her breathing, her sensations, the warmth of the hands of her best friend in the world, existed.

Thank you, she thought, but also said. *Thank you for keeping us safe here. Keeping us dry from the rain. For your thick walls and your soft sounds. Thank you for giving us a place to sleep and survive. To be together. May whoever comes after us, enjoy your protection. May you be well taken care of.*

She squeezed Pinar's hands and they both opened their eyes. Her friend's expression was soft, connected. Another squeeze and they were ready.

"Well," Ash said as she hefted her bag onto her back. "Here goes nothing

* * *

Ash, Pinar, Tania, Yarrow and Cleo stood together, looking back at their building, the curtainless windows on the top floor, their home for years, empty for now. Ash adjusted the rucksack on her back for the third time. The very few things she owned had become inexplicably heavier with every flight of stairs and her shoulders were already chafing.

She turned abruptly away from the building and her bag bumped into Pinar's.

Ash took a small step forward towards the city centre, and the future.

"So," she asked her friends. "What comes next?"

Chapter fifty-one

Radio masts, satellite dishes, antennas. At the top of the tower there were so many good places for a crow to perch. High enough to view the whole neighbourhood and keep an eye out for dropped food, hidden enough for the humans below to never notice. The perfect place to gather with friends, to rest after a morning on the wing. But that day, an enemy had invaded her territory.

A goshawk, pausing on her long hunting path from coast to river had chosen the wrong place to rest. The crow had to attack, she had to make the invader visible for all those at risk. She herself didn't have eggs yet, but she would again soon, and the goshawk wouldn't think twice before killing her young.

She attacked first, swooping and calling with all her force. She dived, claws bared and barely missed the goshawk's arched back. She swooped again and was joined by others. More crows passing by soared down to join the mobbing. They attacked and called as they always had.

They had so little defence against this great predator of squirrels and baby crows, but at least in these collective moments they felt powerful. Defending the eggs and nests yet to come they called and attacked, called and attacked. Their nervous systems in high gear, their bodies filled with adrenaline, they couldn't stop.

Towers had replaced treetops. Satellite dishes were just a toxic mimic of budding branches of pulsing sap and bark. But some survival instincts, some rhythms of this land were too strong to be smothered by cement and asphalt. Down below, the humans of the city barely noticed the drama taking place in the sky above them.

Finally, the goshawk, tired of the disturbance that seemed to follow her wherever she went, took flight. She would have to find a new place to rest

* * *

The demonstration swallowed them before they had even turned the corner. Ash, Pinar and the others were instantly surrounded by what seemed like a good half of the city's population, shouting and banging saucepans with wooden spoons. A *cacerolazo*, Ash noticed. *Because what could be a more accessible protest tool than a saucepan from the kitchen?*

Ash's mind and body were instantly overwhelmed by the noise and so many human bodies in one place. *Me and Pin should probably sit this one out.* She looked around for Pinar, but her friend was being pulled away into the crowd. They reached for each other, just managing to join hands. Pinar pulled her over and with Yarrow and Tania, they formed a small circle of calm in the chaos. *That was too close for comfort*, thought Ash, catching her breath. *We would never find each other again in this mess*

* * *

I'm too late. Fuck, I'm too late.

Twenty metres away from Ash and Pinar's building, standing next to a smashed-up bench and braced against the wind, Finn felt his chest constrict. The building was surrounded on all sides. Through the window of the top floor, he could see troopers moving around inside. Like a line of ants, troopers ran in and out of the main entrance carrying pieces of people's lives in their arms. A clothing rack. A mattress. A vanity mirror. It was clear that this was much more than just an eviction of known organisers; it was a raid. *And they want to make sure Pinar and Ash have nowhere to come back to.*

"Hey you!"

Finn's heart jumped

* * *

"Ash, this is getting pretty wild!" Pinar had to shout just to be heard over the pots and pans. "If we get split up, we need to make a meeting point."

Ash was jostled by a tall man holding up a banner. A whole group of people banging saucepans passed by her on the other side. She couldn't hear herself think.

"*Wait,*" she signed, her eyes brightening. "*Do you remember my favourite spot? With the view?*"

Pinar smiled with recognition. "*Perfect, I love that place. But hon?*" She pulled Ash a little closer. "*Let's just not get split up okay?*"

Ash nodded. "*Good plan*

* * *

"Hey, come over here!" A trooper was running towards Finn. *Should I run? No, that'll only make me more of a target.* Finn stood his ground.

"Yes?" he said as nonchalantly as he could. "Is there a

problem?"

"Shut up. I ask the questions." The trooper couldn't be more than twenty years old, Finn noticed. *And he hasn't even learned to tuck his trousers into his boots properly. A new recruit for sure—so many of them now.*

Finn nodded obediently and waited for a question.

"Do you live here?" the trooper asked, looking Finn up and down.

"I don't...sir."

"Do you know anyone who does?"

Finn shook his head. "I'm just on my way back from the office." Finn said, indicating his suit with his hands. "I work in State...administration. I live in the next neighbourhood. I don't like walking through this area but can't trust the solar trains in this weather. You know how it is."

The trooper took one more look at Finn's well-polished shoes, his pressed shirt collar and said gruffly, "Then get on home, mate. The vergers are being run out today. You don't want to get caught up in this."

Finn nodded and left at a steady pace, risking a quick glance back at the scene. The troopers were now exiting the building with what looked like parts of a kitchen cupboard.

I need to find Pinar

* * *

Someone else banged into Ash's backpack. This time she nearly fell.

"I have to put this down for a minute. Pin, help me?"

Her friend came behind her and helped her to lower the heavy pack onto the asphalt.

"What do you have in here anyway? Rocks?"

Ash stuck her tongue out. "Yours is at least ten times heavier than mine. I don't have a single jar or herb book in mine."

"Well," said Pinar with a smile. "That might be true."

"Tania, would you mind carrying my bag?" Ash asked. Tania smiled and took it from her, hoisting it effortlessly onto her back.

"Here," said Cleo softly to Pinar. "I can take yours too if you like."

Pinar handed her bag over with a smile.

It was then that the loud bangs came from ahead. That the tear gas started to spread and the lines of pepper spray fell from the sky. Like a shoal of fish fleeing a predator, ten thousand people began to run.

Chapter fifty-two

As they ran around a corner, Pinar grabbed Ash's hand and pulled her towards a doorway—*a fire exit*, Ash noticed vaguely. Pinar slammed her weight against the horizontal bar and the door opened, revealing a narrow corridor.

"Ash, quickly."

Pinar practically dragged her through and they ran inside. As the door swung closed behind them, the building became almost completely dark.

"Pin, where are we?" Ash asked breathlessly, but her friend pushed on. They turned a corner, took another corridor past some bathrooms and what looked like a coat check in the dim light.

The space suddenly opened up into a hallway, sunlight streamed in through dusty windows that stretched from floor to ceiling. Pinar crouched down behind some kind of statue and Ash joined her. They huddled together, the statue between them and the front of the building. Beyond the windows, Ash could hear yelling and the occasional explosion. *They gassed us.*

"Pin..." she whispered, holding onto her friend tightly. "What is this place?"

Pinar gave her a tight smile. "You really don't know?"

Ash looked around then at the walls lined with frames, the statues gathered around them, a display of some kind covered in soda cans. "Oh," she gasped. "I've never been in here before!"

After years of intentionally avoiding it, they had taken shelter in the most unlikely of places. The City Gallery of Modern Art.

Chapter fifty-three

A sh stared at the ugly statue looming above them. As her eyes adjusted to the light, she thought she would begin to understand it. She didn't. It seemed to be a concrete bird sculpture embedded with toothbrushes. *Why though?* Kneeling on the floor, Ash looked at the thick dust on her hands. The gallery had been closed for so long, she had forgotten it even existed.

Another explosion drew her eyes to the windows. "Pin," she whispered. "Maybe we'd be safer back in the corridors. We're too exposed here."

Pinar shook her head. "We need to get back out and find Cleo and the others."

Ash's eyes flashed. "Then why are we in here?"

"I wanted to protect you. I didn't have time to think."

"But—"

Something heavy bounced off the outside of one of the windows and they both pulled instinctively back down behind the sculpture.

Pinar stood and grabbed Ash's hand again, pulling her to her feet just as the windows exploded.

Light flooded the gallery. All around them, abstract paintings and sculptures were illuminated. Ash stood and stared at the brightly coloured installations even as the first toxic whiff of tear gas reached them.

"Ash. Ash! Come on!"

Pinar pulled her towards a window, now just a jagged line

of broken glass at knee height. They stepped carefully over it and were back outside. There were people everywhere, running and panicking. Pulled along down the street, away from the building, Ash looked back for a brief second. *What the fuck was that about?*

She felt it almost before it happened. The people around her were pushing forward, pushing her too hard, she couldn't breathe. A bang somewhere ahead made her duck her head instinctively and she felt Pinar's hand slip away. By the time she looked up, her friend was gone, engulfed by the crowd.

Chapter fifty-four

Ash ran. That was all she could do. Her friends lost somewhere in the crowd of thousands of terrified people, her instincts to escape took over. The City, her home for so long, became a blur as she turned corner after corner.

On her daily walks, she loved to take it slow, to reconnect with each special spot along the route, to visit the friends who lived in the trees, the bushes and up high on rooftops. Every street, every neighbourhood held a memory for her.

But, now, blood pounding in her ears, she saw nothing but the street ahead. She knew they were still chasing her. Whenever she paused to catch her breath, it took only a moment before she heard shouts from behind. She didn't dare look back. She pushed on, no destination in mind. She just needed to keep going until she found a way out. Another corner and suddenly she had run out of city. Out of land. She stood at the edge of the cliff that marked the end of the State and the end of the continent. *Nowhere to go but down.*

Ash looked desperately around until she found what had once been a path down to the beach. As she descended, as quickly as she could on loose pebbles, the rocky stairway disappeared into the cliff, giving way to a sheer drop. She looked down, disbelieving. She heard voices from up above.

No way back now.

Braced against the wind and the inevitability of either violence or falling to her death, Ash turned to face the cliff and started lowering herself down, searching for a foothold

* * *

"Ash! Ash! Are you here?"

Pinar's words were lost in what was quickly becoming a full-blown gale. The run up the narrow street and the stairs had been exhausting, and Pinar had to steady herself against the oak tree just to keep from falling over.

She caught her breath and shouted again for her friend, although she could already tell that the park was so small that if Ash was already here, she'd see her for sure.

Pinar stepped over to the rail and looked out from their meeting point. She could see for miles, from the sea, turned white by the storm to the forest that stretched to the horizon. And in between, the streets of the city, which even from this height were clearly filled with rivers of people trying to escape. The gates were open to the north and east and a few dark crowds of people had already been forced out. Just beyond the walls, more gathered. Pinar could only imagine what they were going through. She looked at the sky to get an idea of the time. *God, I hope you're not out there. Ash, where the fuck are you*

* * *

Hanging from the edge of the cliff, Ash couldn't remember a time when she had felt more scared or more focused. Crawling down the rocks, foot by foot, hand by hand, she tried not to look beyond her feet except to see how far she still had to go. *Still ten metres or so. It might as well be a kilometre.* Her hands were beginning to cramp, a muscle in her shoulder was trembling. Against her will, her eyes ran down the cliff face to the rocks beneath. *I won't make it. There's just no way.* Her left leg began shaking too and she tried to adjust her position to make it stop.

Fuck this, just keep going, girl.

Ash found a new foothold, moved her right hand down to a new gap in the rock and lowered herself down another half metre. Despite her focus, an image of Pinar next to her in bed, her hair bedraggled and her breath light and sleepy, flashed through her mind. Ash pushed on.

Finally, she reached the base of the cliff. A sheltered cove, contained by cliffs and the crashing waves, the sand was soft and untouched. At any other time, it would have been a beautiful place to rest, have a picnic, even take a nap. But Ash knew that the troopers wouldn't stop searching for her, even if she had momentarily confused them with her rock-climbing antics. She looked over to the cliff to her left which led out to a small headland. Near the end of the outcrop was an old staircase dug into the rock that wound down to the beach. *Well, I wish I'd known about that twenty minutes ago.*

A gust of wind blew in from the sea. Ash knew she was terribly exposed. She looked around her for a place to hide. The beach was flat and exposed, the rocks on the beach only came up to her knees. *Nowhere here.* She moved around, her body tired and tight, looking for an option. Then she saw it, further up on her right. A large outcrop of rock hid some kind of dark nook behind it; she only noticed it because she had moved from side to side, otherwise the outcrop kept it well hidden. *God, I hope it's big enough to get in.* Ash ran across the sand, shaking out her tired arms as she went. Then she started climbing again

* * *

Pinar withdrew from the edge of the park. She was too high up to see anything from up here anyway and she decided to try to get somewhere more sheltered while she waited. The oak tree, by far the largest tree in the tiny park, got her attention and without thinking she walked over to it. She ran a hand over the course bark. It was cold from the wind, rough, beautiful. *How long have you been here, friend?* Pinar continued to walk around the ancient trunk and gasped as she arrived on the other side. *A cave!* The tree was so old that it had developed a gap of several square metres in its trunk nearly down to ground level. Over the decades, it had been home to foxes and squirrels, several generations of raccoons and for one summer, a colony of hornets. Pinar peered in; apart from a thin layer of moss and a few mushrooms it seemed to be empty. She could already feel how much warmer it was inside. She climbed in

* * *

Ash's cave would barely be big enough. Between the entrance and the rocky outcrop, there was a tiny platform barely half a metre wide. Ash pulled herself up onto it and flopped onto her belly for a moment. She pulled up her legs and caught her balance as pebbles and sand scraped away from the platform and fell back down to the beach. She peered into the nook. She had half a hope that it might be the entrance to a cave. A warm place she could get into to escape the wind and hide from the troopers that she knew would be making their way towards her very soon. *It'll have to do.* Ash turned around and pushed her backside into the shallow nook until she reached the floor. She pulled her knees up in front of her and held them close. The outcrop in front of her gave her a little shelter and the rock beneath her bottom was surprisingly comfortable. She could feel her tired back expanding and her breath slowing. Then she saw the boots and legs of the first trooper appear over the edge of the headland, thirty metres ahead. They had found the staircase.

Chapter fifty-five

in, I need you.

Ash was curled up as small as she could be, barely daring even to breathe. The outcrop in front of her kept her mostly hidden, but if she could see the troopers descending en masse to the beach, then at the right angle, they'd be able to see her too. She knew there was nothing else she could do but to stay still and to hope the troopers weren't paying attention.

No, that's not enough, Ash realised. *Hope is never enough. I need to do something. But what? I'm stuck in a fucking hole between a rock and a hard place. I'm a hundred years old. I can't fight.*

But then Ash knew what she had known for a very long time, but never wanted to admit to herself. Hope may not be enough, but there are always options.

It was then that she left her body behind, curled up tight against the wind and State violence. She left and she knew exactly where she needed to go.

Chapter fifty-six

P in! Are you here?"

"Ash?" Slowly, cautiously, Pinar's head appeared from inside the oak tree. "Ash! Oh my god, you're here, you're okay!"

Ash stood near the entrance to the park, barely ten metres away from her friend. But Pinar had the strangest sensation she was actually so much further.

"Wait..." she said, pulling herself out of the tree. "You're *not* here, are you?"

Ash shook her head.

"When?" asked Pinar as she started walking over to her friend. "For me it's 2035, late January."

Ash smiled then. "For me too."

Pinar paused in her tracks. "Wait...what?"

"I did it, Pin. Somehow, I journeyed by my own will. And apparently not through time." Ash ran her hands over her own head as if checking that she was real.

"Wow, okay. That's new. I lost you in the demo so I came up here. You said we should meet here if we got separated. I've been so worried. Are you okay?"

Ash reached Pinar and took her hand. "I'm not okay. I'm hiding in the cliff and troopers are everywhere."

Pinar's eyes went wide. "*In* the cliff?"

"Yes. The little cove we went to that time. Remember when you brought jam sandwiches and we managed to attract half the wasps in the State?"

"I remember."

"Pin...can you come get me?" Ash seemed to fade for a moment, then her image and the sensation of her hand in Pinar's returned. "I need you."

Pinar nodded with determination. "I've got you."

"Pin," Ash said, fading again. "I think I—"

And she was gone.

Pinar stood alone in the park, accompanied only by the wind. She took barely ten seconds to catch her breath, to process everything. She grit her teeth against the wind, turned towards the sea. She ran.

Chapter fifty-seven

Ash was numb, shutting down. She didn't dare to look out from her nook anymore. *Whatever happens will happen.*

Her body had stopped shaking a while ago. *How long have I been here?* There was only the wind. The sounds of the sea smashing. She wanted to burst out of the tiny hole, to make a run for it. *Hopeless. Just stay. Just stay.* She closed her eyes, there was nothing else to do.

She waited and tried not to hear the troopers calling to each other across the beach or the pounding of her own blood in her ears. At some point, she became aware of a seagull near her. *Herring gull,* she noticed distantly. *A baby.* The gull looked at her curiously and hopped away. Ash felt nothing.

"Ash? Ash?"

Great, now the seagulls know my name. Ash knew she wasn't thinking straight. Her mind was too cold to think. She couldn't.

"Can you hear me? I'm coming up!"

Only her friend's warm hands on her legs brought Ash back.

Pin.

You came.

As Pinar led her back down to the beach, their little cove, empty except for blowing sand, Ash fell to her knees. She felt Pinar wrap herself around her, her body warm and safe. Ash cried. She didn't know if she would ever stop.

"Ash, we need to move. And it's getting dark."

Ash grunted and sniffed loudly, wiping her nose on her sleeve.

"Ash?"

"What? What?" She sat up and glared at Pinar. "I *can't* move! Can't you see? I'm half *dead*. I can't take any more!"

Pinar looked at her with a patient expression. "Darling..."

Ash sighed and looked out over the sea. "I'm sorry Pin. I'm fucked up. The Home, then *our* home, then this. I honestly don't know how much more I can take."

"I know, hon," Pinar's breath was heavy as she rubbed her friend's stubbly head. "It's unbearable. But we *do* need to leave. Up in the park, I saw it. The gates are open, people are already leaving—or being forced out. I guess some people with Protection will stay, but the rest of us...we're not welcome here anymore. We need to leave."

"What do you want us to do, Pin? The State took away our IDs years ago—no-one else will take us! Should we go live in the forest like badgers for fuck's sake?"

Pinar's face was stricken.

Ash paused and took a deep breath. *This isn't her fault. This isn't anyone's fault. It's a system that was designed to destroy us. We should have been dead decades ago.*

She pushed her shoulders back and lifted her chin.

"Okay then. Badgers it is."

Chapter fifty-eight

The City was quiet. The wind had died down and the streets were empty.

Whatever had happened after the demonstration—Ash and Pinar couldn't think about all of the implications—people were staying in their houses where they could. Only every fifth or sixth streetlight was working. The moonlight was barely enough to navigate by. The solar trains had shut down for the night and Ash and Pinar had no choice but to walk. As they passed through the financial district, carefully checking around each corner for troopers, they barely saw a soul.

By any measure, hiking through the city, surrounded by threat, was draining. But somehow, along the way, Ash's exhaustion became determination. A resolute focus on survival. *We have to get out of the city if that's our only option.*

Ash noticed Pinar was quieter than usual. She checked in a couple of times, but her friend was reluctant to speak. *She's processing, adapting,* Ash knew. *We all are.* Their route to the gate took them past the end of a road they now knew very well. At the far end of the cul-de-sac, they saw The Home—their sanctuary for a few days. The lights were off, and curtains were drawn. *Well, that isn't ominous at all.*

Suddenly, two people wearing masks jumped out from behind a dumpster and ran towards them.

Chapter fifty-nine

P in! What the fuck?"

Ash turned to her friend who had already taken a defensive posture, legs slightly apart, fists raised. *Thank god for Tania and her classes.* Ash mimicked her friend, preparing to fight. *Whatever it takes, I will protect us*

* * *

"Ash! Pinar!"

One of the strangers stopped and pulled down their mask. Pinar saw it was Cleo, smiling broadly. Julia pulled down hers as well. "So sorry we startled you," she signed. "Shit's wild today."

Pinar let down her fists, but she saw that Ash was still braced. She put a hand gently on her friend's forearm. "Ash, honey, it's okay."

A look of recognition slowly crossed Ash's face and she came back from wherever she had been. She inhaled deeply and her arms and shoulders dropped.

"Well, fuck," she said louder than she meant to.

"*Can we sign?*" asked Cleo. "*Troopers are everywhere tonight. I barely made it out of the riot. Luckily I found this one—*" she touched Julia's waist "*—on my way out.*"

"*Riot?*" Pinar asked. "*The cacerolazo you mean?*"

Pinar wasn't sure of the sign for cacerolazo, so she imitated hitting a saucepan with a stick.

"*Exactly,*" Cleo replied. "*After the gas started flying, things escalated quickly. The Improvement has become...an exile.*"

Pinar flashed back on what she had seen from the park—hundreds of people running towards the gates, swarms of troopers following them.

"*Exile,*" she signed. She realised she had never used the sign before. She hated it at that moment. "*We're heading to the gates now. Unless there's some other plan?*"

Julia sighed audibly. "*Us too. We're too known here already—hence the masks. As far as we know, people are gathering outside the gates. And then, I don't know. The next right thing I guess?*"

Ash indicated the Home. "*Have you heard anything?*"

"*We were just there. Elias, Oscar and a few others had left already—they're probably at the gates by now.*"

"*This is really happening,*" Pinar signed with a furrowed brow.

"Oh!" Cleo reached into her purse and pulled out a folded piece of paper. "Someone left this for you," she whispered.

Pinar recognised the clean, first-use paper immediately. *From the Accountancy Office. Finn.*

She opened it slowly and noticed her fingers were trembling. She turned her back on the others to read the carefully written words of her sub, and lover.

Mistress,

I'm so sorry to communicate in this clumsy way. I didn't know how else to reach you. I went to Your home, but there was an eviction taking place. I'm so sorry, I wish I could have done more to protect You.

I don't know what to say, this is hard. I think this is goodbye—

Pinar made a sound from deep in her chest and Ash touched her shoulder lightly. "Are you okay babe?"

Pinar didn't respond. She shrugged Ash's hand off and continued reading.

—I've taken care of some things that I could. The Financial Department will take a long time to recover from what I've done. I don't feel guilty, I'm glad that I could do this for You, for all of you. People have told me that the Improvement is exiling Your community and I don't know if I will see you again. I hope that what I've done will at least give you time to escape. I wish I could leave with You, Mistress, but as you know I have ties here, my father is getting sicker. One day maybe we will meet again, in the City, or somewhere else. I pray for that, Mistress. And I hope with all my heart that You will be okay. I'll be here waiting, Mistress; if you need me.

Yours, entirely,
Finn

Pinar folded the paper up and put it carefully into her jeans pocket. After two deep breaths, she turned back to the group.

"Let's go."

* * *

They were close. As the four of them walked down the dark street—eerily quiet as it was—Pinar recognised the rose bush that she had hidden in just a few days before. The sparrows were gone and the last of the flowers had shrivelled on the stem.

The world is a different place now, she thought distantly. *Everything changes tonight.*

"We're nearly there," she said to Ash, trying to gather her strength. There was no response.

"Are you okay?" Pinar asked her.

Ash still didn't answer. Instead, she stopped walking and started tearing off the overlong military sweater she had been wearing for days. Underneath she was wearing her favourite black dress, tucked into her jeans. She pulled it out and let it hang loose around her legs. She dropped the sweater into a puddle on the ground.

"Ash?"

Ash smiled. "Well, we're leaving anyway. We might as well go out in style."

Pinar took her hand and they stepped forward together. One more street and they would be at the wall.

The four of them turned the corner. Even after everything they'd been through, they couldn't have prepared themselves for what they saw. The street leading to the gate was lined on both sides with people, some in uniform, many not. Nearly all were armed with bottles, stones and metal bars.

This is it, Pinar thought as a thick, menacing fog descended upon them.

"What do we do?" Cleo asked, her eyes wide with fear. "We need to get out. And those bastards look like they mean business."

Julia turned back to her. Her expression was pure determination. "How tired are you?"

Cleo looked confused. "Exhausted—but what do you mean?"

"I think we need to run for it."

Ash stepped forward. "Yes."

Pinar stepped closer to her friend. "Okay."

Cleo looked at the gates, and the mob, and turned back to her friends. "Ready."

Already cold, wet and broken-hearted, they had nothing left to lose.

Troopers, some of them citizens barely a day before and the gathered groups of men saw them immediately, despite the thickening fog, running with all their power to freedom. The mob were drawn by a feeling deeper than thought, the impulse to conform to the group, to be a part of something greater, no matter how hateful. Their voices escalated. Their calls of hatred echoed from the buildings around them. From the curbs, they moved towards the centre of the street as one. Their only thought was to eradicate difference. To clean the streets. To protect themselves from the diversity they had been taught to fear. The first bottles started to fly.

Chapter sixty

K eep going!" Julia shouted. She was leading the group but holding herself back. She was by far the fastest of them. *Either we all get out or none of us do.*

Cleo was just behind her and was shouting something over her shoulder. Ash and Pinar couldn't hear either of them over the yells of men. A bag of trash hit Pinar in the side and she nearly fell. Ash stopped immediately.

"I'm okay," Pinar shouted. "Keep going."

They were closer. Maybe twenty metres to go to the gate and whatever awaited them outside. Ash steeled her resolve and pushed on, but her heart skipped. She tripped on a crack in the pavement and the world spun around her.

Through the fog, Ash saw someone standing in the middle of the street. A bald woman, confused, terrified. She was watching the scene as if she was reliving it, as if her only desire was to make it stop. *That makes sense*, Ash thought as she watched herself for a brief second. *I will relive this awful moment until I die—whenever that might be.*

Pinar took her firmly by the shoulder. "Ash, are you okay? We need to keep moving."

Ash brought her gaze back to her best friend. Ahead, she saw that Julia and Cleo were just arriving at the open gate and passing through. Julia looked back at her desperately.

Ash took Pinar's hand and with one final resolute push, they headed for the wall.

They had barely passed through to the other side when the troopers started pulling the gates closed behind them. The sound of the city shutting them out, grinding gears echoing through the fog, was one of the worst things they had ever heard.

Chapter sixty-one

Beyond the walls of the city, the world couldn't have been more different. Ash and her friends stood for a moment, catching their breath, taking in the scene.

The ground they stood on had been cleared of trees and life. Naked soil striped with lines of erosion from the winter rains surrounded them for hundreds of metres. A dirt highway trailed away from the gates towards the north—one of the last trade routes still open with other states.

And then, just beyond the fog in every other direction, forest. The State Forest. Kilometres of woodland, virtually untouched since the State had withdrawn to its ever-growing walls and lost contact with the outside world. They had all heard rumours of Resistance groups forming out there, but Ash couldn't imagine how they survived. *Or how we will, for that matter.* As much as she hated it, the City and others like it, had been her life for a very long time.

The fog was clearing and the line of trees ahead of them came into view. Grouped there, at the edge between forest and bare earth, a group of some thirty individuals gathered, waiting for them. She recognised Tania, Elias and Oscar among them. The exiled. The marginalised. *The vergers*, Ash thought sadly.

Without a word, they started walking toward the group. *This is our life now.*

6. Resilience

Chapter sixty-two

Ash felt nothing. The fog was lifting but part of her ached for it to return. She was exposed, standing between worlds, between what she knew would be two eras of her life. City and forest. Past and future. She knew there was no way back. *They literally closed the door on us.*

But she wasn't ready to go forward either. Instead, her nervous system did what it often did in emergencies; it disconnected from the people around her and dived into the land. Into the rattling sounds of a wren far away. Into the smell of leaves carried out from the forest ahead. Ash felt her chest expanding, her breathing slowing.

Then, abruptly, she tensed back up.

Her heart raced erratically. *I can't relax. We're in danger.*

"We're moving out," announced Pinar.

Coming back, Ash noticed her friend's tone and the effect it had on her body.

She's cold, disconnected. Her entire focus is on problem-solving now. Ash pushed away the sensations.

"Pin, where the heck are we going to 'move out' to?" Ash asked, barely controlling her voice. "The next town is hundreds of kilometres from here. Me and you couldn't make that. Much less Oscar."

Just then Oscar came over to them. Ash saw he was already having difficulty on the rough ground. *And we're not even in the forest yet.*

"Sorry Oscar," she said, her hands out in apology.

Putting on his brakes, Oscar shook his head. "Don't be. It's okay to say it—having me along will limit our options. We can't travel as far for sure. And I have no idea how far I can go out here. Apart from occasional parks, I've never ridden on anything other than asphalt."

Pinar put her hands on her hips. "Fuck that. We'll find a way. And there are plenty of young, strong people here to push you, when you want that." She looked over to the others who were gathered near the treeline. "Cleo says she swiped a bunch of tyre repair kits and a bike pump—don't ask me where from, she produces things out of pure air, that one. We'll find a fucking way. We have to."

Ash noticed how much her friend was swearing.

"So, yes Ash, we're moving out, right now." Pinar had a hand on her belly, caught herself and put it firmly back on her hip. "We can't stand out here in the cold all night and Julia says she might know a building, some abandoned something or other, a couple of hours walk—or roll—from here."

Oscar released his brakes. "Well, alright then. That sounds like a plan." He pushed his wheels and started moving into the treeline. "Come on then!" he called back.

It took five minutes before his left wheel got stuck in a rut.

"Babe!" Oscar called over his shoulder and Elias appeared immediately.

"Need a push?" he asked over Oscar's shoulder.

"I'm in a rut."

"I see that—are you doing okay?"

"I will be when we arrive at whatever this building is. Give me a big push and I'll take it from there."

"Here goes."

Elias and Oscar were used to speaking to each other in this way. Both facing forward, without the possibility to see each other's faces, they were perfectly able to tell how the other was feeling just from their intonations. Oscar knew Elias was deeply exhausted and Elias in turn could tell Oscar was scared but being stoic. *Sometimes I wish he'd just admit he's afraid. But I get it. Our dignity is everything.*

Oscar's wheel was soon free and Elias pushed the chair for a while. They were making slow progress through the forest, but at least the soil was fairly dry. Pinar, near the back of the group ahead, turned her head and saw they were falling behind. She whistled through her fingers and the thirty of them immediately stopped for Oscar to catch up.

"Uff," Elias grumbled over Oscar's shoulder. "Way to make you the centre of attention."

Oscar turned his head slightly and Elias could see he was smiling. "I mean, I am literally the only person here in a wheelchair babe. I'd much rather people wait for me than leave the two of us alone out here in the forest. Thank you though."

Elias said something that Oscar didn't quite make out and they pushed on to catch up with Pinar and the others.

Three hours later, their collective nerves frayed, the group arrived at Julia's mysterious building. Only as Ash got closer did she understand just how big it actually was. An enormous veranda opened up onto what had been a tributary of the river but was now just a small, rocky creek. Many of the windows were broken, but from what she could see, a lot of the building was intact.

"Welcome to our home away from home," Julia announced, her arms opened dramatically. Despite her playful tone, Ash could see she was exhausted.

"What is this place?"

"A hunting lodge," Julia explained. "From decades back, before the crash I guess. Rich tourists from the City and other places would come to spend time killing things. A few of us runners use it as a sleep-over point when we're going into the forest, or bringing medicine from the border."

Ash wasn't surprised to hear that runners sometimes left the City—a good part of the materials they had relied on in the Clinic came from outside. As she thought about the Clinic, she felt her chest compressing.

Pinar came over. "Let's get in, Ash. You must be exhausted."

"Do you think there are beds?"

"I mean, tourists must have *great* beds, right?"

For the first time that evening, Ash smiled.

Their room wasn't in great condition. The window was intact, but it was still barely warmer than the cold woods outside. Ash dropped her bag and collapsed onto the bed. The mattress squeaked and she could feel a spring poking in her back.

"Get off there!" Pinar demanded. "Julia packed us some extra sleeping bags." She opened a backpack and pulled out two sleeping bags in compression sacks. "I don't want to think about how long that mattress has been hanging around collecting mould."

Ash started pulling hers, fluorescent pink, out of its sack.

"This place is weird, Pin. It's like some ghost ship where the kettle's still warm and toast has just been buttered, but they never found the crew."

Pinar gave her a confused look. "What are you even talking about? Buttered toast?"

Ash threw her sleeping bag onto the bed and snuggled inside it. It smelt vaguely of laundry powder. "Maybe I'm hungry!" she chuckled. Pinar arrived next to her, the bed squeaking loudly as she got into the sleeping bag.

"Shall I get us a snack, love? We've been through so much and I don't remember the last time we ate. I think I still have some Nutrition bars and if not, I can see how much is in the stock the others brought."

Ash didn't respond. Pinar pulled down the edge of her friend's bag and chuckled. Her friend was already fast asleep. Pinar sighed lovingly, and as best as she could, curled up to spoon her through the sleeping bags

* * *

I'm not at home. Ash woke with a start.

Where are we? She reached out automatically and found Pinar's hair splayed out next to her in the bed. She wiggled her feet and felt the cocoon of plastic around her. She opened one eye and saw the terrifying head of a deer staring at her from the wall. *The hunting lodge. The forest.*

She screwed her eyes closed and tried to relax her legs, her arms, to stay perfectly still and maybe just fall back asleep. It was no use. She needed the bathroom and knew there was no way back from that. A yawn took her, and she stretched her arms. But the manoeuvre of wiggling out of a sleeping bag on an over-soft mattress without making a sound was too complicated. The more she tried, the more noise she made. Suddenly, with no friction to keep her bag on the mattress, Ash skidded right off the bed and landed with a crash onto the wooden floor.

"Ow. And fuck."

"Ash," Pinar mumbled sleepily. "Are you okay?"

"Blurgh," Ash replied. "Go back to sleep. I was just trying to pee."

"On the floor?" Pinar was only half awake.

"What? No, Pin. I'm stuck in my fucking sleeping bag."

Pinar shuffled over to the side of the bed and couldn't suppress a giggle at the sight of her friend trapped in her neon pink bag.

"You look like a caterpillar!"

Ash wasn't impressed. She was battling with the bag's zip which appeared to be broken. "If you're not going to sleep, can you at least help me out of this thing before I pee in it?"

"Do you know where the bathroom actually is?" Pinar slid elegantly out of her own sleeping bag without a sound.

Ash shook her head.

"Well, then let's find it together." Pinar bent over and unzipped Ash's bag in one easy move.

"I hate you sometimes," Ash grumbled.

"I love you too."

They made their way down a dingy corridor lined with dead animals mounted on the walls. Pinar realised it might be later in the day than they had thought, the light was already bright enough to be midday. The corridor opened to the right into a massive salon complete with a cozy fireplace. Gathered around in concentric half circles, sat most of the people they had arrived with. Sunlight poured in through the French windows. *It's beautiful*, Pinar noticed. *Or it used to be. How did they ever let this place go?*

"Pin..." Ash was physically wiggling next to her. "Let's admire the view later."

"Right," Pin chuckled. "Down there!" A sign for toilets with an arrow hung at an angle on the wall. Above it a taxidermy squirrel sat in a dusty glass box. "Run, run...I'll go in after you."

Ash didn't need to be told twice, she dashed down the corridor and disappeared around the corner.

Pinar stepped into the salon to wait. The room was strangely quiet, just a few small conversations happening. Everyone seemed tired and the atmosphere was heavy. She knew that she, Ash, Elias and Oscar had been given the best rooms and the others had made do, some three or four to a bed. From the sleeping mats piled up near the fireplace, she guessed a few people had also slept here. *There are just so many of us. How are we going to make this work?*

"Morning everyone," she said brightly, trying to push away her worries. She saw Tania and came over to her, glad to see her friend's face. "Did you sleep okay?"

Tania gave her a wane smile. "As well as could be expected. But thank god for this fireplace, it would have been freezing without it." She stretched her arms. "Did the heat reach you and Ash?"

Always thinking of others, Pinar noticed.

"We were comfortable, thank you." Pinar sat down cross-legged next to her friend.

"Elias and Oscar are still sleeping. We had some problems with the bathroom in the night—of course the cubicles are too small. But we worked it out." Tania yawned and covered her mouth automatically. "Sorry, it's been a night..."

Pinar touched her leg gently. "Come sleep with me and Ash if you need to tonight. Ash snores a bit, but you can just give her a little kick and she rolls over every time. Apparently I steal the duvet, but as we have sleeping bags it should be okay."

Tania smiled at the image.

"I mean, unless we're moving on today?" Pinar's expression grew serious. "What's the plan actually?"

Tania sighed audibly. "Well, we already tried to discuss that. But everyone's so tired we couldn't really think straight. And without you four, obviously we weren't going to make any decisions." She looked at Pinar directly, her forehead furrowed. "Honestly, I don't know what happens next."

"We'll work something out. Have you eaten?"

Tania shook her head. "Not yet. I hadn't gotten that far."

"You don't need to. There are thirty of us—you don't have to bottom-line everything."

Tania laughed then. "You're one to talk! Let's fucking delegate it. Someone else can definitely take care of breakfast for a change."

Within ten minutes, there was a kitchen working group, an access and cleaning working group for the bathrooms, and a committee to organise sleeping-solutions. Within an hour, food was served: a mishmash of things people had brought in their backpacks and some long-life tins that had been left by the tourists. Pinar and Tania sat back against a wall enjoying the warmth from the fire. They were soon joined by Ash, Elias and Oscar.

"Now that's the way to do it," said Tania, leaning back with her fingers interlaced behind her head.

Pinar smiled. "I couldn't agree more."

The arguments began just after breakfast.

Chapter sixty-three

The raised voices overlapping each other, the acidic smell of stress fogging up the air, it all became too much and halfway through the second hour of trying to make impossible decisions, Ash needed to get away. Without excusing herself, she stood up, flung open the French windows and stormed onto the deck. The windows banged closed behind her, but she didn't look back. She needed to connect with something that wasn't tension and panic, fear and confusion. She stared at a distant poplar tree on the edge of the clearing, its highest branches bending in the wind. The leaves whispered into her nervous system and she sighed.

A while later, Pinar appeared next to her. "Babe? Are you doing okay?"

Ash took her time coming back. She unconsciously picked at her nails.

"I'm okay, Pin. It's just a lot, you know?"

"It is."

"It shouldn't be this hard to come to a decision. We either stay or we move on. We either go north and hope we make it to the State border—which is possibly the most absurd thing I've ever heard. Or we head out into the forest and search for your mysterious friends in their magical land of unicorns and free snacks."

Pinar gave her a stern look and crossed her arms. "They're not mysterious, or unicorns. And I've told you about Dee and Rob at least a hundred times. We've known each other for years. You just don't pay attention when I'm talking about people you don't know."

Ash shrugged. "Well, that might be true. You know so many people—you can't expect me to also remember the semi-existing people I haven't met yet."

"Well, *I've* met them."

"But only online right?"

Pinar sighed. "Yes. I worked with Dee online for a few years and we stayed in touch. I've told you this."

"Online!" Ash threw up her hands. "Those were the days! All of us shouting at our laptops saying 'hello hello, can you hear me?' until we gave up and went back to bed."

Pinar suppressed a smile. "Yes, exactly. Me and Dee shouted 'hello hello' at each other for many years because she was sick during that time and couldn't leave the house or travel much. Also, as we know, travel wasn't the same after the 20s. Then she met Rob and they left their home during the collapse."

"And they ended up in the State forest."

"They did."

"And you've been relaying messages to them through the runner network."

"Yes."

"In the middle of the forest."

"Yes, Ash. Oh my god! Do you not believe me, or what?"

"Of course I believe you. I'm just not sure if I believe that we should be putting all our eggs in some mysterious basket that we've never met before who chose to live out in the middle of nothing, doing whatever it is they're doing out there." Ash waved dramatically towards the forest. "I mean, it's a bit weird. And it'll split the group for sure. Elias and Oscar will come with us, maybe Cleo and whats-her-name and Tania. But the others will want to head north, I'm sure. Are you sure we can trust your internet-forest friends?"

"They're both trans and working-class if that helps?"

"It doesn't." Ash pouted. "People of all kinds can suck."

Pinar tucked her hair back in desperation. "Would *you* like to go north?"

"We'll never make it."

"Stay here?"

"Amongst all the dead squirrels and stuffed badgers? No, thank you."

Pinar stared at her friend for a good long moment, trying and failing to control her anger.

"Ash," she said, her voice hard.

"Mm?"

"You're pushing me too hard. I know you're tired and stressed by everything that's happening, but I don't feel so great either."

"But—"

Pinar put up a hand. "Let me finish. I spend a great deal of time listening to you. Understanding what you're going through. Forgiving you. It wouldn't kill you to think about me more, to ask me what *I* need. You're not the only one in this movie, you know."

Ash looked forlorn and Pinar could see her hands were shaking. They both hated to fight.

"Ash...hug me."

Ash looked confused but complied. Pinar pulled her in, embracing her a little too hard and causing her back to crack.

"Pin," said Ash, her voice muffled by Pinar's shoulder in her face. "Pin, I need to breathe."

Finally, her friend released her, stepped back and wiped her eyes.

"I love you," she declared.

Ash smiled and gave her a wink. "I love you too, honey. Even though you make decisions *so difficult* sometimes."

They stood quietly for a moment, looking out over the lush forest ahead of them.

"Let's go back in," Pinar commanded as she turned her back on the forest and led her friend back inside.

Inside the salon, the tense discussions continued and finally after three more hours of speaking, the group realised that it would be impossible to stay together in the long term. They wanted different things and trying to find a single plan for the group would just lead to more conflict that no-one had energy for. They would stay a few days, then would split into two and make their own choices.

That evening, as Ash and Pinar collapsed onto their squeaky mattress, they lay in silence for a while. It was already dark and they were too tired to talk. Ash stared at the ceiling, trying to process the day. *I'm not sure how long we can do this for.*

Living collectively exhausted her. For the most part, it was better than isolation, better than nuclear families, or places like the Home. But sometimes, it took everything Ash had and didn't feel worth it at all.

Chapter sixty-four

One week later, they left the derelict lodge. Ash, Pinar, Elias, Oscar, Tania, Cleo and Julia formed a loose circle in front of the building. The rest formed a larger group that stood nervously off near the edge of the trees. There was nothing left to say that hadn't been said, and after some hushed goodbyes, they moved off out into the forest.

Now that the day had arrived, reality was beginning to sink in. Ash could feel anxiety permeating her body. Her throat had closed up. Her heart was pounding. *I hate this.*

She paused for a moment by a straggly lavender, planted by the entrance to the building. She opened her water bottle and poured a few drops around the desiccated stems.

Pinar arrived with her rucksack on her back. "Let's go?"

Ash sighed and walked with her to the edge of the woods. Elias, Cleo and Julia were ahead, clearing the way of obstacles for Oscar. Pinar's jaw was set in determination.

They had travelled just a few kilometres when the sky opened.

Chapter sixty-five

Everything's soaked!"

"Pin! Help me with the tent! Where does this fucking pole go?"

"Oscar, are we missing a sleeping mat? I can't find it anywhere!"

"Oh my god, it has to stop raining!"

They set up an emergency camp between two grand oaks, which gave them some slight protection from the rain. It wasn't enough. The deluge had turned the soil to thick, sticky mud. In the time that it took Ash, Elias and Julia to set up the tents, they were already wet through. Oscar climbed in first. Cleo jumped in after to help set up the beds for him and Elias. He was shivering, she noticed, as she helped him get into his sleeping bag.

"I'm going to get you some tea," she promised. *Although fuck knows how we'll make a fire tonight.* "Or at least a snack. Do you need anything else?"

Oscar shook his head. His teeth were chattering.

Cleo emerged from the tent bottom first and bumped into Elias.

"How is he?"

"He's got a chill, I think. He's wrapped up warm, but we should find a way to dry out his clothes. All of our clothes for that matter. Any idea how we make a fire? All the wood must be wet."

A stream of water dripped from a branch of the tree directly down Elias' collar. He shuddered.

"No fucking clue. I'm not built for this life. I've never even been camping. Wait though—"

Elias turned and pointed at Tania as she stood back from a fire circle she had improvised with stones and thick branches. There was already a small fire blazing inside the circle and Elias let out a sound of admiration. "Well, there we go."

A while later, having thoroughly soaked the forest, the rain began to slow and fade. The sun burst out so abruptly that Elias had to shield his eyes. The clouds quickly burned away, and the spring sky was left a perfect blue.

Chapter sixty-six

That evening, drying his feet by the fire while his friends busied themselves preparing the food and camp for the night, Oscar sat with an unzipped sleeping bag draped over his shoulders.

Once he started coughing, he couldn't stop. He bent over hacking until his throat was raw. Elias was by his side immediately, rubbing his back and pulling the sleeping bag tighter around him.

Though he knew it had to be a cold that he'd picked up from all the changes and stress—not to mention getting soaked—Oscar couldn't help but flashback to the early 2020s.

We lost so many, locked away in camps for the old and the sick, coughing until we died, discarded by the healthy. Me and Elias were really the lucky ones.

Elias spoke, his voice deadly serious.

"Babe, what do you need? Should we get you back in your tent?"

Between coughs, Oscar nodded. With help from Pinar and Tania, Elias efficiently got him back into their tent where they wrapped him in a sleeping bag and several fleece blankets.

Elias sat next to Oscar as he finished another bout of coughing. Even in the growing darkness, Oscar could tell his expression was one of worry, even panic.

"I'm okay," Oscar said weakly, his voice hoarse.

"You're really not." Elias crossed his arms. "This was the worst idea. What are we even doing out here?"

Oscar lay back on his pillow and pulled a blanket up under his chin.

"It's just a cold, hon. I'll be fine."

Elias' tone was adamant. "We're going back to the hunting lodge. At least we had a bed there."

Oscar nodded. "Well, we'll need to reach consensus but—"

"Fuck consensus. You're sick. I love you. First thing tomorrow we're going back."

In the flickering light from the fire, Elias saw that Oscar was smiling. "I want to kiss you so bad."

Elias smiled too. "Get better first and you can kiss me all you want."

Oscar nodded in agreement and snuggled down deeply.

Just like 2020, he thought as he dropped off to sleep.

"We're going back," Elias announced to the circle gathered around the fire. His arms were crossed, his lips thin. He was braced to defend himself. "Oscar is sick, and we need to go back to the lodge—at least for a few nights. It's the only smart thing we can do."

He looked around at his friends, waiting for the pushback, anticipating some interminable discussion. Instead, he saw only nods and sympathetic smiles.

"Well...good," he huffed at them. "We leave at first light, or whenever Oscar is ready."

He turned abruptly and headed back to the tent for the night.

I guess we finally learned to centre the needs of the right people, he thought as he unzipped the tent, slipped off his boots and climbed in next to his lover. *Took us fucking long enough.*

Oscar was snoring softly.

* * *

As Elias had demanded, they were ready to leave just after first light. Pinar and Ash organised breakfast while Julia, Tania and Cleo took down the camp. They were an efficient team.

Oscar's cough was no better, but he looked rested as he sat in his chair folding tent poles. Elias paced up and down the clearing as if his feet were on fire.

"Let's go already," he mumbled as Oscar rolled up next to him.

Oscar put his arm on Elias' hip. "We're going. Stop worrying—I'm going to be okay. It's all going to be fine."

Within one hour of leaving the camp, Tania paused suddenly and turned to the group following her closely behind.

Pinar noticed her expression immediately and came to stand next to her. "What's up?"

Tania shook her head, then looked down at her feet.

"We're...lost

* * *

"I don't understand." Elias' voice was escalating. "We only went a few kilometres at most. How hard can it be to find a giant ass tourist resort?"

Tania shook her head again. She was trying hard not to cry.

"We should never have left!" Elias practically shouted. "You said it would be an easy route to find the river and Pinar's friends. Whoever the hell they are. Yet here we are—" He spread his hands in fury. "—with Oscar sick and nothing but three stupid leaky fucking tents and—"

"Elias, stop." Pinar's voice cut right through his panicked tirade.

"But—"

"Stop. You're not helping. It's no-one's fault that it rained. And your complaining isn't going to get us on track." She turned to Tania. "What do you need?"

Tania looked up and caught her eye contact. "A minute...to think. There has to be a way to work out where we are."

Cleo left for a moment then reappeared with a flask. She poured Tania a steaming cup of coffee from a flask. "Here, this should help."

Tania took the plastic cup with a look of total confusion. "But how...?"

Cleo smiled. "Let's call it magic."

Tania took a sip. She could practically feel her neurons firing, the fog of her panic clearing.

"Okay," she declared, passing Cleo back the empty cup. "I have a plan

* * *

The neon yellow walky-talky in Oscar's hand squeaked as Julia's disembodied voice pushed out of its ancient little speaker. "Badger one, this is squirrel one, there's nothing out this way but trees forever. The ground is rising here so the river probably isn't this way. We're turning back now."

Oscar pushed the plastic button and replied. "Roger that, squirrel one. See you soon."

He put the walky-talky on his lap. Elias was staring at him in disbelief. "'Roger that, squirrel one?' What the hell is happening to our lives?"

Oscar shrugged. "I mean, maybe the State is listening. Or it's just cute. What do you care anyway? You *are* kind of a grumpy badger after all."

Elias ignored that. Another of the walky-talkies squeaked and Elias picked it up.

"Erm...Hedgehog...six to Badger...oh my god, Pin what was it again?"

Elias pushed the reply button. "Ash. It's me. Can we please stop with the goddamned woodland animals?"

"Hey Elias..."

"Hey yourself. Any news?"

There was a short moment of silence and Elias wondered if they'd lost the connection or if Ash's batteries had given out. A loud squeak and scratchy interference suddenly rang out and Elias almost dropped the bright plastic device.

"Ash?"

"...we...ducks...to the east and..."

"What? Ash what are you even saying?"

"Pin didn't...in the oak tree."

Elias glared at the anachronistic toy as if he was ready to throw it into the forest. Oscar gently took it from him and pushed the reply button.

"Ash, we can't hear you properly. You're out of range. Can you come back towards us?"

More squeaking, more silence and then finally Pinar's voice rang out clearly.

"Elias, Oscar... we found the river."

* * *

Elias could hear the sounds of water long before they arrived.

After creating a gap through a particularly thick line of brambles for Oscar's chair to pass through, the world suddenly opened. They found themselves at the edge of a wide, slow river. Ash, Pinar and the others were gathered at the bank. Cleo had taken her shoes off and was paddling around at the shallow water's edge.

Oscar pulled up and put his brakes on. Elias was surprised to see him untying his shoes.

"Oscar?"

His partner smiled. "I'm so ready for a wash, even if it's just a paddle."

"But you're sick." Elias gave him a look of concern and desperation. "And isn't the water cold?"

Oscar was already working on his socks.

The seven of them spent that afternoon at the river. The sun was bright and the water was warm enough that they could paddle around for a good while before flopping out onto the beach to heat back up. Elias and Ash stayed with Oscar in the shallows while Cleo and Julia made out on the sand. In the deeper water, Tania and Pinar were having some kind of loud splashing fight.

We're all in denial, Elias thought to himself as he, Oscar and Ash got out of the water and back onto their towels.

We've been evicted from our lives and here we are carrying on like kids on a holiday. And we still need to set up camp for the night. Who knows how far upriver these friends of Pinar's are? We have no idea if—

Oscar took his hand and as they lay there, the warm sun drying their bodies, Elias couldn't help but feel himself relax a little, his worries trailing off.

Amazing what some water and sun can do.

That evening the group set up camp near the river and after a quick meal, they all retired to their tents. Pinar fell asleep quickly but Ash lay awake listening to the sounds around her.

She noticed that the tent closest to theirs was silent, which meant that Oscar had stopped coughing. *Thank god.* After a few indiscrete sounds from the third tent, Julia and Cleo had also quietened down. Tania's hammock, as usual, was hung up just outside the camp, as she kept half an eye open in case of unexpected visitors.

Without the disturbance of human sounds—save Pinar's tiny breaths as she slept—Ash could tune into the night music of the forest.

An owl was calling to its mate somewhere to the left. Some heavy insects plopped down on the tent fabric then continued their journey.

At some point, someone big, maybe a fox or a badger, came to snuffle around between their tents. Ash sniffed the air instinctively. *Fox, definitely.*

She knew she was being seduced by the sensations permeating her body. Since she was young, she had consciously made her life in cities, but every time she had spent any real amount of time in nature, she realised just how much she was sacrificing. Now, the world had forced her decision and there was no way back. *I will never return to the City, or any other. This is my world now.*

Next to her, Pinar gave a contented sigh and Ash could no longer resist the warmth of her body. She curled up against her friend and closed her eyes

* * *

The next morning, as the sun was just beginning to warm up the air, Ash unzipped the tent and crawled out. Shafts of light through the trees illuminated the first clouds of nettle pollen. Her friends were already up, heating water, cooking flatbreads on a pan, and taking down tents. Ash stood and stretched, a beam of light filtering down directly onto her face.

Okay, she thought. *This could be worse*

* * *

After a couple of hours following the river, the group arrived at a gap in the forest, some twenty metres wide.

Ash could already see that it was different. Unlike the devastated clear-cuts of the State, this space had been planned, had been created with care. Around the edge she saw young fruit trees planted next to vegetable beds. There was the slightest bitter-sweet odour of compost in the air. *This isn't a clearing, it's a garden.*

"We've arrived," Pinar said, with a voice both weary and proud. "We made it."

It was then, standing cautiously at the edge of the forest, looking out over the open space, that Ash noticed the blue transit van, partially covered in camouflage netting. *A vehicle, out here? This I've got to see.*

Elias arrived next to her and Ash heard him inhale sharply. "What is this?"

Out of the back of the van, two people emerged from under the netting and the group unconsciously stepped backwards. Ash read them as a man and woman, both white, *both pretty intense-looking*. Their body language struck her as hostile, their expressions stern.

Ash saw that the woman was holding what looked like a bottle of pepper spray in her left hand and the man had something behind his back. The way he held it, she guessed it was some kind of bar or stick. The couple stood and stared at them for a good ten seconds.

Oh Pin, what have we gotten ourselves into now?

Just then, Pinar began to run forward. "Dee! Rob!" she shouted.

As Pinar approached them, the couple threw down their weapons—the metal bar clanged as it hit the dirt. Ash's heart jumped with the sudden noise.

The couple scooped her friend up into a hug. Even from the edge of the clearing, Ash could hear that the woman—Dee—was crying.

"Oh my fucking god," she was saying. "It's so good to see you!"

"It's been so long!" the man said, his low voice somewhere between a reprimand and joy.

Breaking their hug, Pinar stood back and turned to indicate the rest of the group. Oscar, Elias and Ash all hovered cautiously near the fruit trees. Elias looked defensive, Oscar was yawning and rubbing his tired arms.

"Actually," Pinar said with a broad smile. "It's a bit more than just a social visit."

"Ash?" Elias whispered to her. "Where the heck are we?"

"Home," she whispered back. *Well, someone's home at least.*

Chapter sixty-seven

H ere, let me bring you something to sit on," Rob hefted a log onto his shoulder and placed it down next to the fire. "Sorry, we don't often have guests."

Ash sat down. The log was wobbly, but she was glad to take the weight off her feet. Rob arrived with another log for Pinar and she gave him a grateful smile. "It's perfect, thank you."

Elias and Oscar were having trouble getting across the clearing—Oscar's wheel was stuck on yet another root. Rob reacted immediately. "Dee? Do we still have the tarp somewhere?"

Dee appeared from the back of the van with a bundle of plastic in her arms. "Already on it," she said with a smile as she took it over to Oscar and lay it down on the ground ahead of him. "If you're okay to try this it might help with the roots a bit. Sorry, it's the fucking kudzu, no matter how much we dig them up, they always come back."

Oscar gave a nod and with a little push from Elias, his chair rolled onto the tarp. Oscar rolled to the end until they reached dirt. "Here, let's do that again." Dee pulled the tarp ahead of Oscar again and his chair rolled all the way to the campfire this time. Ash noticed that Dee was very careful not to touch Oscar, or his chair, and checked consent for everything. *I already like her*, she thought.

"My name's Dee, by the way."

"D, like the letter?" asked Elias.

"D-E-E. I never understood that State one-letter-per-citizen thing."

"One more thing they could take from us. I'm Elias."

"And I'm Oscar. Do you do cheek kisses down south?"

Dee nodded. "I think it's four now. But could we just fist bump? I guess I never got out of the habit."

Oscar nodded and after a round of the hygienic greetings, they joined the others gathered around the smouldering ashes of the previous night's campfire. Rob brought two more logs for himself and Dee and they completed the circle.

"Welcome," he announced in his husky voice. "I'm Rob. Erm...this is...pretty overwhelming and unexpected, but I'm really glad you made it out here to visit us."

"We're here because the State destroyed our lives. And we were forced out of the City," announced Elias with his usual bluntness.

"Oh." Dee poked at the embers with a stick. "Fuck, I'm so sorry. We knew things were bad, but..." She didn't finish the thought. They all knew that things had been bad for a very long time.

"And you?" asked Ash. "How did you come to be out here, with all this..." She gestured towards the van and gardens. "How long have you been here?"

"It's been..." Rob looked at Dee for confirmation. "A few months? Nearly a year?"

"Eleven months, two weeks. But it feels like a lot longer. We've been on the road since the first pandemic."

Oscar blew out air. "That was a while ago."

"It was. City life was getting harder for us anyway down south. So, one day, we got our licenses, bought a van with all our savings and left."

"And you chose to live out the apocalypse in the State forest?" Ash's voice was more cynical than she meant it to be.

"Of all places…"

Dee played with her hair. "Honestly, the rest of Europe isn't so much better."

Ash believed her. With climate change, migration crises and pandemics, things had gone downhill quickly.

"After Hungary it all went to shit, didn't it?"

Ash recalled the day clearly, fifteen years before, when she and Pinar, locked down along with the rest of the city, had heard the news: Hungary's government had passed a law for the prime minister to rule by decree. The very next day, using these new powers—ostensibly to fight coronavirus—Orbán submitted a bill to illegalize the recognition of trans people.

"I mean…" Ash said gently. "Things were also bad before dictatorships spread across Europe." *Scapegoating and disaster capitalism have been with us for a long time.*

Dee nodded. "True. You know, we even spent a few months in Espera on the way here. Now that's a weird-ass place."

"Espera?" Pinar looked confused. "Never heard of it."

Dee sighed. "Next state down the river. It wasn't called that before of course. Just like the State had another name before Europe disintegrated into a thousand pieces and it all went to hell. Anyway, you wouldn't like it. We couldn't make our life there, so we hit the road again, stealing and turning tricks as we went. One day we started driving along the river and, well, we ended up here."

"And the State?"

"No sign of them so far. At some point they'll find us, but I guess they have better things to do—"

"—like exiling all of us," said Elias, his voice heavy.

"Sorry," replied Dee, looking down at the cold fire and poking at it absently. "It sounds awful."

"It was awful," Pinar agreed. "But we survived."

"Well, queer and trans people are good at that," agreed Rob.

"I mean, haven't we always been? Always looking for ways to get our meds, hormones and rent. Staying alive in prison." He looked off into the woods for a moment. "I guess creating community and networks of support is built in for people like us."

"All true." Ash nodded. "I mean some really bougie queers got into joining the army for a while, but the rest of us know a thing or two about surviving in the margins."

Elias spoke again. "So...speaking of community. We're looking for a new home."

He doesn't fuck around, thought Ash. *That's why I love him.*

Rob sat up straight. "Yes. I wanted to ask about that. I mean, we'll need to discuss it, of course." He looked at Dee, who returned a soft glance. "But we'll do whatever we can to help."

Dee stood up. "How about some tea?"

Pinar stood too. "Can I help?"

Dee flashed her a smile and they headed to the van

* * *

While they drank their tea, the group chatted amiably. Dee and Rob were surprisingly open about their past, living from sex work and the occasional theft from grocery stores and petrol stations—and more recently the State supply houses near the border. Ash found them easy to talk to, she was already beginning to trust them more than she would have expected. She could see why Pinar had stayed in touch.

"And you don't have internet out here we noticed, is that all across the State?"

"Not for years," Ash explained. "They cut it off at some point although I never really understood how. The City barely has electricity to be honest. And the little there is is mostly reserved for the richer neighbourhoods."

"Where did you all live, I mean, if you want to talk about that?"

Oscar and Elias shared a glance.

"We've been locked away in a care home for quite a long time." Elias' voice was tight. "Apart from some...recent developments...it's been rough."

"Sorry," Dee repeated. "I'm so sorry."

Chapter sixty-eight

The group fell quiet and listened to the sounds of the forest for a while. A wren's call rattled through the trees and several bumblebees, emerging early from hibernation, buzzed through their camp.

After a while, Rob stretched and turned to Dee. "Babe, should we head out and get some more nettles for tea and soup? Our State supplies are running a bit low."

Dee knew very well that their 'supplies' were fine—in coordination with a forest resistance band, they had raided a warehouse only a week before. *He wants to talk. I know him so well.*

"Sure. Let's head out." She turned to her new friends. "We'll be back in a while—eat anything you find in the van. Please make yourselves comfortable."

* * *

"So...what do you think?" Rob asked as they walked through the forest. Dee ran her fingers over the cool bark of a beech tree. *Grounding*, she noticed. *I need that.*

"It's a lot," she replied.

They arrived at a fallen tree trunk and Rob hopped over and offered his hand to Dee. She was more than used to navigating forest obstacles in heels, but always appreciated Rob's gallant side.

Despite their rural lifestyle, Dee only owned heels. They had left their previous life in the south so quickly, she hadn't had time to pack anything else. And her selection of three pairs had proven themselves very useful for their financial survival. *It's been the two of us for a long time now. This will change everything. Again.*

"I mean," he said as if reading her thoughts. "I think we're both assuming that they will stay for a while. But we don't have to say yes. There are other options."

There are no other options, Dee thought but didn't need to say. *It's a miracle they made it this far.*

She paused and turned to look her lover in the eye. "Clearly they're staying. And to be honest, we could use the company. Some collective care and help getting resources wouldn't be the worst thing." *I'm not half the thief that you are and you're the worst gardener of all time.* Dee tucked her hair behind her shoulders. "Don't get me wrong. This has been incredibly romantic. The two of us eking out an existence, escaping oppression and building our life in the woods together. But it was never meant to be a long-term solution." She took his hand. "And if it doesn't work out, we can move again." *God knows we're good at it.*

Rob gave her hand a little squeeze. "I love you, babe."

Dee squeezed him back. "So they stay?" she asked for confirmation.

"Absolutely. And so do we—at least for now."

"Should we actually get some nettles on this walk then? We have a lot more mouths to feed now."

With a smile, Rob pulled a tote bag and a pair of scissors out of his pocket. Hand in hand, they continued into the woods.

* * *

"I don't fully understand to be honest." Elias sipped his tea and looked around at his friends, all perched on their logs. Why would anyone *choose* to live out here in the middle of nowhere?"

"I mean, *we're* here," Pinar said softly. "And *you* just asked them if we could stay."

"What fucking choice do we have? But it's not the same as doing this voluntarily."

"Maybe they didn't leave their home by choice either."

"Well, that might be true. But is this it then?" Elias' voice was rising. "Are we going to live out here forever, eating sticks and berries?"

Oscar put his hand on Elias' leg.

"Babe, what else is there?" Oscar asked softly. "I mean the City was no picnic either—especially in the Home."

Elias swallowed. "How can we though? I mean, just a few days out here nearly killed us. We have almost no food left, no water. And I smell like a rat's ass."

Oscar smiled. "You smell perfect babe. And besides, there's the river."

"And it's basically spring," said Pinar in a brighter tone than she felt. "In February, but still...Dee and Rob must have somewhere they're getting fresh water from. And I guess they've been raiding State food reserves somehow—"

"*If* they let us stay. Maybe they don't want a bunch of elderly queers crashing their party." Elias sighed dramatically.

"—the other *exiliadas* will find us at some point." Pinar continued. "I mean, this forest isn't *so* big."

Elias gave her a look. "*Exiliadas*, is that what we are now?"

Pinar shrugged again and gave him a look.

Elias sighed and threw up his hands. "Fine, fine. I'll eat sticks and berries and become a frikking woodland animal. But you're all going to have to feed me and build a nice bed of pine needles for us."

Oscar gave him a smile. "You'll be such a cute woodland animal."

Elias tutted at him.

"Speaking of which," Ash stood and stretched. "Did you see that there are badger setts all around here? I've never seen so many in one place! It's kind of beautiful. Not the worst place in the world to start a new life."

"The Sett," said Pinar in a strange tone Ash hadn't heard before. "It's the perfect name

* * *

Dee and Rob returned soon after with a bag full of nettles and some more wood for the fire.

"Hi everyone," Dee said cheerfully as she put down the branches near the fire. "We chatted a bit and if you'd like to stay, we'd love to have you."

"We don't have much to offer," said Rob apologetically. "But what resources we have are yours to share."

"And more hands make light work," Dee added.

Pinar stood and gave her friends another hug.

"Thank you," she whispered. "I have a feeling this is the start of something beautiful." She turned back to the circle. "Ash, would you mind giving me a hand organising our stuff?" Ash stood and nodded.

Elias stretched and stood too. "I can help out with the food."

"I'll join you," said Oscar, releasing the brakes of his chair.

Tania stood and brushed off her jeans. "Dee, Rob—need some help with firewood?

And with that, out of solidarity and care, on a warm day in February, the Sett was founded.

Chapter sixty-nine

J ulia could you help me set up the tent?" Cleo stood at the edge of the clearing surrounded by various poles and pegs, hands on her hips. "I'm still not sure how this all goes together."

Julia flashed her a smile and stepped closer. "You've totally got this, but it's more fun to do it together."

As they worked straightening pegs and clearing the ground of stones, a ray of sun caught Julia's hair. Cleo noticed a bead of sweat on her upper arm. *You're still magnificent*, she thought and almost said.

After the ground was clear, Julia stood back and looked at their work. "There, I think that'll make a good spot for our new home, don't you think?"

Cleo moved closer and put a hand gently on Julia's hip. "It's perfect. This is perfect."

* * *

Oscar and Elias were cooking. Elias stirred the pot he had balanced on a grill over the fire. Oscar cut vegetables on a chopping board on his lap. Neither one spoke as they focused on their tasks.

Without a word, Oscar passed Elias the board and he added the diced beets to the soup. Elias passed back the board with some leaves of cabbage to chop. Once the pot was full, Elias dragged his log a little closer and sat down.

"Are we okay?" he asked abruptly. "Is this—" Elias looked around at the camp; the van, the vegetable beds and the tents. "—is all of this alright for us?"

Oscar took his hand and gave it a squeeze. "It will be."

Ash and Pinar sat cross-legged in a circle of backpacks. Everything the group had brought with them was organised into tidy little piles. They had chosen a particularly sunny spot to work and Ash leaned back onto her hands, enjoying the warmth.

"It's nice here," she said softly. Pinar nodded and leaned back too. Ash thought her friend's eyes looked a little wet. *Or it might just be the light.* "I'm sorry," Ash continued. "About our fight at the lodge."

Pinar sat up straight. "I'm sorry too."

"I don't mean to ignore your needs." Ash looked down at the ground and sighed. "I'm working on it."

Pinar stood and moved over to sit next to her friend. She pulled her into an embrace and said something Ash didn't quite hear.

"I love you too," she whispered back.

Chapter seventy

A n hour later, Ash stood at the edge of the clearing looking over the camp. The tents were up, Rob, Dee and Tania were behind the van preparing firewood, Oscar and Elias were in bed resting and Julia and Cleo had gone off for a swim in the river. *It already looks like home.* And yet Ash noticed a sense of incompleteness rippling through her, begging for her attention.

What? What is it? she asked herself. *What do I need?*

The land itself whispered a response.

She turned her back on the others for a moment and without thinking, stepped back into the forest. She had walked barely twenty metres when her legs gave way beneath her and she fell to her knees on a deep pile of moss and leaves.

She inhaled the scent of the earth, her hands digging into the dirt as they would a thousand times more. The smell of pollen and bark and pine leaves seduced her into her senses. The sounds of her friends were all around her—human, and non-human—going about their days.

Ash said a silent thank you then. For companionship, and for the adventures she now trusted lay ahead of them.

I'm ready, she thought as she stared at her dirty hands. *As long as I can keep this balance.*

She stood, brushed off her knees, and went back to join her community.

About the author:

Otter Lieffe is a working class, chronically ill, femme, trans woman and the author of two other trans feminist novels—*Margins and Murmurations* (2017) and *Conserve and Control* (2018). *Dignity* is the third part of the series and is a prequel to the others.

In 2019 her short story *Synergy* was published in *Our Entangled Future,* an anthology on social change and the climate crisis. In 2020 she released a colouring zine called *Queer Animals* published by Microcosm Publishing and illustrated by Anja Van Geert. Otter's short story, *Soft,* (featuring characters from *Dignity*) can be found in the upcoming publication *Glitter and Ashes: Queer Tales of a World That Wouldn't Die.*

A grassroots community organiser for over two decades, Otter has worked and organised in Europe, the Middle East and Latin America with a particular focus on the intersection of gender, queerness and environmental struggles.

Since publishing her first novel in 2017, Otter has been building networks to counter the systemic oppressions faced by working-class trans women. In 2018, she helped establish Books Beyond Bars UK, an LGBTQIA prisoner support group in the UK and in 2019 she launched a new organisation, Trans Feminism International, organising to meet the material needs of trans women.

www.otterlieffe.com
www.transfeminism.net

Bookshops are disappearing. Small stores are being consumed by giant corporations, independent businesses are being centralized and assimilated. We all know this: we see it with our own eyes. But what does it really mean to lose these places? What does it mean when autonomous bookstores turn into just one more homogeneous warehouse driven by decisions a million miles away? For me, among many things, it's a question of space.

I spent a good part of my twenties in independent and radical spaces of all kinds. Bookstores and libraries that would become migrant language classes and queer self-defence dojos in the blink of an eye. And then a café, a bar, a meeting place and back to a bookstore again. I felt like these spaces were not only holding books as a product on a shelf, they were held by the books themselves. Every meal or evening conversation was watched over by a hundred titles who slipped themselves into our conversation. "That reminds me of something I read," says one person over dinner as she gets up and flicks to the right page. "Here, look." That sensuality, the availability of words on pages on shelves in collective spaces, is one of the things we lose when all our books come from the internet.

Printing and distributing online has opened a world of possibilities to self-publishers like me (where there are profits to be made, capitalism will always find a way). Without a certain giant multinational how else would I—a completely unknown author— have gotten my book to twenty something countries, even into prisons on the other side of the world? And for some the internet is more accessible than radical bookstores. But the work of non-profit groups like Active Distribution, printing books like this one to be put onto real shelves in real spaces, is world-creating. And with the books, come the spaces themselves and the communities that they gather. I am honoured to be a part of that.